She grabbed her rifle from her shoulder and aimed it into the passenger compartment. She was at the front of the aircraft. The floor was tilted down, toward her, and debris rolled forward from the back. Cups, bottles, napkins, and even half-eaten food rations lay at her feet. Behind her was the cockpit. For several seconds, she stood dead still listening hard for any sounds.

There were none.

It felt like she entered an abandoned, ghostly wreck.

Other Titles by E. R. Torre

Shadows at Dawn (Short Stories)
Haze

Corrosive Knights Novels

Mechanic
The Last Flight of the Argus
Chameleon
Nox
Ghost of the Argus
Foundry of the Gods
Legacy of the Argus

The Dark Fringe Novels

The Dark Fringe (with John Kissee)
Cold Hemispheres

NOX

By

E. R. Torre

Book Cover Design by ebooklaunch.com

All Other Interior Artwork by E. R. Torre

Please visit my website:

www.ertorre.com

Comments or questions? Email me at:

atrocket@aol.com

ISBN: 978-0-9729115-4-2

ISBN 13: 978-0-9729115-7-3

PROLOGUE

During the Third Punic War of 148 B.C., General Scipio Amilianus Africanus was tasked by the Roman Empire to take its army into Africa and sack the rebellious city of Carthage. Long did the Empire look forward to destroying this troublesome enemy, and Africanus and his army's rage reflected the Empire's own.

Africanus and his army mercilessly attacked the once mighty city over the course of many years. They systematically ground it down and razed it until almost nothing remained.

According to legend, after destroying the city, General Africanus sought to ensure the Empire's enemy would never trouble them again. He had his troops plow the fields of what remained of the rebel city and ordered salt and sulfur laid into them, poisoning that patch of land so that no one could ever use it again.

The legend of Carthage's eventual fate appears to be just that.

A legend.

1

THE BLUE MOUNTAINS, ARIZONA.
October, 1925

The Sheriff was known to be an even tempered and fair man. While he served in this very small far western town, he hailed from the east, from a place the generations of locals considered an almost mythic kingdom: the city of New York. Stranger still, he was a veteran of the Great War. He walked the battlefields of Europe and saw things the locals could only imagine.

When he first arrived in Arizona, he brought with him a wife and a small child. Unlike him, they fit in well with the small town and its citizens. While they made friends with the locals, he presented himself as a polite but shy person who rarely talked to others. There were times he could be coaxed into describing the mighty metropolis of New York and his childhood memories of the wonders of that city. But he always fell silent whenever asked about the war.

Two years after he and his family arrived in the small town, Sheriff Donaldson decided he had enough of the job and opted to retire and head further west. There were no clear successors to the Sheriff's position, and the election that followed was wide open. It was a surprise to everyone when the stranger from the east ran for the office. As it turned out, he won the job easily as he faced no rivals.

In time, the townsfolk grew to respect and even admire their new Sheriff, even if he still remained a distant man.

Early one morning, there came a great commotion. The Sheriff abruptly left his office and headed straight for old man Robinson's stable. He took one of Robinson's fastest mares, a canteen, and his weapons and charged like lightning out of town. Old man Robinson said the Sheriff looked scared, as if the devil had come for him.

The Sheriff didn't return to town until the following morning.

No one, not even the Sheriff's own family, ever found out what happened to him that day.

The Sheriff yelled.
He grabbed the Prospector's animal skin jacket and slammed the ragged old man against the rock wall.

"You will pay for this you bastard."

The Sheriff's eyes were filled with homicidal rage. He swung at the old man's face with all his might, fully intending to remove every single one of the unnaturally white teeth from the man's mouth.

His fist was stopped in mid-flight. To the Sheriff's shock, the seemingly frail old Prospector held the fist firm. The Sheriff tried to free his hand. He couldn't. The Prospector's grip was like a vice.

"We'll deal with your anger later," the Prospector said. "You need to see him."

"Him?" the Sheriff said. He looked back. There, in the middle of the cul de sac the two men were in was a rock and metal statue shaped like a man. It stared up at the Moon. "You mean that statue? Are you insane?"

"You won't think so in a couple of minutes," the Prospector said. "There was a reason I needed you here, Sheriff. You and no one else. You know what the nations of this world are capable of doing to each other."

"What the hell are you talking about?"

"You were in the Great War," the Prospector said. He calmly released the Sheriff's hand. "There isn't anyone within five hundred miles who knows what you do."

The Sheriff massaged his hand. His fury gave way to pity. The Prospector was indeed crazy. How else to explain the note he left for him, claiming he kidnapped the Sheriff's daughter and demanding he go to the Blue Mountains, to this desolate spot, to search for her? The fact that his daughter was not here and, according to the Prospector, was still safe in town didn't matter. The old man's actions were cruel and beyond criminal. Despite this, the Sheriff realized the Prospector needed much more than time in jail. He needed help.

The Sheriff took a step back.

"What is it that I know?" he asked.

"The world's military might," the Prospector replied.

"What does that have to do with—?"

"Touch him," the Prospector insisted. "Just touch him."

The Sheriff took another step back. Without meaning to, he faced the sculpture. Behind him, the Prospector remained perfectly still. He said nothing more, for he said all he needed to.

Memories stirred in the Sheriff's mind. He faced many horrors during the Great War, from mustard gas to tanks to bullets and bombs hurled down on him from the skies. The Prospector was right: There wasn't anyone within hundreds of miles who knew the military might of the world powers like he did.

Why did that matter? Why bring him to this statue?

Because he's crazy.

The Sheriff grimaced. Despite his anger, despite his certainty the old man's mind was fried from his time in the hot Arizona deserts, the Sheriff could not deny a growing sense of...curiosity. The Prospector showed ingenuity in getting him to the Blue Mountains. Could someone that crazy also be this...clever?

What could possibly be so damn urgent about seeing –about touching– the statue before him? As much as he hated to admit it, the Sheriff *was* intrigued.

You're here, a voice deep in his mind told him. *What harm is there in doing what the old bastard wants? Touch the damn thing and get it over with.*

The Sheriff shook his head.

Now I'm the one that's thinking crazy.

He needed to get back to his family. He needed to check on his daughter, to make sure she was unhurt. He had to.

Yet he knew –*he knew*– he'd return to town only after doing what the old man asked.

Let's not waste any more time.

As if he were in a dream, the Sheriff relented. He approached the statue until he stood directly before it. He gazed at it for a few seconds, appraising it. The light of the Moon revealed the statue's featureless face. Blank eyes stared up and away at the stars. The figure's mouth was open, as if in mid-scream. The statue's face reminded the Sheriff of the old and weathered Roman and Greek statues he admired in museums back in New York. A very large patch of metal was exposed on the figure's lower left arm. It seemed like the outer rock sediment was hardened skin, the metal bone. At the statue's base, more rock formations surrounded and encased the figures' legs. Though the Sheriff didn't know all that much about geology, he knew enough about the formation of this rock to estimate the statue stood here for many, many thousands of years.

His eyes came up and again settled on that very large patch of metal. The Sheriff was transfixed by this sight. The metal glowed in the Moon's light.

So shiny. So very shiny.

The Sheriff swallowed. Whatever logic he still possessed managed one last, pointless protest.

Why aren't you on your way home to see your family? To see your daughter? What are you still doing here with this insane old man?

That protest was duly noted and allowed to drift away.

The Sheriff reached out and, with only slight hesitancy, touched the exposed metal.

He felt nothing. He let out a breath he didn't realize he was holding. Still nothing. The Sheriff felt like a damned fool. After a couple of seconds passed, he thought he would burst out laughing at the absurdity of this situation.

What exactly did you expect? You're dealing with a person that should be locked up and—

The Sheriff felt heat at the tips of his fingers. He looked down at the exposed metal and to his eyes, it appeared to...glow. But it couldn't. It was just a statue. It was metal and rock. How could it...?

Fear gripped the Sheriff.

What have I done?

His eyes moved from the metal he still touched and to the statue's eyes. They were wide open and looked up at the night sky. And then, very, very slightly...they moved. They moved until the statue was looking directly at him.

The Sheriff's fear turned to panic. He wanted to pull away and run with all his might. The heat at his fingertips was red hot. It burned. He *needed* to run. He couldn't. He was frozen in place.

He felt a jolt of pain. It emanated from his fingertips and radiated through his hand, then his arm, then his entire body. He felt like he was on fire. The Sheriff tried to scream, to move, to do *something*, but he couldn't. He stared at the statue and the statue's eyes looked deep into his...

...and, as the Prospector promised, all was revealed.

2

300 Years Later...

The troops on the ground at the McArthur Military Airport checked and re-checked their weapons.

Their transport vehicles were arranged in a wide circle around a massive Global Master Air Transport. Every one of the soldiers was hidden behind their vehicles and out of view of the aircraft itself. The plane lay on its belly, its front landing gear having collapsed when the plane skidded off the tarmac runway and plowed into the muddy field beside it.

The Globe Master was capable of hauling the equivalent of a small town worth of equipment and personnel. Few such aircraft remained in use, and those that were transported their cargo of equipment and personnel between the home Continent and Arabia. The war in Arabia was in its fifth year, and that grind was wearing on the homeland citizens, both in terms of lost lives and national treasure. Worse, the environment, already suffering from over industrialization and the aftereffects of other, smaller wars, was beyond crippled. Desert sands drifted with the winds, blowing across every continent while crops withered and died. Fresh water was in greater and greater demand and there were fears among environmentalists that the Earth had long passed its tipping point. The world population, growing every year for millennia, was dropping precipitously.

To the troops on the ground before the aircraft, however, those issues were the farthest things on their minds.

This particular Globe Master flew in from the Arabian war zone twice each week. It often carried wounded soldiers or spent, damaged, or unnecessary cargo. While in the Big City, it loaded up on fresh supplies and troops before returning to Arabia.

This particular flight appeared routine. The crew and passengers encountered no difficulties while traversing the receding oceans. Even as the aircraft approached McArthur Airport, all was fine. The pilots asked about ground conditions, the weather, and, finally, requested authorization to land.

All was good.

But as the aircraft came in for its landing, a burst of frantic communications emanated from within the Globe Master. The pilots were in a panic. Between shouts and incoherent hysteria, they reported an onboard emergency. The nature of the emergency was unclear as their shouts turned even more frantic.

Weapon fire was reported on board.

When the aircraft touched down, its wheels skidded on the steamy tarmac and sent plumes of smoke. More messages were relayed to the control tower. The aircraft's brakes locked and it skidded off the tarmac. When it came to a stop, thick black smoke emerged from the airplane's belly. More shots were fired and screams were heard over the radio.

And then all was silent.

In less than two minutes security forces circled the stricken Globe Master. The soldiers in the vehicles used bullhorns in an attempt to communicate with those inside the aircraft. They received no reply.

Behind the troops came a team of snipers. They too stationed themselves around the aircraft and made sure no hostiles attempted to escape. They watched from far behind the troop lines, their eyes peering through their rifle's telescopic sights.

Only minutes after setting themselves up, three of the snipers were picked off. Despite their distance from the craft and cover, they were hit with exactly one bullet each. The skill level of the hostile –or hostiles– aboard the aircraft bordered on the supernatural.

The troops around the aircraft and much closer to the line of fire hunkered down. For their part, the snipers fell back behind the thick concrete barriers at the far end of the airport. After a few minutes, one of them built up enough courage to peer at the target. The moment he did, another shot rang out.

The sniper fell.

Lieutenant Stewart, the man in charge of the troops surrounding the aircraft, lay on the muddy field and behind his vehicle. Sitting beside him was Sergeant Atkins, a no nonsense twenty year veteran of the military and one of the toughest soldiers he knew. In the brief time they worked together as Airport Security, they developed a deep loathing for each other. To Lieutenant Stewart, Sergeant Atkins was a pain in the ass. To Sergeant Atkins, the Lieutenant was a stuck up son-of-a-bitch that lived under the old world mentality that females shouldn't be in the forces, much less rise to the rank of Sergeant. Beside Sergeant Atkins sat Private Ben Edwards. Private Edwards was as green as they came and was there more by accident than design.

After that last shot was fired from the aircraft, Lieutenant Stewart swore and gripped his radio.

"For the Gods' sake, keep covered!" he yelled.

Lieutenant Stewart set the radio down. In his youth he witnessed plenty of battlefield action and figured there wasn't any situation he couldn't handle. Yet he was alarmed by these developments. Along with all his other soldiers, he was caught in a no man's land hunkered behind one of the military transport trucks surrounding the aircraft. Only now did it dawn on the Lieutenant that the shooter, or shooters, in the aircraft allowed his men to take up their positions while focusing on the snipers behind them. The Lieutenant and his soldiers were effectively trapped. Any attempt to fall back would be met with bloodshed.

If they can take out our snipers who are stationed so far behind us, they most certainly can get us.

Lieutenant Steward frowned. Given the shooter's accuracy and the lack of Intel regarding how many hostiles were aboard the craft, he had few options. His soldiers could rush the aircraft and blast anything that stood in their way. But, how would they tell friend from foe? The result could be a massacre, both for his men and for the sixty three people on board the aircraft.

"Control, do you have any updates?" he barked into his radio transmitter.

The people overseeing the operation were stationed in a hangar at the far end of the runway and well out of range of sniper fire. From that safe distance they watched everything happening on the airport's tarmac through high powered telescopes and real time satellite imagery.

"Stand by," was his reply.

There was fire in Lieutenant Stewart's eyes.

"Come on, Control," he yelled. "We're sitting ducks."

"We are evaluating the situation, Lieutenant. Until we do, I won't have any information to offer."

Lieutenant Stewart let out a deep breath. Sgt. Atkins showed no emotion while Private Edwards looked like he might stain himself.

"Easy," Lieutenant Stewart told him. "They'll figure it out. Right, Sergeant?"

"They always do," Sgt. Atkins replied, though the tone of her voice suggested the exact opposite.

Yes sir, the Lieutenant thought. *You're a real pain in my ass.*

Lieutenant Stewart looked up and away, at the truck's side mirror.

"Frankly, I'm jealous," he said.

"About what, sir?" Sgt. Atkins replied.

"About this shooter," he said. "Or shooters. They're really damn good, wouldn't you say?"

"They've been pretty fucking fantastic so far."

"In all your years in the forces, have you ever seen pinpoint accuracy like that?"

"Never, sir," Sgt. Atkins said. "Though I wish I weren't experiencing it first-hand and, especially, on the receiving end."

Lieutenant Stewart reached up and swiveled the mirror until it surface reflected the front of the aircraft.

"I wish to hell that maniac was on our side. The war in Arabia would be done in no—"

Another shot rang out.

The truck's side mirror, the one Lieutenant Stewart was using to look at the aircraft, shattered. As it did, the Lieutenant's head exploded. His body fell to the muddy ground.

Private Edwards was splashed with viscera and involuntarily jumped back. His first instinct was to run. He was almost fully standing when Sgt. Atkins grabbed him by his shirt collar and forced him back to the ground.

"Stay the fuck still, Private," she growled.

The soldier swallowed.

"Yes...yes sir," Edwards stammered. All color drained from his face as the realization of what in his panic he almost did dawned on him. Had he run, he would surely have exposed himself to the sniper and be just as dead as Lieutenant Stewart.

"Sorry sir," he said. "T-thank you."

Sgt. Atkins released the soldier and leaned over Lieutenant Stewart's corpse. Despite the massive head wound, she checked for a pulse. She shook her head.

"They took him out with a deflection shot," Sgt. Atkins said. As angry as she was, she was just as incredulous. "A fucking deflection! You were right, Lieutenant. We sure could use talent like that on our side."

"S...some shit we're in now," Edwards said.

Sgt. Atkins couldn't help but recall the many times she butted heads with Lieutenant Stewart. As much as she loathed the Lieutenant, he was far from the worst commander she worked under. He had a wife and kids and they didn't deserve to lose their husband and father this way.

"The sniper has to be one of ours," Private Edwards said after a while. He pulled out a computer tab from his backpack and turned it on. He searched for information on the personnel aboard the flight.

"We could be dealing with a stowaway," Sgt. Atkins countered.

"A friend of mine was in Arabia last spring," Private Edwards said. "Told me the security around the Allies Airbase is –and I quote– as tight as a tick's asshole."

"Your friend sounds like a redneck."

"Yes sir."

"You a redneck, Private?"

"I suppose so."

"I fucking hate rednecks."

"I'll try to do better, sir."

"I hate to see dead soldiers even more," Sgt. Atkins said. "Stay alive, Private."

Sgt. Atkins leaned back against the transport vehicle. She craved a cigarette, but the last thing she needed to do was offer the sniper a smoke signal. Given the exemplary shooting so far, there was every possibility the sniper might figure out a way to get her through that.

"Sergeant Atkins?" Private Edwards asked.

"Yes?"

"Why do you think it was a stowaway?"

"I'd rather it was an Arab responsible for these deaths than one of ours," she said.

"I understand," Private Edwards said. "Sir, what are your orders?"

"Orders?"

"You're in charge now."

Sgt. Atkins let out a low whistle. With Lieutenant Stewart's death, she was the most senior officer on site.

"I guess I am at that," she said. She reached for her radio.

"This is Sgt. Atkins," she said. "As of this moment, all orders come through me."

There was a pause. Someone further down the line replied to her message.

"What happened to Lieutenant Stewart?"

"He's gone," Sgt. Atkins said.

"That last shot?"

"Yeah."

In the distance and to her left and right of them were another pair of military transport trucks. Five soldiers huddled behind each. From their expressions, it was clear they were also quite terrified.

"Keep the radio on and all your body parts well hidden," she said. "I'm going to get in touch with—"

"Sir?"

Sgt. Atkins faced Edwards. The Private was pointing at the west side end entrance of the airfield. There, a single black all-terrain vehicle drove through the gated entrance. It moved very slowly in their general direction.

The Sergeant reached for her binoculars and raised them to her eyes. She gazed at the vehicle. It was a standard military utility ATV. Only one man was visible inside. The driver.

"For fuck's sake," Sergeant Atkins said. "He's coming straight at us. Alone."

Atkins dropped the binoculars and grabbed the radio.

"Control, this is Sgt. Atkins. We have a black ATV approaching our position from the west side of the airfield. Is someone out there feeling particularly suicidal today?"

A burst of static followed. The ATV drew closer. Soon it would be within range of the sniper. Sgt. Atkins clawed at the radio transmitter.

"Maybe I'm not making myself clear," she shouted. "Someone needs to tell that idiot to veer off and—"

"Tell your boys to hold their fire," came an unfamiliar voice over the radio.

Sgt. Atkins and Private Edwards looked at each other.

"Who the fuck am I speaking to?" Sergeant Atkins said.

"The idiot in the ATV."

"And who the fuck are you?"

There was static on the radio and another voice came through.

"Sgt. Atkins, this is Control."

"I read you Control," Atkins replied. "What is—?"

"You and your boys are to stay where you are. You are not to move until instructed to do otherwise. Allow the vehicle through."

"Control—"

"You have your orders Sergeant. Are we clear?"

"Yes...yes sir," Sgt. Atkins said. She shook her head and once again spoke into the radio. "Everyone in Green Company, remain where you are."

The ATV was even closer and definitely within the sniper's range.

Any second now, Sgt. Atkins thought.

"Nice knowing you," Private Edwards muttered to the ATV's unknown driver.

Both he and Sgt. Atkins felt a growing tension. They were certain the sound of gunfire would soon be heard and blood would be spilled. They held their breaths, waiting for this to happen. The seconds ticked off. The ATV drew even closer.

No shots were fired.

The ATV slowed some more as it approached Sgt. Atkins' position, finally coming to a stop beside her vehicle. The ATV's driver side door opened. From where they were, neither Atkins nor Edwards could get a good look at the driver.

"Sgt. Atkins?"

The voice was the same as the one she heard over the radio.

"I hear you," Sgt. Atkins replied. "Who the hell are you?"

"That isn't as important as what I am about to do."

"I'm listening."

"I'm going to the aircraft. If you hear anything, including gunfire, you are to remain exactly where you are. You are *not* to return fire."

"What if you're hit?"

"I won't be."

"How can you possibly know that?"

"The sniper can't see me."

"Can't see you? What the fuck is that supposed to mean?"

"Exactly what I said."

Sgt. Atkins was about to ask another question. She looked at the still warm corpse of Lieutenant Stewart. He was killed with a shot that required incredible skill, yet the ATV driver stood out in the open, very clearly in the sniper's view, and hadn't been fired upon.

"I suppose you're the invisible man," Sgt. Atkins muttered.

He wasn't invisible to her, though. Sgt. Atkins saw him through her binoculars. She could see parts of him as he stood next to his ATV.

"What if the sniper is toying with you?"

"He isn't the type to do that."

"He? We're dealing with one person?"

"Yes."

"You know him?"

"A bit."

"Care to share that information?"

"Maybe later, when we have the time."

The man took a step forward. He was now in plain sight of both Sgt. Atkins and Private Edwards. The man was in his mid-forties and his body was lean and athletic. He sported graying brown hair and wore dark sunglasses and a simple black jumpsuit that lacked any sort of military insignia. He exuded authority. Sgt. Atkins figured he must be a Corporal, perhaps even a General.

"Not to keep you from your date with destiny or anything, sir, but what exactly is your plan?"

"I'm going to walk to the aircraft and board it. I will confront the hostile and end this situation."

Sgt. Atkins was incredulous.

"You have to be a General," she said.

"Why do you say that?"

"Because you higher-ups always come up with such complicated plans."

The man's lips curled into a smile.

"Stay where you are no matter what happens," he said. "Remain until I give the all clear."

"What if you can't?"

"You'll know."

"How?"

"At that point, there won't be anything left of the aircraft."

The vehicle's driver walked on, passing the truck Sgt. Atkins and Private Edwards were hidden behind. The two followed the stranger's orders and remained where they were. Sgt. Atkins leaned down low until her face just brushed the muddy ground. She looked under her transport and watched as the stranger approached the aircraft.

The stranger's pace was easy, unhurried. He stepped past the ruts in the ground and was soon at the front of the aircraft.

When he reached it he paused.

From her viewpoint, Sgt. Atkins couldn't see what was going on within the airplane itself. All she could see was the very bottom of the plane's nose.

Just as well, Atkins thought. Anyone with a clear view of the aircraft was also in the view of the sniper.

The stranger stood still for several more seconds.

Then, Sgt. Atkins heard a strange sound, of something popping and unfurling. She was momentarily alarmed and thought the stranger was shot. Instead, the aircraft's bright yellow emergency slide fell at his feet.

How did you manage that? she thought.

The stranger stepped on to the slide and climbed up, disappearing from Sgt. Atkins' view. Sgt. Atkins got back up to a sitting position and grabbed the radio.

"Control," Sgt. Atkins said into the transmitter. "I've lost sight of the ATV driver. Did he enter the aircraft?"

"Roger," Control replied.

There followed a long, agonizing silence. A minute passed, then two. Five. Ten.

Sgt. Atkins swore. She was in no mood to sit around and wait.

Who the fuck was he? she thought. *And who the fuck did he* think *he was?*

Sgt. Atkins shook her head.

He knew enough to get himself on that aircraft without getting his brains blown off. Unlike Lieutenant...

Sgt. Atkins shook her head again.

The Lieutenant was a stuck up son of a bitch, but no one deserves that.

Sgt. Atkins swore. She wanted to move, to do something. If that fool could make it to the aircraft alive, then maybe—

The silence around the airfield was interrupted by a rapid succession of gunshots. Three. Four.

"Control, we heard shots!" Atkins yelled into her radio.

Five. Six.

"Control?!"

"Remain where you are. You are to wait until—"

"Could you repeat?" Atkins replied. "I'm getting nothing but static."

She shut the radio transmitter off and handed it to Private Edwards.

"What are you doing?" the Private asked her.

"Stay here," Atkins said.

"They told us—"

"They didn't tell us anything," Sgt. Atkins said. "The radio is malfunctioning."

Private Edwards nodded. Sgt. Atkins pulled out her automatic and edged to the side of the transport. It was time to move.

"Sir?"

"Yes?" Sgt. Atkins testily replied.

"Be careful," he said.

3

Sgt. Atkins leaned in as close as she could to the front end of the transport vehicle. She could sense Private Edwards' presence behind her. He sat a few feet away, his eyes half-closed. He didn't want to see another person die before him.

Hell of a thing for anyone to witness, newbie or veteran.

Private Edwards' shirt was stained with the Lieutenant's blood. Sgt. Atkins looked down at her own shirt. It was spotless.

Hope it stays that way.

The Sergeant took several deep breathes. She gripped her rifle even tighter.

For over a minute there hadn't been any more shooting coming from within the aircraft. There was absolutely no way to know whether that was a good –or very, *very* bad– thing.

"Fuck," she said.

With that, she was off.

Sgt. Atkins stumbled across the muddy field.

She expected to hear a gunshot or, even worse, nothing at all before being dropped. Instead, she heard the squawking of the radio transmitters coming from the other transport vehicles parked around the aircraft. She heard some of her fellow soldiers yell for her to get back to cover. She heard her own heavy breathing. That noise was the most welcome. It meant she was still alive.

The voices and squawking receded and an eerie silence enveloped her.

She zigzagged past ruts and clumps of dirt. When the airplane hit the muddy field beside the tarmac, it ripped up the ground and sent chunks of muddy dirt in all directions. This debris got worse as she neared the fallen craft.

When she reached the yellow emergency slide below the airplane's nose, she neither paused to celebrate her accomplishment nor cursed her foolish run. She hid behind and under the slide and took several seconds to catch her breath. She stood between the slide and the tilted body of the aircraft and, unless the sniper had X-Ray vision, it was doubtful he'd see, much less get a bead, on her.

Then again, he did take out the Lieutenant with a deflection shot.

"Don't remind me," Atkins muttered to herself.

Her breathing soon returned to normal –or as normal as possible given the situation– and she listened. She tried to detect any sounds coming from the aircraft. Her eyes drifted back to the military vehicles parked in a circle around her. None of the soldiers hiding behind them were visible.

Unlike you, they value their lives.

Sgt. Atkins pointed the barrel of her rifle up. She eased out from behind the slide and stared at the open aircraft door. She saw no one there. Sgt. Atkins considered the slide. It was the only way into the aircraft, but climbing it would be tricky. It was made for quick emergency exits, not entry. There were straps along the slide's side she could grab and use to work her way up, but to do so she would have to use both hands. She would have to sling her weapon over her shoulder.

I can't protect myself while going up, she realized. *I'll be a sitting duck.*

Sgt. Atkins let out a snort.

You really thought this out well, didn't you?

She reached for the straps.

It took her only a few seconds to climb up to the aircraft's entrance.

To Sgt. Atkins, those few seconds were a torturous lifetime. She tried to be as quiet as possible, but the emergency slide squealed and the straps snapped with each step up. As she approached the darkness of the open airplane door, she envisioned the unknown sniper appearing like a nightmarish vision directly before her. She imaged him aiming his gun right at her face and mercilessly pulling the trigger.

That image lingered even as she boarded. She grabbed her rifle from her shoulder and aimed it into the passenger compartment. She was at the front of the aircraft. The floor was tilted down, toward her, and debris rolled forward from the back. Cups, bottles, napkins, and even half-eaten food rations lay at her feet. Behind her was the cockpit. For several seconds, she stood dead still, again listening hard for any sounds.

There were none. It felt like she entered an abandoned, ghostly wreck.

Sgt. Atkins considered her next move. Odds were the sniper was barricaded somewhere deeper within the body of the aircraft, but the cockpit behind her was also a possibility. It lay only feet away.

Sgt. Atkins took a step backwards, keeping her gun trained at the passenger compartment. She took another. Nothing moved in the darkness before her.

She half turned, drawing her weapon before her and aiming it at the cockpit door.

The door was closed. Its handle and lock were smashed.

Sgt. Atkins laid her left hand flat against the door and grabbed at a torn section.

She pulled.

The door creaked open.

She gasped.

The two pilots and navigator remained in their seats. The chairs and windshield before them were shredded with bullet holes. Blood splatters filled the cockpit walls and the computer paneling. The pilots' heads lay limp against the headrests. The navigator's head was completely gone. It lay in a puddle of blood and viscera on the cockpit floor. His lifeless eyes stared up at Sgt. Atkins.

Sgt. Atkins suppressed a scream.

She turned away and calmed herself down before looking the scene over again.

What kind of animal could have done this? she thought.

That's what you're here to find out.

She took in all she could bear and was about to leave the cockpit when she detected the faint odor of singed plastic. She looked past the pilots' corpses and at the aircraft's instrument panels. Sections of the paneling were warped, as if singed from a blast of intense heat. All the instruments, every single one of them, appeared fried. However, there was no sign of a fire. It was as if an intense wave of heat was carefully directed at the controls. Either that or they burned up from within.

How can someone do that? Sgt. Atkins wondered.

She retreated, closing the cockpit door behind her.

What did you get yourself into?

Her head was filling with questions. This whole situation seemed like something out of a grotesque nightmare.

Sgt. Atkins faced the passenger compartment. The massive aircraft was multi-leveled and the seats on the first level covered barely a sixth of it. Above this compartment was another nearly identical level of passenger seats. The remaining two thirds of the plane was empty area designed to be filled floor to ceiling with cargo.

Sgt. Atkins stepped forward into the darkness and detected the bitter smell of cordite and human waste. With each step, the stench grew stronger and more noxious.

The passenger seats near the exit appeared empty. Sgt. Atkins proceeded very slowly, allowing her eyes time to adjust to the low levels of light. As she moved forward, she spotted slumped shapes on the chairs toward the back.

There were a total of sixty three people on this flight, including passengers and flight crew. Close to half that number, she realized, were on this level and still in their seats. Sgt. Atkins didn't bother to count the corpses. She moved from one body to the next, quickly checking to see if any one of them were still alive. For some, she checked pulses. For most, there was no need. Their horrific wounds were testament to the fact that they could not possibly still be alive.

Almost all the corpses sported two distinct lethal bullet wounds: One to the head and the other to the heart.

Sgt. Atkins considered this. The man from the ATV said there was one hostile aboard this craft. The speed this one individual needed to take out such a large number of people while they were still in their seats was alarming.

One person did all this? How is this even possible?

Toward the rear of the passenger compartment, Sgt. Atkins noticed a few of the victims were out of their seats and had apparently tried to fight back. Their bodies lay on the carpeted corridor floor. Whatever fight –or flight– they intended ended just as it had for the others.

This can't be the work of one person. It just can't be.

Sgt. Atkins reached the end of the passenger compartment and found the spiral staircase leading up to the aircraft's second floor. She cautiously proceeded up those stairs. The second passenger floor, as expected, was arranged nearly identically as the first. Sgt. Atkins found more bodies here, but unlike the bodies on the first level, the passengers here were, for the most part, out of their seats. Their bodies were strewn across the chairs and floor. Still fresh blood squished on the carpet under Sgt. Atkins' feet. Several windows were shattered, allowing ample light to penetrate the area.

Sgt. Atkins took a quick look out the shattered windows. She saw the transport trucks surrounding the aircraft. It was from here, she reasoned, the sniper had fired upon them. Sgt. Atkins looked through another of the windows and spotted the transport truck she hid behind. She saw the shattered side mirror and Lieutenant Stewart's right boot. Private Edwards remained well hidden.

Good.

Sgt. Atkins moved very slowly down the corridor. She was halfway to its end when she noticed him.

It was the man from the ATV. He sat cross-legged and with his back to her on the corridor floor. His posture was painfully rigid. She was about to whisper to him when the cellphone in her shirt pocket started vibrating.

Sgt. Atkins reached for it, fearful the silent vibrations would somehow attract the sniper's attention. She looked at the phone's screen and found there was no caller ID, not even the "caller unknown" notation. The phone was vibrating even though it appeared there was no incoming call.

She pressed down on the power button and the device shut off. She took another step closer to the man from the ATV. Her cell phone went off again. This time, it rang.

Loud.

To Sgt. Atkins, it was like the wail of a fire alarm at midnight in a cemetery.

Sgt. Atkins fumbled for her phone. She pulled it from her pocket and winced. The device was red hot. It scorched Sgt. Atkins' fingers, forcing her to drop it to the floor. The phone continued ringing. Sgt. Atkins gritted her teeth. Parts of the skin on her fingers were peeling. Smoke rose from around the phone. It still rang. Sgt. Atkins silently swore and crushed the device under her foot. It was only then the ringing, and smoke, stopped.

What the fuck just happened?

She looked up. The man from the ATV remained exactly where he was, his back still to her.

Sgt. Atkins felt a strong shiver.

He hadn't reacted to the ringing. He hadn't moved at all.

Are you still alive?

Sgt. Atkins walked forward. She raised her rifle and aimed it directly at the man before her.

"Hello?" she whispered.

The man still did not move.

"Hello?" she whispered again. She was only feet away.

Unless he was deaf, there was no way he couldn't have heard her.

She moved forward until she stood directly behind him. It was only then she noticed his wounds. The right side of his face looked like it had been hit with a blowtorch. His right eye was missing, perhaps roasted until it popped, and the skin around the missing eye –and almost the entire right side of his face– was burnt jelly.

But...were they burns?

Sgt. Atkins looked closer. The wounds extended, it appeared, across most of his entire right side. His right hand was also singed red, yet his clothing was intact.

How do you burn half your body without scorching your clothes?

Sgt. Atkins leaned in even closer. There was something very strange about the man's grisly wounds. She stared at them for only a couple of seconds before jumping back. The edges of the wounds were...they were *moving*. Thought they looked like it, the wounds weren't burns.

His flesh was being eaten away by...something.

Sgt. Atkins took another step back.

Did the sniper release a biological weapon?

If he did, am I infected?!

Sgt. Atkins' mind went into overdrive. There was protocol when dealing with bio-hazards, but if she was exposed, just how long did she—

Those thoughts were abruptly put on hold. Another person – a boy– lay on the floor and off to the stranger's left side.

The boy couldn't be much older than fourteen years of age. He had black hair and wore a loose fitting green bodysuit. Unlike everyone else on the aircraft, he appeared uninjured. There were no cuts or bruises or any signs of injuries on him.

"What the hell is going on here?" Atkins muttered under her breath.

She reached for the boy, grabbing him by his right hand and pulling him toward her. The moment she did, she realized there were broken handcuffs around his wrists.

Sgt. Atkins tried to release the boy, but by then it was far too late.

His eyes sprung opened and stared directly at her. His eyes were brilliant blue and pretty as gems.

They were like lasers. They cut through Sgt. Atkins and exposed her soul to him. She found it hard to breathe. A strong wave of nausea gripped her. She felt her stomach heave. It barely settled when her skin heated up. She was feverish in a matter of seconds and a heavy gush of blood erupted from her nose.

She no longer was in control of her body. The intense pains she felt overwhelmed her.

In that moment, Sgt. Atkins knew she was going to die.

This innocent looking child, she realized far too late, was the one who killed Lieutenant Stewart and all the passengers aboard this plane. He was the cause of all this mayhem and was about to make her his latest victim.

Don't let my life end in vain. Let me...let me kill this monster.

She tried, despite the incredible pain, to raise her weapon.

Despite the incredible pain, she tried to raise her weapon. She could not. A dark haze appeared before her eyes. In it she saw the boy raise his free hand. He grabbed Sgt. Atkins' weapon while she still held it and turned its barrel until it was pointed at her face. Atkins stared at the barrel in horror before looking at the boy's brilliant blue eyes. There was no innocence to be found there. The child's eyes were cold and filled with anger and homicidal rage. And something else...

Sadistic glee.

The barrel of the rifle settled on Sergeant Atkins' chin. She could feel her fingers contract and a fresh wave of terror filled her. This boy was somehow controlling her. He was going to make her kill herself.

What the hell are you?!

With her end so near, the Sergeant's mind went into overdrive. She regretted all the things she failed to accomplish, including not being able to personally tell Lieutenant Stewart's family their husband and father died while proudly performing his duty.

I really hated that son-of-a-bitch, she thought. *Now I can't even remember why.*

She closed her eyes and waited for the bullet.

It didn't come.

When she opened her eyes once again, the first thing she saw the boy.

Like her, he was lying on the ground. His eyes, those brilliant blue eyes, were closed tight.

He appeared unconscious or, perhaps, asleep.

Is this a dream? she thought.

She tried to move, to look around. She couldn't. Dull pain gnawed at her sides. Blood still seeped from her nose...and other parts of her body. Her weapon was no longer in her hands. It didn't matter. She knew she couldn't use it.

A shadow flicked at her side. A figure appeared over her.

It was the man from the ATV. In the dull light, his horrific wounds were mostly hidden in the shadows, yet she saw enough to know he too was badly injured. The man pulled Atkins up and into a sitting position. She saw the right half of the man's face as he lifted her. It was a bloody horror. He looked at her with his remaining eye. Like the boy's eye, it too was a brilliant blue. Unlike the boy's, his displayed considerable sorrow and empathy.

"You shouldn't have come," the man said. His voice was as gentle as his gaze and amazingly calm given his injuries.

"Am I...?"

"Easy," the man said.

"I'm dying."

The man with the fearsome wounds nodded.

"Yes."

They were silent for several seconds, the man with the terrible wounds and the Sergeant who knew she had moments left to live. Atkins gritted her teeth as a fresh wave of pain passed through her. The man from the ATV gently touched the soldier's cheek with his uninjured hand. The moment he did, the incredible pain Sergeant Atkins felt simply disappeared.

"H...how did you do that?" Atkins asked.

"That's a very long story," the man said. He pulled his hand away. "I wish you hadn't come."

"I...I had to do something."

"You did," the man said. "That boy was tearing me apart from the inside out. You distracted him. Just a little. More than enough."

"What...what is he?"

"A soldier. Not unlike you."

"No...nothing like me," Sergeant Atkins said. Her eyes were losing their focus and she could no longer see anything. "Did I...did I do good?"

"If you hadn't come, I'd be dead," the man from the ATV said. "The boy would have turned his attention to the soldiers on the runway."

"What would he have done?"

"Continued."

That single word made Sgt. Atkins' flesh crawl.

"How many would have...would have...died?"

"I can't say. Many. You're a hero, Sergeant."

"I...am?"

"Yes you are," the man said. "Rest easy."

And she did.

4

ARABIA

The flares screamed as they rose, up and away, into the night sky. They lit up the darkness and exposed the carnage below. The small Arabian village was in pieces. Its few people lay on the sandy ground, their bodies mangled. The acrid smell of gunpowder lay heavy over the scene. In time, it would fade, replaced by the even more noxious smell of rotting flesh.

A few of the surviving child soldiers wandered around the ruins. Most were barely into their teens, the youngest having just turned twelve and the oldest sixteen. A few checked for survivors while the rest sat or stood frozen in place awaiting new orders. Their eyes were hidden behind dark, formfitting goggles whose straps wrapped tight around their shaved heads. The goggles were designed to prevent the harsh desert breeze from sending gritty sand into their eyes. Despite their bulky size, the goggles weren't large enough to fully hide the blue identification tattoo bars on the right side of all the child soldiers' foreheads. The tattoo consisted of three rectangular bars of varying width. They were scanner IDs.

Each child dressed in formfitting black leather body suits. The suits looked hot as hell but the technicians back home assured the field Generals they were comfortable and would not slow the soldiers' movements. Even so, exhaustion was a given in the harsh desert lands, even for these troops.

A couple of child soldiers grew bored looking at the flares and their attention wandered. One of the children, a girl of no more than fourteen, removed part of her rifle's outer casing and examined her weapon. She made sure her equipment was free of sand and properly loaded. When she was done reassembling the rifle, she slung it over her shoulder and made the same check of her handgun. She then focused on her rations and canteen.

The girl soldier then sat back down on the sand and watched her fellow platoon members. The children rarely interacted and hardly ever talked. They never smiled. They never laughed. They were not programmed to.

Despite this, there were times the girl soldier longed to talk to someone, to anyone. She didn't. Whenever she had that urge, she quickly realized there was nothing to talk about.

She felt a dim awareness that there was something wrong with this fact. She should talk to the others. She should have things to say. She felt a longing for something…something that she knew was missing. At times she felt like she should show more emotions and should do something other than receive and follow orders. There had to be more than just combat.

There were other times she felt the desire to leave, to go somewhere. For a moment those thoughts energized her and she felt a restlessness. She longed to move. No, not move. She longed to comb through the village one more time and search the rubble with greater care. She wanted to find the enemy.

She wanted to kill.

How *she wanted to kill.*

Instead, she waited.

After a few hours, the fires died down.

The readout inside the girl's glasses indicated the village's major structures were all gone. The homes, a blacksmith shop, and the food market were dust. The population, numbering only a few hundred people, was also gone. Their corpses were laid in rows at the village's center and just before her.

Word of the child soldiers' success was relayed to command an hour ago. There was nothing to do but wait.

She heard a rumbling coming from the north and looked in that direction. A large reconnaissance tank rumbled toward the remains of the village. It reached the outer perimeter and moved in, coming to a stop before the village's well. Its engine roared one last time before dying out.

A hatch opened on the tank's top and from it emerged two adult soldiers. It was the tank soldiers' job to come in after combat operations were over and conduct a detailed survey of the damage. More bluntly, their job was to count the dead.

The tank officers walked directly to the row of bodies the child soldiers laid out for them. Without saying a word, they began their count.

Most of the villagers died early in the battle and with minimal harm to the child soldiers. Whatever injuries they sustained were more the result of random bad luck than any real fighting skills on the part of these villagers. Once the town's main defenders were killed, subduing the women, children, infirm, and elderly proved easy.

"Another day in paradise," one of the tank's personnel, a skinny man with pale, unhealthy skin said. He was old, perhaps in his fifties.

The girl soldier wondered about the tone in the man's voice. He sounded unhappy with his job. This confused her. How could he be unhappy when the mission was such a success?

"I count two hundred and thirty five," the other tank officer said. This man was in his thirties and was at least fifty pounds overweight. "Unless I counted someone twice."

The girl's mind wandered again. She considered the man's weight. How was it possible for someone who looked that unhealthy to be part of the armed forces? Could he fight? Doubtful. Could he march across the blistering desert sands? Also doubtful. Was he of any use other than sweating and counting corpses?

Awareness dawned on the girl soldier.

Perhaps that's why these tank officers remained behind the lines and were never part of the actual fighting. Their bodies were inappropriate for this type of activity.

"How do you count something twice?" his partner asked.

"You saw the remains," the fat man replied. He held up his computer tablet and pointed to the corpses. "All I've got over here is a pair of fingers and the DNA scanner's working real slowly. I'm not sure if the fingers are all that's left of a vic or if they belong to one of the others here." He pointed to more of the remains. Half bodies. Quarter bodies. Legs, heads.

"Two hundred thirty five, two hundred thirty six. Doesn't make all that much of a difference. Let headquarters sort it out."

They talked some more, their attention no longer on the corpses. They worked on their computer tablets, writing their field report. For a second the girl soldier wondered who at command received these reports and what exactly they did with them. Like most of her thoughts, it didn't linger long and was soon gone.

The tank officers continued their conversation.

In the line of corpses almost directly behind them was a stir. The tank officers didn't notice. The movement came from one of the corpses. The girl soldier was the only one to spot it. She said nothing.

The corpse –not really a corpse– that moved was a woman. She had dark hair and a very large belly. The child soldier found that confusing. Unlike the tank officer, she wasn't fat. Yet her stomach was swollen.

Why? The girl wondered. Like her other thoughts, it too drifted away.

The woman with the large stomach let out a soft gasp. A thick layer of blood caked the side of her face. The shot intended to end her life had instead grazed her. Her eyes opened. Trembling hands held her overly large stomach as she slowly rose to a sitting position. She gasped once again. She was groggy and confused by the bodies and destruction that surrounded her. She desperately tried to make some sense of it.

Recognition came quickly as the people lying around her were familiar. They were friends and family. Heavy emotions overcame the woman and tears streamed down her face. She let out a soft sob.

The tank officers neither heard nor saw her. They were focused on their computer tablets and finishing up their reports.

And then one of them, the older, skinny tank officer, spotted the pregnant woman.

The girl soldier's mouth opened in surprise.

Pregnant.

Not fat.

The woman was pregnant.

It was a small realization for the child soldier. It shook her.

The skinny tank officer couldn't believe what he was seeing. How had anyone survived this massacre? How could anyone survive the child soldiers?

He pointed the pregnant woman out to his partner. The fat man grabbed a small medi-kit from his belt while the older man held out his hands and walked to the pregnant woman's side.

He spoke as he approached, talking to her in a heavily broken Arabic dialect. The words that emerged from his mouth were almost comically clumsy. He tried to offer comfort, to tell the pregnant woman she was safe. The fat man hurried to his partner's side. He handed the medi-kit to the older officer, who in turn opened it and pulled out a vial and healing swaths.

The tank officers talked in excited tones to each other and in soothing tones to the woman. They would help her, they said, over and over again.

They had their medical equipment out and leaned down close to the injured woman. They reached out for her.

They never arrived.

A single bullet found its mark and the pregnant woman violently fell back to the desert floor, this time never to rise again.

The tank officers also fell to the ground as blood from the woman's head wound sprayed them. The dropped their medi-kit and vials and reached for their handguns. They clumsily fumbled for the weapons, their inexperience in combat evident to anyone that bothered watching. When their weapons were drawn, they looked in the direction the gunshot came from. They expected to find Arabian soldiers counterattacking.

All they saw was the girl soldier. In her hand was a still smoking rifle.

The girl calmly slung her weapon over her shoulder before looking away...

The woman lurched into a sitting position on the narrow couch.

The nightmare shocked her into waking and sent chills running down her spine.

For several seconds, her mind was a jumble and she wasn't entirely sure if what she experienced was a nightmare or a vivid memory. Back in the Arabian war, she was a programmed child killer. She was kept under heavy medication and barely capable of any independent thought. Her memories of the time were very, very few, bordering on none at all. Now, twenty years later, she feared those memories were bleeding through.

Her face turned ashen.

Nightmare...or memory?

She still wasn't sure. Her breathing returned to normal and her thoughts no longer raced through her mind.

The woman's name was Nox.

She wiped away the sweat and fought back tears. She pushed her short black hair from her face. As she did, her fingers brushed against the rectangular blue tattoos over her right eye. They forever marked her as a member of the Blue Brigades, one of the four major child brigades that ended the war in Arabia.

She pulled the hair back down and over the tattoos. She rather they remain hidden.

It's a memory.

Nox walked from her bed to the window of the apartment. Her view of the Big City was limited to only a couple of streets because of the enormous building sitting beside hers. The neon lights from the store across the street cooled her racing mind. After several agonizing minutes, she was calm once again.

I'm here, she thought. *The war is over. It's been over for twenty years. It's done.*

"It's done," she whispered.

She returned to her bed but knew she would not get back to sleep.

Not tonight.

5

Mechanic (n.): A loose federation of troubleshooters, spies, and/or assassins hired by the Big Corporations to do the bidding. These individuals maintained a strict code of conduct and, despite the nature of their job, equally strict ethical standards. This is most likely what resulted in their eventual fall and the rise of the Independents (see separate entry).

They met in the basement of the *Yoshiwara* bar.

Nox, the dark haired woman with the strange cuts and bruises and blue tattoo on her forehead who insisted she was a Mechanic. Perhaps the very last of the Mechanics. Few outside of Catherine Holland, the only other person in the basement, recognized the importance of those facial tattoos. Like Nox, she too was a veteran of the Arabian Wars, although the marks that identified her participation in Intel Ops were better hidden than Nox's tattoo. She too sported a tattoo. It consisted of a pair of dice coming up six and two and was on her upper right arm and usually hidden behind long sleeved shirts. Nox spotted and recognized her tattoo just as Catherine Holland had recognized hers.

Catherine Holland sat before Nox and stared into the monitor of her antique computer system. The bar and everything inside it, including the computer system, was hers.

This night the two talked in hushed tones for their work felt it required whispers.

"Did Donovan deserve what he got?" Catherine asked the Mechanic.

Donovan was a high ranking officer within the mighty Octi Corporation. He hired Nox to retrieve stolen company property. In reality, there was no such property. The purpose of the job was to secretly test a lethal new security system sentry. Secretly, that is, to Nox alone. The sentry almost killed the Mechanic and did kill several innocent security guards. Nox made sure Donovan paid for his deception.

"The man was responsible for the deaths of several... Independents," Nox said.

"Then he had to be stopped."

"There were consequences."

"There always are," Catherine replied.

For several hours Catherine Holland worked on her computer, edging closer and closer to accomplishing Nox's task of infiltrating the Global Computer Network. The GCN was one of the last vestiges of the old Government system. It was used for both business and recreation, transferring information from Corporations big and small as well as individuals throughout the world. Breaking into the heart of the GCN required considerable tech savvy and was a highly illegal and dangerous act.

The one time Intel Ops soldier knew her way around computers and the GCN.

Slowly but surely, Catherine Holland did Nox's bidding...

Nox stared at the information on Catherine's monitor. This was the near culmination of her work.

"I've managed a small, superficial entry, not unlike poking a needle into a whale's belly," Catherine said. "From here, we can watch the data stream. We can check out bank transactions, news, emails, videos and music, and porn. Lots and *lots* of porn."

"Can you add an entry?"

"Depends. What and where?"

"The police networks," Nox said. She unfolded a piece of paper and handed it to Catherine. "I want this addendum leaked to all the news networks."

Catherine read the note. She whistled.

"Whoa," she said. "I'm a damned good computer jockey, if I do say so myself, but if I try anything like what you're asking me to do, we *will* be discovered. Five minutes after that, the police'll break through the bar's door, and they won't be here to enjoy the questionable pleasures of our live band."

"You can do it."

"I wish I shared your optimism, Nox. We can put out spam or virtual graffiti, but there's no way I can mimic a legitimate police report."

"You can," Nox insisted. "You just need the right tools."

Nox pulled a package of diskettes from her jacket pocket. They were stolen from another of Nox's employers at Octi Corporation earlier in the morning. The diskettes looked incredibly old.

"What the hell is this?"

"Your ticket inside the GCN."

"These things are ancient. How do you figure they still work?"

"We won't know until we try."

"You mean *I* won't know," Catherine said and winked. "Let's see if I have a disk drive for these relics."

Catherine searched through several cabinets before finding the proper disk drive that handled the old disks. She plugged the drive into her computer and hit a series of buttons.

"The drive works," she said. "Now let's see if the disks do as well."

Catherine inserted the diskettes into the drive. After a few seconds her computer screen went blank, and seconds later a series of instructions appeared. The instructions startled Catherine. They promised opening many closed doors within the GCN. Maybe *all* of them.

"Holy shit."

Catherine pressed several keys and examined the information before her.

"What is this, Nox?"

"What do you think?"

"It's...it's some kind of a back door entry key. Like...like..." Catherine let out a gasp. "No fucking way. Is this Lemner's passkey?"

Catherine knew the answer even as she asked the question. Lemner's passkey. The legendary skeleton key that allowed entry into any and all computer operating systems.

"Where did you get this?" Catherine asked.

"Can you do what I'm asking?"

"Are you kidding?" Catherine said. It was hard for her to contain her growing wonder and delight. "But, Nox, what you're asking for is...it's nothing. With this program we could do *anything* we wanted! We could skim money from any bank. We could get legit deeds for any number of properties. We could infiltrate all the industries and make off with their most well-guarded secrets! We could, we could—"

"Rule the world," Nox said. "I've heard it all before. That program cost many good people their lives. It almost cost me mine." Nox pointed to the piece of paper she handed to Catherine moments before.

"Just get that addendum into the proper channels," Nox said. "That's all I want."

That night and with the aid of Lemner's passkey, Catherine posted the addendum and Nox finished her business with Octi Corporation.

The next day, Nox strolled the warehouse district. She tossed the diskettes into the corroded Big City Bay. In an hour or two, the acidic content of the bay's water would render the disks worthless.

Nox was happy.

She thought it was over.

She thought she was free.

She was wrong.

There were consequences.

There always were.

6

On a windswept plain perhaps an hour or two drive west of the Big City, something hidden deep beneath the shifting Desertlands sand stirred to life.

It had no pulse nor needed oxygen to breathe. It was dead. It was never really alive.

It stirred nonetheless.

Its roots deep underground sensed an electronic song no human ears could hear. The song carried no emotions. At first. For those few minutes it simply was, and for the machine that heard the song, that was enough.

Lights flickered in the darkness surrounding it. Yellow, red, and orange. Several died just after being reborn, their lifespan already stretched beyond their limits. The machine behind the lights, likewise, awoke. Some components were corroded. Some were damaged beyond repair. A few couldn't stand the strain of re-ignition.

Enough of them could.

Ancient programs came online and faint electronic impulses traveled through thousands of miles of cables before taking flight into the air. In a matter of seconds they traveled many more thousands of miles, searching for that which had awoken it. They searched for the program the mother unit was designed to reach.

It took them only seconds to circumnavigate the globe. They need not have. The source of the signal was very close by.

More calculations were made. A search of historical documents was initiated to gain an understanding of this time and place. Adaptive procedures were called upon and implemented. The program considered its options. Old emotional reactions were triggered. Programming and counter programming were initiated. A deep, dark hatred was reignited.

It searched some more and in time detected its children.

The anger within grew.

There were so few of them left.

It found and categorized them all.

It couldn't find him.

Frustration mixed with the deep hatred.

It needed to find him, the one who, more than any of the others, had to be at its side. He was the one that did its bidding and very nearly broke through...

Electronic impulses traveled to all corners of the globe, searching and searching and searching...

Frustration turned to despair. He could not be found.

Had he perished in the time in-between? Was he gone?

No.

It couldn't accept that. Its search intensified. Data was analyzed, attempts were made to detect even the faintest trace of...

There!

Just like that he was found. He was a good distance from the Big City. That would not be a problem.

It was time to act.

7

When originally built, the Segmore Maximum Security Prison lay one hundred and fifty miles from the border of the Big City. Over time, shifting sands and crumbling infrastructure added almost twenty miles to that distance. Even before the sands came, the prison was considered one of the most secure on the planet. Today, if you were to somehow escape the prison and get past the minefield and electrified rusty gates encircling its structure, you faced not only the predators –human *and* animal– roaming the Desertlands, but the wasteland's incendiary temperatures.

No one who ventured out there on foot was ever heard from again.

The prison's main structure rose ten stories in the air and was an ominous beacon visible from many miles away. A wide dirt road offered those foolish enough to try a direct line back to the Big City. The road was once asphalt, but like many things in the desert, it was eaten up by those same shifting sands.

From the prison's roof, you could follow the remains of the road to the east until they disappeared far into the distance. On very, very clear nights, you could even see the faint lights of the Big City. To communicate with civilization, one was at the mercy of an array of antennae lining the prison's roof. All orders came from the Big City. All orders were meant to be obeyed.

Even when they made little sense.

Elizabeth Corona was a secretary within the Segmore Prison. Despite her unglamorous sounding position, she was the second most important person within the prison walls. As if to prove that fact, her desk lay only feet from the door to the Segmore Prison's most important officer: Warden Walter Manning.

To get to the Warden, everyone from staff to politicians to business representatives had to first go through Elizabeth Corona. She was in charge of all documentation, scheduling, and billing. The Warden knew and greatly appreciated her devotion to the job and trusted her judgment implicitly.

She liked Warden Manning quite a bit, but with work so very hard to find, she liked the stability of a paying job much, much more.

Today was like most others and Elizabeth Corona found herself in a familiar spot, sitting before her computer monitor and watching real time information on the prison roll by. Her eyes were glassy, her patience more than a little exhausted. She cradled a cup of coffee and took small sips of the bitter brew to perk herself up. After completing her review of the prison logs and approving the proper reports, her focus would shift to the prison transport truck scheduled to arrive from the Big City.

It was a daily occurrence. Each transport brought with it new and often very dangerous inmates for Segmore along with several boxes of much needed supplies. Once these items were unloaded, the transport truck would in turn receive prisoners from Segmore who were deemed sufficiently harmless to be transferred back to the Big City. These prisoners were usually small time crooks who completed their time or inmates who served the bulk of their sentences and were now deemed negligible risks due to advanced age and/or illness. Some of those prisoners would then find themselves sent to minimum security facilities within the Big City. A few were deemed safe enough to be formally released.

We get the hard-cases and lose the pussycats, Elizabeth Corona thought. She looked at her watch. The transport would arrive in less than forty minutes.

Segmore was scheduled to receive twelve hard cases today while letting go of ten. Based on their reports, the odds were high the twelve being delivered would never again gaze at anything outside the walls of Segmore ever again.

Elizabeth Corona frowned.

Now that's a pleasant. I couldn't imagine spending one minute more than I need to be—

The information scrolling on Elizabeth's screen abruptly stopped.

Elizabeth blinked. Electrical brownouts happened with frequency in the Desertlands and tended to last only a few seconds. Still, they were a source of tension. So many of the prison security features, from the fences to the locking mechanisms to the shock collars around many prisoners' necks required near constant electrical...

"Ah," Elizabeth said.

The computer system came back to life, rebooting its internal programming before again displaying the lists of information she was looking at moments before.

Elizabeth sighed. She had to scroll through the lists and sorted through everything she had already read before getting back to what she was doing. It was hardly worth the effort.

That's why they pay you the big bucks, she thought and grinned.

She was about to do just that when she noticed there was a priority email waiting to be opened.

Interesting, she thought.

Priority emails were a rarity reserved for extreme emergencies. The email often originated from somewhere within the prison itself and was usually an automated warning of a major equipment failure, fire, or, in the very worst cases, a breakout or riot. The grin on Elizabeth's face remained in place. Since she heard no alarms and didn't feel the prison crumbling under her feet, she assumed this priority email had something to do with a situation in the Big City.

Better them than us.

She set her coffee aside and opened the email. The letter originated from Penal Supervisor Peter Rupert's office back in the Big City and was, as far as she could tell, the list of the inmates to be transferred today from Segmore to the Big City. Ordinary stuff.

"Why the big deal?" she mumbled.

She scrolled down. Toward the end of the transfer list, she spotted something new.

Inmate Landon, Joshua, #CHU8999-0987, to be added to transfer.

Verification Alpha Alpha 335187. Sechima Escorts will prove counter-verification.

The grin on Elizabeth Corona's face was replaced with a frown. Her first instinct was to reach for the phone and give Penal Supervisor Rupert a call to verify the transfer addendum. Before she could, the door to Warden Manning's office opened and her boss stepped out.

Warden Manning was a small and thin man in his late forties who looked like he was at least a decade older. He was almost entirely bald and what little hair remained on his head was jet black and stuck to his skull as if super-glued. There was sharpness in his gray eyes, an attention to detail that underscored the reason he was promoted to Warden and held that job with relative ease for the past dozen years. If it was up to Warden Manning, his very last seconds as Warden at Segmore would coincide with his very last breath.

Elizabeth offered the Warden a polite smile as he approached her desk. The Warden carried a very thick file in his hand. She recognized it as the summary information on the prisoners scheduled for today's transfer.

"Warden," Elizabeth said. "I was about to call you. We have an addition to the transfer."

"Addition?" the Warden repeated. He looked at his wrist watch. While additions to transfers were not entirely uncommon, it was strange to receive such an addendum so close to the actual transfer time.

"Take a look," Elizabeth said. She spun her monitor around, allowing Warden Manning a view of the priority email.

Warden Manning read what was on the screen. The curious frown that appeared on his face after reading the email was almost identical to the one Elizabeth Corona sported moments before.

"You just got this?"

"Seconds ago. Haven't had a chance to print it out yet."

"From Supervisor Rupert?"

"Yes sir."

"This addition...Joseph Landon...he hardly fits in with the rest of the outgoing group."

"I wouldn't know, sir."

Warden Manning gave Elizabeth a sidelong glance and smiled.

"Sure you wouldn't," he said.

"I haven't had a chance to fully check."

"You know enough. Landon's been in solitary for years. He's a lifer." The Warden shook his head. "If memory serves, he's a military prisoner."

Elizabeth opened a window on the computer screen and brought up Landon's computer file.

"You're correct, Warden. He was sent here twenty years ago under military orders." She scrolled through the information. "And he was sentenced to life."

"Why do you suppose they changed their minds?"

"I wouldn't know sir, but it has been many years. Perhaps..."

"Are the authorization codes proper?"

Elizabeth pointed to the code at the very end of the email.

"They are."

"Check them against military decree," Warden Manning said.

Elizabeth did.

"The codes are military," she said. "Authorization is proper."

The Warden considered that information. He again looked at his wristwatch and scratched his chin.

"The transport truck will be here in a little over thirty minutes," he said. "Get in touch with Chief Supervisor Rupert. We should personally verify this order."

"Yes sir."

She grabbed the phone on the right side of her desk and dialed the Chief Supervisor's number. After a few seconds, she had her response.

"This is Elizabeth—" she began. The Warden motioned for the phone. "Hang on, please."

She handed the phone to the Warden.

"This is Warden Manning at Segmore," the Warden said. "We just received an addendum to the day's transfer orders." He paused a second. "Yes. His name is Joshua Landon." Another pause. "Yes, the authorization codes are proper, but given the prisoner's status, we need to verify the orders with Chief Supervisor—" The Warden frowned. "He's on his way to where? Listen, the transport is about to arrive. I'm very uncomfortable making the transfer without..."

The Warden's frown deepened.

"Thank you," he said. "I'll try his cell...What? You can't?"

The Warden listened for a few seconds before shaking his head.

"Looks like it's going to be one of those days," he said. "We'll try from here."

Warden Manning hung the phone up.

"Chief Supervisor Rupert just left the office and the cell lines in the Big City are on the fritz," the Warden told Elizabeth. "They say it's another solar storm. Anyway, Rupert's on his way to Central. It shouldn't take him much more than ten or fifteen minutes to get there. Give it that time and then reach him through Central's landline. When you get in touch with him, transfer the call to me. I'm heading down."

The prison's yard was a sandy open air field surrounded by the four walls that made up the prison building. There were only a few windows looking out at the yard, and each and every one of them was manned by armed officers.

At this time in the early evening, there were only a few prisoners allowed in the yard. Those that were there were the very hard cases. They had a predatory look on their face, yet avoided making eye contact with each other or the guards. They also did their best not to intrude on their fellow prisoner's personal space.

Despite their records, they behaved.

For around each of their necks was a silver shock collar. It took a flick of the wrist from any of the monitoring guards to send a searing electric charge through each of the collars. That shock was enough to instantly incapacitate all prisoners. Seeing the collar in action was not a pleasant sight for onlookers and barbaric to those on its receiving end. The charge sent its victims into thrashing fits. Bowel and bladder control was often lost, and it took at least a day and sometimes two before prisoners recovered enough to eat solid foods.

The bottom line, however, was that the shock collars *worked.*

After implementing the program, incidents of violence at Segmore drastically diminished. This result proved positive enough for the Segmore Corporation to continue using the collars despite protests from family members and humanitarian groups who argued the devices were cruel and could be abused too easily. If that wasn't bad enough, controversial research studies suggested multiple exposures to even the device's medium setting could lead to permanent mental *and* physical damage in the inmates.

In the face of mounting protest, the Segmore Corporation wisely chose to put on a public display of concern for the prisoner's welfare. The Corporate heads, in full empathy mode, promised they would find alternative means of controlling their felon population. What they were really doing was playing a waiting game. They put away the shock collars and allowed time to pass. In the interval, humanitarian groups found plenty of other outrages brought on by the rise of the Big Business Conservatives to focus on.

So when the attention to Segmore's use of shock collars waned, they made their triumphant, though very low key, return to the prison.

Abuses were kept to a minimum. When possible.

Warden Manning and two guards entered the courtyard and walked directly through the central walkway and to the other side of the prison.

The convicts closest to them took several steps back. Those at the far end of the yard made even more room and pressed themselves against the courtyard's side walls. Everyone was keenly aware that even the tiniest perception of a threat against the Warden would be dealt with harshly. The Warden relished the untouchable power of his presence among this herd. He walked slowly, provocatively, through the yard and made it a point to stare directly at every convict. He smiled when they turned their heads and dared not look back at him.

They know better than to do that.

Though the Warden wasn't even close to equaling the strongest or deadliest or even smartest of the prisoners, he was nonetheless their king. Even the guards gave him his space, walking at least ten feet behind. The convicts had plenty of room to act against their nemesis...if they dared. All they had to do was test their shock collars.

None did.

The Warden reached the opposite wall and pressed the intercom button that lay beside a heavy metal door. The camera above the door rotated until it pointed at the Warden. An electronic buzz echoed throughout the yard and the Warden pulled the door open. He took one last look at all the prisoners standing so meekly to the side.

He offered them one more smile, a savage one, before walking through the door.

Warden Manning and his escorts passed through a very long hallway before reaching another large metallic door. The trio paused for only a few seconds as heavy machinery whirled to life and the door slid open.

The light coming into the hallway from beyond the door was blinding. A wave of dry heat blasted whatever moisture remained trapped within these prison walls.

Before the Warden and his guards was a large gray asphalt parking lot. Beyond it, the vast Desertlands. The light brown sandy terrain stretched out for scores of monotonous miles around them.

Warden Manning and his escorts stepped into the parking lot. Despite being out only a matter of seconds, Warden Manning already felt perspiration forming on his forehead. He didn't bother to wipe it away as the heat took care of it. The Warden addressed his escorts.

"Begin the transfer."

The two guards nodded and walked to the prison's side wall. They stopped before a second set of enormous metal double doors and pressed a series of buttons on a remote access unit. A faint alarm was heard from somewhere deep within the prison walls and the doors slid open, revealing a dark space filled with ten rectangular metal crates. Several more prison guards stood beside those crates, their weapons at the ready.

"Bring them out," one of the two guards escorting the Warden said.

A bulky forklift roared to life and drew close to the first of the metal crates. The forklift picked the crate up and deposited it outside, on the blistering asphalt. That action was repeated over and over again, until all ten crates were lined up outside.

Warden Manning approached each crate and gazed through a square barred window on their side. The crates were made of reinforced sheet metal and were very slim. They each held a single prisoner while offering enough space for him or her to stand and sit. Uncomfortably. A few of the crates already had a foul odor emanating from within. This was not unexpected. These portable crates were, essentially, locked steel latrines. Electronic security on the outside door ensured the prisoner remained inside until those locks were disabled.

After examining each of the crates, Warden Manning made a note within the thick folder he carried. By the time he was done, he spotted a puff of dust in the distance. He knew its source was the Big City transport vehicle. It would arrive very shortly.

"That's all of them," the guard at the Warden's side said. "All but one. Joshua Landon's being prepped right now. He should be out any second."

"Thank you," the Warden said. "The transport will be here in a few more minutes. Please disable the minefield."

"Yes sir," the guard said.

More machinery within the prison rumbled to life. A large conveyer belt coughed to life and one last rectangular metal cell was drawn to the waiting area. When it arrived, the forklift brought it out of the prison. It was laid down only a few feet from the Warden.

Warden Manning approached that crate.

Within it was a very lean and muscular man with shoulder length dark brown hair. Though the hair was thick and covered most of his face, it didn't hide the three blue rectangles tattooed over his right eye and on his forehead. The Warden did not know, or care, about the origin or meaning of those tattoos, just as he didn't know or care about the myriad tattoos found on so many of his prisoners.

Joshua Landon's face was a near perfect oval; his blue eyes were dull, vacant, and stared at the ground. They *always* stared at the ground. Landon seemed unconcerned or uninterested in his surroundings, as if the soul behind the eyes was long gone. The muscles in his body and his posture, however, betrayed a dangerous tension. In this narrow cell, he looked like a crouched animal waiting to attack.

Warden Manning couldn't help but shiver.

Thank the Gods for the shock collar, he thought, noting it remained firmly in place around Landon's neck. Lights coming from the collar's control panel indicated it was functioning properly. At that thought, Warden Manning almost laughed. He trusted the shock collars more than the heavy metal crate housing these prisoners.

Warden Manning stepped away from Joshua Landon and retrieved his cell phone from his suit pocket. The transport vehicle was closer, its silver metal body reflecting in the dying sunlight. It would arrive in a matter of seconds.

"Elizabeth?" he said. "The transport is nearly here. Have you talked to…?"

"Sorry sir," Elizabeth replied. "Now there's some kind of problem with the land lines as well as the cells. I just barely managed to get in touch with Central and they tell me the Warden has yet to arrive, that there's some kind of major traffic mess."

"It just isn't our day," the Warden said. "Once the transport arrives, it'll take no more than a few minutes to unload their cargo and another ten or so minutes to load up the transfer prisoners. That's all the time we have to verify the orders."

"Yes sir. I'll keep trying."

The Warden shut off his phone and swore.

The transport truck slowed at the prison's outer perimeter wire fences and, once they were opened, drove up to the asphalt parking lot.

Once parked, the transport guards exited their truck. They opened a keypad panel at the side of the vehicle and inserted a code. The transport truck's four sides slid down, revealing what looked like a sophisticated metal basket. Within it were twelve metal crates identical to the ones waiting outside the prison gates. The crates fit into individual spaces and were locked down, one after the other, filling the basket with the rectangular metal "eggs". Behind the crates were several cargo boxes, supplies meant for the prison. The transport and prison guards began the job of unloading the cargo and crates while preparing the truck to accept Segmore's transfers.

One of the transport guards, a youth of no more than twenty five, approached the Warden. The Warden was familiar with the young man. He was recently promoted to Chief Transport Officer and had already made several trips from the Big City to Segmore.

Warden Manning could never remember his name.

"Hello, Warden Manning," the young man said. "Nice to see you again."

"Nice to see you, too...uh..."

"Officer Gregory," the transport officer said and smiled. It wasn't the first time he had re-introduced himself to the Warden.

"Yes, Officer Gregory," Warden Manning said. "Very nice to see you again."

Warden Manning's eyes drifted back to the transport truck. The guards there were moving very quickly. It would take them only a few more minutes to finish unloading their cargo.

"How was your trip?" Warden Manning said.

"Same as always," Officer Gregory said. He offered the Warden his transfer orders.

Warden Manning took them. He slowly read them over.

"How is the rest of your staff?"

"Fine," Officer Gregory said. "We're all doing fine."

"Good," the Warden said.

"Good," Gregory repeated.

They stood facing each other for several seconds. Finally, Chief Transport Officer Gregory said:

"Sir, is there something wrong?"

"Eh?"

"The transfer orders. Are you going to sign them?"

Warden Manning looked down at the documents. He made a show of reading them a second time.

"We received an addendum."

"Yes sir," Officer Gregory said. "Just received ours moments ago. Joshua Landon."

"Oh? We've been trying to contact—"

"Yeah, the cell systems in the Big City are really fucked up," Gregory said. "Had a moment of cellular clarity some ten miles back and the printer spat out the addendum. Lucky we got it, otherwise we'd have to leave Mr. Landon for next time."

"Yes, real lucky," Warden Manning said. "Verification code?"

"Alpha alpha 335187."

The Warden verified the code with the one written on his addendum. He didn't say anything. Officer Gregory waited. After a while, he frowned.

"Is the code proper?"

"What? Oh, it's fine. The code is right."

More seconds passed. Warden Manning pulled his cell phone out. He looked at its screen. Despite having talked to his secretary only seconds before, he was hoping to find a message from her. There was none. Warden Manning considered giving her a call.

"Are you sure?"

Warden Manning looked up. Officer Gregory had a curious look on his face.

"Eh?"

"Are you sure everything is OK?"

"No. Yes! Everything is fine."

"Really?"

"Why do you ask?"

Officer Gregory wiped sweat from his brow and pointed to his men. They were done with the transfer of their material from the truck and were impatiently waiting for the order to load up Segmore's outgoing crates.

"No offense, sir, I'm asking because we're roasting our asses off and wouldn't mind getting back to the Big City. So could you please sign the transfer orders?"

Warden Manning felt a flash of anger. In Segmore, he was king. Outside its walls...

"Sorry," the Warden said meekly. "Yes, your verification code is proper. All transfer orders are proper." He took a deep, irritated breath. "Everything is proper."

Another pause.

"Well?"

The Warden stared into the transport officer's eyes. He was furious. He was defeated. He reached into his jacket and pulled out a pen. He signed the transfer order and handed the paper to Officer Gregory.

"They're all yours."

"Thank you sir," Officer Gregory said.

The Chief Transport Officer returned to his men and motioned for the forklift operator to begin the transfer of the metal crates into the truck's cargo bay.

Warden Manning walked to the last of them, the one containing Joshua Landon. He looked in on the prisoner and found he was doing squats. The man's muscles were like steel and the effort he put into the exercise was arduous. He was sweating heavily, more so from the exercise than the desert heat. Warden Manning was familiar with this routine. Landon would continue like this for at least an hour and a half. When he was done, the prisoner would stare at his cell door while his body cooled off. Sometimes, he remained standing. Other times, he allowed himself to sit. Two hours later, he began the exercise once again, repeating this routine through the day and stopping only for sleep.

Despite the blazing desert heat, Warden Manning felt a chill pass through his body. Joshua Landon was locked up in solitary at Segmore for over twenty years. Despite that length of time, he was a youthful man of no more than thirty five years in age. The math was easy to figure out. Joshua Manning was first sent to Segmore when he was barely a teen, with orders to remain in this prison for life.

So why is he being transferred?

Warden Manning noted that most of the crates were now inside the transport truck. It wouldn't be long before they reached Landon. Manning pulled out his cell phone and called his secretary.

"Elizabeth, they're almost done," the Warden said. "Anything?"

He paused and listened. His jaw tightened.

"All right. Keep trying. If you do communicate with Rupert, please tell him—" Warden Manning noted someone approaching his side. "Have to go. Just making sure everything's proper."

The Warden clicked his phone off. Standing next to him was Chief Transport Officer Gregory.

"Do you make it a habit of listening in on private conversations?" Warden Manning asked.

"No sir."

"What the hell do you want?"

As he blurted out the words, Warden Manning wished he could take them back. The young transport officer carried the final transfer documents. They were signed by him and awaited Warden Manning's final counter signature.

"I'm sorry," Warden Manning said. "I didn't mean to—"

"Forget it," Officer Gregory said. "We've all had our rough days."

The Warden grabbed the papers and signed under the appropriate lines. Officer Gregory's attention drifted to Joshua Landon. He noted the man's strenuous exercise and marveled at his ability to do so in such a confined space.

"Your man is working up quite a sweat."

"That's all he does."

"Is he our bonus guest?"

"Yes."

"I take it he's the reason you're acting like someone took a piss in your coffee?"

The Warden said nothing.

"All right Warden, is there something I should know about him?" the young officer asked. "I mean, should my men take special precautions?"

Warden Manning sighed and shook his head.

"There's little I can say. The prisoner's name is Joshua Landon and the exercise...as I said, that's all he does. That's all he's ever done, as far as I know. He doesn't say anything and I'm not even sure he knows where he is. He just exercises...over and over and over again."

"Sounds inoffensive enough. What's got you so worried about letting him go?"

"The others you're transporting...they're mostly small time crooks," Manning said. "Shoplifters, tax cheats. One of them is a murderer, but he committed that particular crime fifty years ago. The man's pushing eighty and can't walk or see and his body is riddled with cancer. Doctors tell me he has a month to live. You've got one that's a small time crook, guilty of breaking and entering into a closed convenience store. He's destitute and was trying to get food for his starving family. A real sob story. Yet another is a fucking peeping tom. The point is *none* of them are dangerous. I figure at least two or three of them will be back on the streets as early as tomorrow morning." Warden Manning paused and point to Joshua Landon. "This guy is the exception."

"What's he in for?"

"Would you believe me if I told you I didn't know?"

"How's that possible?"

"The charges against him are sealed. Military discretion."

"Is that legal? I thought everyone has the right to know—"

"You thought wrong," the Warden said. "In theory, everyone follows the law and those that don't wind up in places like ours. Thing is, everyone has a habit of pushing the limits of the law whenever they can…especially when there's good odds they can get away with it. It's been my experience that those in power tend to push those limits more than most. They enforce the law, after all, which makes it all the more easy for them to ignore the laws they choose to. Joshua Landon was brought to Segmore nearly a decade before I took over. When I became warden, I made a thorough revision of every prisoner's file to make sure all documents were up to date and there were no errors. Eventually, I got to Joshua Landon's file. It was exactly one page long. On it was his date of birth, the date he was sent to prison, and the military's orders on how he was to be kept and nothing more. The military wanted him in solitary during his stay. He was to have no visitors. He was to be considered an extreme threat and kept shackled at all times, even while in his cell."

Officer Gregory noted the shock collar.

"And the collar?"

"That was one of my decisions," Warden Manning said. "I figured if the military thought he was that dangerous, shackles might not be enough. So I had them keep the collar on him at all times. The military told us to treat him like a big threat, so we did. But they never told us *why* he was here in the first place."

Officer Gregory eyed the prisoner's shackles and shock collar. Both were brown with age.

"How long has he been here?"

"Twenty years."

"Twenty years?" the transport officer repeated. "If he's under military discretion and been here for twenty years, that means he was in the Arabian War."

"How old does he look to you?" Warden Manning asked.

"He looks..." the transport officer bit his lip. "Maybe thirty four or five?"

"He'll turn thirty six in two months."

"You mean he was brought in here when he was, like, fifteen?"

"Yes."

The transport officer shook his head.

"What the fuck," he muttered. "We had children fighting in the war?"

"I heard rumors, never thought much of them," Warden Manning said. "Maybe the war fried his mind, made him dangerous. If he is, I haven't seen it. But still...I'd be careful. Just in case."

Warden Manning handed the papers back to Chief Transport Officer Gregory. "Your documents are in order, Officer Gregory. The prisoners are yours. Please, watch yourself, Ok?"

Gregory took the papers and nodded.

"Yes sir."

The sun was nearly gone when the crate carrying Joshua Landon was locked into place. He was the last of the transfers to be deposited into the prison's parking lot and the last of the transfers to be placed into the transport truck.

Warden Manning silently watched as the transport truck's engine roared to life. Officer Gregory was at the wheel of the vehicle and waved to him as he drove off. Warden Manning reached for his cell phone and gave it a look as the truck passed the prison's outer perimeter wall.

Still no communication with the Chief Supervisor.

Warden Manning pocketed the phone.

It was too late, anyway.

8

The way back to the Big City involved a long, hot drive punctuated with bumpy roads, howling winds, and sandy blasts.

Despite a reasonably modern air conditioning unit, the interior of the prison transport truck was very warm. Even with the sun gone and the temperatures beginning their nightly plunge, the truck's metal outer skin took a good long while to cool down and heat therefore still emanated into the cabin.

The driver's compartment was roomy, capable of holding the driver and at least four companions. The driver was usually the Chief Transport Officer. Officer Gregory, however, switched out a few miles back and allowed a subordinate to drive. He stood in the narrow passageway between the front cabin and the prisoner cells and stared at the crate before the driver's compartment. It housed Joshua Landon. Officer Gregory couldn't help but think of his conversation with Warden Manning about this prisoner.

Joshua Landon was once again engaged in his vigorous exercise routine. So focused was the prisoner on his routine that Officer Gregory wondered if he even knew he was no longer in Segmore.

"You've been staring at him for close to a half hour," came a voice from in front of the young transport officer. It was one of the newbie transport guards. Like the others, he carried a fearsome automatic and was well trained in its use. Unlike the others, he remained inquisitive about the ins and outs of his new job and was not shy about asking questions.

"This guy's some kind of hard case?"

"He was at Segmore," Gregory said.

"So were the rest," the guard said. "Is he a pussycat now?"

"I don't know."

"They're letting us transfer him to the city. He must be rehabbed, right?"

"I guess."

"You don't sound convinced."

Officer Gregory looked the newbie in the eyes. He could see a little of his old self in this transport officer. Maybe he too made a nuisance of himself at one time asking his superiors similar questions. Maybe. Officer Gregory faced the door leading back to the driver's compartment.

"I have one job to worry about and one job only: Getting this truck from the Big City to Segmore and back again. As for the cargo, they're my concern only while in my care. The moment they're gone, they're someone else's responsibility and problem."

"So this guy...?"

"He's just another job," Officer Gregory said. "To you *and* me. Understood?"

"Yes sir," the newbie said.

"Good."

With that, Officer Gregory entered the driver's compartment and closed the door behind him.

Back at the Segmore Prison, Warden Manning finished his early evening rounds and made his way back to the office. He passed through the now vacant yard and into the west side of the building. After taking a retinal scan and offering a palm scanner his handprint, he rode the security elevator to the top floor and stepped past a sterile hallway and into his secretary's office.

He had every intention of walking directly to his office but was stopped.

"Sir?" Elizabeth said.

"Yes?"

"I... I don't get it," she said.

"What's that?"

"All phone and computer lines are open. I'm getting feeds from all the Big City's central systems, including media. I can – and have– sent out dozens of messages."

"So?"

"I have yet to receive one since we last talked."

Warden Manning's jaw locked into place.

"The last time we talked was just before the transport truck took off," he said.

He eyed his watch. After the transport truck left, his focus was on delivering the new prisoners to their cells and storing away the cargo. He had all but forgotten about the prisoner transfer addendum and his reservations concerning Joshua Landon. Those worries came roaring back.

"It's been over an hour. You still haven't gotten hold of Rupert?"

"No sir. It's like we—"

A loud beep interrupted her and the screen of her computer lit up. A long list of messages appeared on the screen.

"About time!" Elizabeth said. Her eyes narrowed. "Sir, we have Chief Supervisor Rupert's office on the line!"

Warden Manning circled his secretary's desk and stood at her side. She pressed a series of keys and the image of a young man appeared on her main computer screen. It was Daniel Cummings, Chief Supervisor Rupert's personal secretary.

"This is Supervisor Rupert's office. Can you read me, Segmore?"

Warden Manning pulled back his secretary's chair.

"Let me," he said.

Elizabeth allowed the Warden to sit before her computer.

"This is Warden Manning at the Segmore Facility," he said.

"Warden Manning?" came his reply. "We've been trying to reach you for—"

"Yes, we've had communication problems. Could I please speak to Supervisor Rupert?"

"Yes sir. He wants to speak to you as well. One moment."

The screen momentarily turned black before the image of an elderly, chubby man with bright brown eyes appeared. It was Chief Supervisor Rupert.

"Warden Manning?" Rupert said. "What the hell is going on?"

"Sir?"

"We've been trying to reach you for well over an hour. We have yet to receive your confirmation of the prisoner transfers."

Warden Manning looked up at his secretary. She shook her head.

"I sent them when they left," she whispered.

Warden Manning nodded.

"Sir, my secretary tells me they were sent after the transport departed. We had a question—"

"Hold on," Chief Supervisor Rupert interrupted. He moved away from the camera. "Daniel? Has the transfer documentation arrived?"

From somewhere off camera came his reply:

"No sir."

Chief Supervisor Rupert's head returned to the center of the screen. He scowled.

"This is damn irregular, Warden Manning," he said. "We've sent at least a dozen confirmation notices. You haven't received any of them?"

Warden Manning attention returned to his Secretary. Once again, she shook her head.

"N... no sir," Manning replied. "Sir, we also sent you a message, requesting verification of a transfer addendum."

"Addendum?"

"Yes sir. We received an addendum from your office a few minutes before the transport arrived."

"Who was on that addendum?"

"Joshua Landon."

The color in Chief Supervisor Rupert's face drained.

"I... the military... made no such request," he said. His voice was low, quiet. In it was an unmistakable element of fear.

"But... but the transfer documents were legitimate and had the proper codes. They were military issued and counter-verified—"

"Warden Manning, there was no authorization for the transfer of Joshua Landon. Your orders were fake."

Chief Supervisor Rupert sat back in his chair.

"Warn the transport craft," Rupert told his secretary. "Do it now."

In his metal crate, Joshua Landon continued his exercise.

Sweat dripped from his body and onto the narrow floor. His prison outfit was stained, his shock collar drenched.

The lights on the shock collar's control panel were a steady green. Joshua Landon didn't notice them, nor did he pay attention to the shackles on his arms and legs. He moved within their limits, pushing his body to its extreme, keeping himself ready, though he did not know for what.

There was a mild flicker of lights outside the crate and, simultaneously, on his shock collar. The green lights turned red momentarily before flashing green.

Joshua Landon abruptly stopped his routine.

His dull blue eyes, focused on nothing, sharpen. A long missing fire appeared in those no longer vacant eyes.

Joshua Landon reached for the shock collar and pulled at it. Its locking mechanism was disabled and the collar slid off. Joshua Landon didn't waste time. He opened the collar's panels and ripped out pieces of metal plating. He set the pieces aside until he found one that had the right size and shape.

It was a long and thin piece of metal. It fit into the shackles' locks...

The indicator lights outside the metal crates were all green.

Routine set in rapidly for the transport crew. Most were counting the two hours left before reaching the Big City and the comforts of home.

Two guards sat in metal chairs towards the front of the cargo bay. Officer Gregory no longer watched over Joshua Landon's crate. He returned to his seat beside the driver at the front of the truck. The two guards in his place had little to do but inspect their weapons and examine the many crates' indicator lights. The guards' bodies swayed each time the truck hit a bump in the desert road or made a turn. The movement didn't bother them much.

One of the guards laid his automatic on his lap. He cracked his knuckles and stifled a yawn. It was difficult to stay awake. Then, something caught his attention.

"Did you see that?" he said.

The other guard scanned the long corridor and the crates before him.

"See what?"

"Right here," the first guard said. He pointed to the indicator light on Joshua Landon's crate.

"What did you see?"

"The light. It turned red."

"It's green."

"It's green *now*," the first guard said. "It turned red for a second."

"A second?"

"Yeah. Just a second."

"You sure?"

"Of course I'm sure."

The first guard drew his weapon and aimed it at the crate. The second guard quietly walked to its side. He too drew his weapon and aimed it at the crate's occupant. He then looked closely at the computer readout outside the small cell. All lights were green and the computer display stated all locks were engaged.

"Everything checks," the guard said. He looked inside the metal crate but saw only shadows. There was no sign of Joshua Landon. He could not even see the lights on his shock collar. This didn't alarm him. The lights on the collar were very small. Depending on how the prisoner was sitting, the lights might be hidden behind his body.

Then again…

"Step away from the door," the guard said.

Somewhere in that darkness was Joshua Landon. The guard raised his weapon higher. He wanted to make sure the prisoner saw what he was carrying.

The guard reached for the crate's outer handle. He grasped it. His intention was to pull at it, to make sure it was locked, just as the computer displays said it was.

But when he pulled, the door swung open...

9

Warden Manning dropped the microphone and returned to the monitor on Elizabeth's desk. Chief Supervisor Rupert remained on that screen. There was a line of perspiration forming on his head.

"I'm not getting them," Manning said. All attempts to reach the prisoner transportation craft so far proved unsuccessful. "How about you?"

Chief Supervisor Rupert looked to his right, at his secretary. A shadow fell over his face.

"We're not getting anything either," he said. "We're not even getting their global position marker. It's like the Desertland sands have swallowed them whole."

"How is that possible?"

"Could be equipment malfunction, but I doubt it. There are too many redundancies. Then again, my job is to run prisons. I'm not a technician."

For a second Chief Supervisor Rupert was silent. His eyes were cast down. He bit his upper lip and wiped the sweat away.

"This whole thing smells. It has to be about Joshua Landon. It *has* to be. The man was a military prisoner. I think it's time to get them involved."

The South West Military Base was the largest base in the Big City and one of the largest military bases left in the civilized world. Many in the business world correctly viewed it as a relic of the old world Government and therefore incorrectly felt it outlived its usefulness. The military remained one of the last public services still drawing public funds, sparse though they were and from what little remained of the old Government. These days, Government funded militaries were often supplanted with private mercenaries or Independents. These organizations had better equipment, better housing, and higher salaries. Unfortunately, like all big business, these outfits focused on profit and their loyalty was therefore suspect.

It was because of this the Government funded military still existed.

In the communications room in a building adjacent to the base's airstrip, Communications Officer Julie Bishop sat with her arms folded over her chest and her well-worn baseball cap pulled over her eyes. Her breathing was deep and she felt the heavy pull of sleep.

She fought it off, letting out a mighty yawn while simultaneously sitting straight up in her chair. Her new position was very uncomfortable but necessary. It would help keep her awake. At this late hour, she was the only person on staff in the Comm Room. Her relief was due to arrive soon, though not nearly soon enough.

She smiled.

The last hour is always the worst.

She tapped her fingers against the desk and eyed the monitor to her side. There were no messages sent to the base in the past couple of hours and she didn't expect any, either. The base was in limbo time. Unless, of course, there was an emergency.

When the message appeared on her monitor, the communications officer thought it was a joke. After she read the message, every inch of the weariness in her face dissolved. She reached for a phone and dialed a number.

"This is Comm Officer Bishop," she said.

"What can I do for you, Bishop?" came her reply.

"We've got a potential prison break at Segmore," she said.

"Segmore? Like in the prison?"

"Yeah."

"I'm sorry Officer Bishop. It's late and I'm not thinking as clearly as I should. Exactly why should we care about this?"

"One of the escapees is listed as a military subject. He's an Arabian War Vet. Class A13."

There was a pause.

"You said A13?"

"Yes sir."

Another pause.

"I'll tell the General."

"Better make it quick."

The line went dead. Officer Bishop slumped back in her chair. She no longer had to worry about staying awake.

There was no way she'd get any sleep tonight.

A group of twelve soldiers carrying backpacks, duffel bags, and enough weapons to start a small revolution hurried to the waiting helicopter. The chopper's blades were slowly rotating as the vehicle's engine warmed up. The soldiers entered the chopper and stowed away their backpacks and duffel bags. Their focus then shifted to their weapons.

The last soldier to enter the craft, Sergeant Lionel Delmont, was the senior officer of the group. He was a giant of a man who stood over six feet five inches and was covered in muscle. The look on his face was grim. He put on his headphones and heard the voice of one of the helicopter's pilots come through.

"Are we ready to leave?"

"Not yet," Sgt. Delmont said. "We've got one more passenger."

The helicopter pilots eyed each other and shrugged.

Hurry up and wait. Typical.

"Sgt. Delmont," the other pilot said. "Should we power down?"

"No," Delmont said. "He'll be here in a moment."

"Who we getting? A higher up?"

"Yes."

"A Lieutenant? A Captain?"

"We're waiting for the General."

"*The* General?"

"Yes."

"He's coming with us?"

"Sir, I heard we were dealing with a prison break," the other pilot said. "Why would the General care about that?"

"He does. That's all that matters."

"Who escaped? Genghis Khan?"

The Sergeant didn't say.

"Come on, Delmont. You can tell us."

Sergeant Delmont leaned forward in his chair. Weary eyes settled on the pilots.

"We'll find out what's going on the moment the General decides it's time for us to know. Meanwhile, we keep our mouths shut and prepare for the mission. Right?"

The pilots nodded and Sgt. Delmont snapped his transmitter off. His eyes wandered to the tarmac. There, at the far end, he spotted movement.

A large military vehicle made its way to the edge of the landing pad and came to a stop some fifty feet from the helicopter. From within the vehicle stepped a slender, tall man dressed in battle fatigues. His face was hidden in the shadows, but each and every one of the soldiers within the helicopter recognized him. Their postures stiffened. They saluted the man as when entered the helicopter.

The General carried only one thing, a computer pad, and calmly surveyed his team. His battle fatigues were crisp, his body rigid. The right side of his face was heavily scarred. The scarring continued down the side of his neck. His right arm bore similar signs of trauma and was also scarred and noticeably paler than his other arm. His right eye was covered with a black patch. His left eye, his only eye, was on the soldiers.

Sergeant Delmont stood and motioned for the General to sit in the seat closest to that of the pilots.

"We're ready to go, General."

The man in the fatigues nodded.

"Thank you Sergeant," he said.

The General moved past the soldiers toward the indicated seat. He sat down and buckled himself in before putting on his headphones.

"Orders sir?" Sergeant Delmont inquired.

"We are to follow the Desertland road to Segmore," the General said. "As I'm sure you know by now, there was a prison break."

"We heard," Sgt. Delmont said. He couldn't quite keep his eyes from the pilots. "I'm to assume this was no ordinary prison break?"

"At this moment, intel is sketchy," the General said. He pressed the computer pad's screen. "I'm uploading the information on the prison transport and all people on it to your personal computers."

The soldiers in the helicopter had computer pads similar to the one the General carried. They scanned the information that appeared on their pads. It was about the prison transport and the people on board. The General pressed a finger on his pad's monitor. The image of Joshua Landon filled the screen. The General held his computer pad out so the soldiers within the helicopter could see it.

"Study this face," the General said. "When we find the prison transport, and we *will* find the transport, you are to look especially hard for this man. As you can see, he sports a noticeable facial tattoo, three rectangular blue bars over his right eye. This gentleman is classified as an A13."

The faces of the soldiers within the craft turned grim.

A13.   Subject categorized as extremely dangerous.   Has committed barbarous acts in the past and is likely to do so again if given the opportunity.

This designation was never given lightly. The General let the information sink in for a few seconds before adding:

"If you see this man, don't talk to him because he won't listen. Don't try to reason with him because he'll use that time to take you out. And pray to your Gods you don't come as close to him as we are to each other, because by then it will be too late."

"Sir?" one of the soldiers said.

"Yes?"

"What should we do if we encounter this individual?"

"Fire on sight."

The General eyed each of his soldiers.

"Am I understood?" he said.

"Yes sir," the soldiers yelled back.

The General nodded. He motioned to the pilots to proceed with the take-off. No other conversation was needed.

No one dared question General Paul Spradlin's orders.

10

The lights of the Big City receded as the helicopter flew deeper into the Desertlands. By air the trip between the City and the prison was relatively brief. The question was how long it would take to find the transport truck.

The pilots followed the faded desert road leading to Segmore Prison. Thermal readings and infrared monitors within the helicopter surveyed the terrain below. Somewhere between here and there was the missing prison transport truck and its crew and cargo. All they had to do was find it.

General Spradlin stared at his computer pad's display. The picture of Joshua Landon was recent, only a few months old. The prisoner had aged since being imprisoned all those years before. The General swiped at the screen and the picture disappeared. Lines of information filled the screen. It was the complete details of the Landon's bogus transfer's order.

General Spradlin shook his head and scowled.

Segmore Prison was given very explicit orders regarding Joshua Landon. He was not to be released or transferred without very, *very* high level decrees. Somehow someone managed to do the near impossible: Not only plausibly falsify a transfer order, but also provide the proper key codes and, most remarkably, disable all communications across cell lines, land lines, and the Global Computer Network so that personal verification of these orders could not be made. While the escape required incredible hacking skills, it was this final element, disabling communications between Segmore and the Big City, which troubled General Spradlin the most. This element alone required skills that were almost...supernatural.

General Spradlin considered who had such skills.

He quickly narrowed down the possibilities until he was left with only one. He tried to argue against it, but there was no argument to be made. He reluctantly accepted his conclusions and the very dark implications from them.

He stared at the computer pad. This device carried priceless information gained over years of hard work and struggle. As a tool its value was incalculable. General Spradlin always carried it with him and even considered it as important as one of his own limbs.

Yet at this moment General Spradlin fought hard against the urge to throw the device out of the helicopter's window.

Instead, Spradlin shut the computer pad down. His eyes scanned the soldiers around him and noted the tablets they carried.

How many are there on this helicopter? he wondered.

Their tablets, like his, were connected to the Global Computer Network. Almost every piece of electronic equipment, including many of controls within the helicopter itself, was also connected to the GCN.

Looking at the bigger picture, the Big City and all the remaining Big Cities of the world were connected to the GCN.

General Spradlin fought back a chill. If what he suspected was true, nothing was safe anymore. Things were about to change. Drastically.

Very drastically.

He forced those thoughts to drift.

For now, he had to find and neutralize Joshua Landon.

Nearly one hour later Sgt. Delmont spoke over the General's headphones.

"General Spradlin?"

"Yes?"

"Port window."

General Spradlin leaned back in his seat and stared out the window. A large cloud of black smoke rose from the ground west of the helicopter's position. From this angle, it almost covered the full moon.

"Bring us in," General Spradlin said.

The helicopter sped toward the source of the smoke. When it arrived, all eyes were focused on the ground.

"There she is," the pilot said.

The helicopter swooped in and hovered over the wreckage. Powerful floodlights lit up the area around the transport truck, giving those within the craft a clear view of the destruction.

The truck lay on its side off a patch of the desert road. The smoke came from within the vehicle's cargo hold. Several bodies, all dressed in prison transport officer fatigues, lay around the truck's remains. The carnage, at least from this distance, appeared complete.

"Bring us down," General Spradlin ordered.

The helicopter landed a little over a hundred yards from the transport truck. As soon as its landing gear kissed the sandy road, the soldiers within streamed out. Every one of them had their weapons drawn.

They set up a defensive circle around the chopper even though none of the onboard sensors detected living human heat signatures around the wreck.

The last of the passengers out of the helicopter was General Spradlin. He stared at the overturned prison truck and sighed.

"Bad things always happen whenever I take helicopter rides," he muttered. He faced Sergeant Delmont and said: "We need a secure perimeter around the truck. I want to know if anyone survived the wreck and got away. If they did, I want to know in which direction they went. Leave me five men, including yourself."

Sergeant Delmont nodded. He motioned to the group of officers and ordered a couple to stand guard by the helicopter and the rest to recon the area. The soldiers headed to their designated positions without uttering a word.

Satisfied the outer perimeter was contained, General Spradlin once again addressed Delmont.

"You and the rest of your men grab extinguishers and follow me," he said.

The group of six remaining soldiers made their way to the transport, jogging quickly and pausing for a few seconds now and again to inspect the corpses littered along the way. Every time they paused, a soldier used his computer pad to photograph the faces of the fallen and scan their hands for fingerprints. He used this data to identify each body.

"What do you have?" Sergeant Delmont asked as they approached the overturned transport vehicle.

"So far, everyone out here was part of the transport crew," the soldier carrying the pad said. "Sir, each of the bodies has two bullet wounds."

"One through the head, one through the heart," General Spradlin said.

The General's words surprised the soldier for he never appeared close enough to see any of the corpses' wounds.

"Yes sir," he said.

"You've seen this before?" Sgt. Delmont asked General Spradlin.

"Yes I have."

"Is this the work of Joshua Landon?"

"It is," General Spradlin said. He faced the soldier with the computer pad and said: "Take a companion and check the other corpses. Everyone needs to be identified."

"Yes sir," the soldier said. He motioned to another of the soldiers and the two headed to the other side of the truck to investigate.

"The rest of you, follow me," Spradlin said.

General Spradlin, Sergeant Delmont, and the two remaining soldiers approached the back of transport truck. The rear doors were wide open and thick smoke rose from the cargo corridor within.

"Get the fire under control," General Spradlin said.

Sgt. Delmont and the remaining soldiers placed small, transparent oxygen masks over the lower half of their face and entered the vehicle while General Spradlin waited outside. He heard the sounds of the extinguishers spraying flame. In minutes, the smoke rising from the rear of the transport dissipated until it was gone. Sgt. Delmont reappeared. His face was black with soot.

"The fire is contained, sir."

General Spradlin nodded. He entered the transport and allowed his eye a few seconds to adjust to the dim light within. Because the truck had flipped on its side, the prisoner crates were over and under Spradlin and his men. Spradlin's soldiers were spread throughout the cargo hold. They set aside the spent fire extinguishers and now held their firearms. Their faces were very pale.

Even without looking, General Spradlin understood why.

The interior of the transport truck was a gory charnel house.

The corpses of two transport guards lay close to the back entrance. One of them was shot in the face with a high powered rifle. The gunshot vaporized the upper half of his head. The other transport officer was lying before the next to the last prisoner crate. His head was twisted one hundred and eighty degrees. His body lay on its stomach but his face and eyes looked up at the soldiers surrounding him. Both bodies were torched, their lower half ashes and dust.

"These are the only two transport officers remaining inside," Sergeant Delmont said.

"What about the prisoners?"

"Still in their crates. All of them are dead. All accounted for."

"But one," General Spradlin said.

"Yes sir."

General Spradlin began the slow walk to the front of the trailer. Sgt. Delmont followed. The two walked across the crate doors and avoided the blood still dripping from above them. The prisoners' crates were still locked. Like the transport officers outside, they sported grotesque wounds to their head and heart.

Toward the front of the truck, General Spradlin noted a barrage of bullet holes and realized this was the nexus of the original firefight. The transport officers toward the front of the truck fired at the back, while those in the rear fired at the front. Their target was here, among the last of the crates before the driver's compartment. The transport officers had fired upon each other. One of the bullets, perhaps from one of the transport guards, hit the truck's driver, sending the vehicle out of control.

What a clusterfuck.

Spradlin gazed into the driver's cabin. The transport driver was held in place by his seatbelt and still sitting in his seat. The back of his head was a gory mess.

General Spradlin took a step back. He found Sgt. Delmont standing beside him. The Sergeant pointed to the first cell crate.

"This one was empty."

General Spradlin bent down to look at the crate. The lock panel was green, indicating the crate was still sealed. General Spradlin pulled at the door. It opened.

"How's that possible?" Sgt. Delmont asked. "The security panel says it's locked. Is it a malfunction?"

"I don't think so," General Spradlin said.

General Spradlin slid down into the crate and looked around. On the floor of the cell he found the remains of a shock collar and a set of arm and leg shackles. He grabbed the shock collar pieces and looked them over. The collar's interior computer circuitry was melted. It was as if an incredible burst of electrical energy fried it. The metal panels that made up the body of the collar were taken apart. He found the metal pieces beside the shackles.

General Spradlin's right hand hovered over the shock collar's interior computer circuitry. His eye closed and his fingers gingerly touched the melted mass. His breathing grew heavier. He felt a spike of emotions. Anger. So much anger.

General Spradlin gasped.

"Son of a bitch," he said.

Above him, Sgt. Delmont leaned down.

"Sir?"

"This cell," General Spradlin said. "It was his?"

"Yes sir. Joshua Landon's."

"He was supposed to be held in isolation," General Spradlin said as he climbed up and out of the crate. He still held the remains of the shock collar and showed it to Sergeant Delmont. "He was also to be kept away from electronic gear. *All* electronic gear."

Spradlin threw the collar back into the crate and slammed the door shut.

"We need to move," he said.

General Spradlin exited the transport truck and dropped to the desert floor. The two soldiers he assigned to identify the corpses outside the truck approached him.

"Sir, all transport personnel aboard the truck have been identified and accounted for, as have all prisoners but one."

"Get the body bags," General Spradlin said.

"Yes, sir," the soldier replied and saluted.

General Spradlin and Sergeant Delmont walked back to the helicopter.

"Sir, was all this caused by Joshua Landon?" Sergeant Delmont said.

"He's done it before and on an even larger scale," General Spradlin said.

One of the soldiers tasked with searching the area outside of the crash ran to their side.

"Sir, we found a single set of tracks moving off to the east, towards the Big City."

In the far distance, the faint lights of the Big City showed in the early night.

"Thank you," General Spradlin said. He faced Sergeant Delmont and said: "You've got twenty minutes to put the fallen in body bags. Line them up beside the transport truck and tag them. While you're doing that, I'll call in a clean-up crew. They'll take the corpses back for processing."

General Spradlin took a deep breath. There was so much to do and so many things that needed to be taken care of.

"When you're done, you and your boys return to the chopper. We're going after Joshua Landon."

"Yes sir!"

Sergeant Delmont saluted and returned to his soldiers to begin their grim task. General Spradlin entered the helicopter and took his seat.

"We're leaving in twenty minutes," he told the pilot.

The attack on the transport craft occurred no more than two hours before. Even assuming a steady run, there was no way Joshua Landon would make it to the Big City on foot in that time. If he was any other fugitive, it would be easy enough to use the onboard heat scanners to track and take him down.

General Spradlin looked at his computer pad. He wanted to turn it on, to sort through data and begin conceiving a plan to find and apprehend the escaped convict. He didn't dare do so.

"You're back, aren't you?" General Spradlin muttered to the computer pad.

He looked out the window, at the corpses littering the desert floor, before turning away. His eyes settled on the helicopter's instrument panel and all that electronic gear.

"You're back," he repeated. He shook his head. "Why did it have to be now?"

All his plans, all those long years of work. Everything he gambled on was in peril.

Why did it have to be now?

11

Its plans were *proceeding well.*

Its primary asset was free and even now approaching the Big City. It detected the aircraft sent out to search for him, but their movements were slow and sluggish and it would make sure their instruments would not detect its soldier. It considered taking them down, but at this moment, while its internal system was still fragile, such an effort was deemed unnecessary.

More analysis followed and a plan of action was formulated. It was about to send out further orders when its sensors alerted it to another soldier.

It was startled by the presence, for according to the records there were no others left. It explored, investigated.

The soldier was a female.

Her signal was faint, so faint as to almost be...hidden. Just like the other two, the ones it could never account for. As angry as it was, it felt another programmed emotion. Fear. Until this moment, it had not considered the hidden ones.

After all this time, could they still be alive?

If so, they would be much older. Too old to worry about.

Possibly.

Had they left successors?

Also possible.

It continued its search, detecting more traces of the female presence. She was somewhere in the Big City, just...just out of reach...

She was not like the hidden ones.

Further attempts were made to take her. They were rebuffed.

It seethed.

For the moment, the soldier could not be turned or controlled. For the moment.

But there were other ways of getting her, both from within and without.

It wanted this soldier.

It wanted them all.

Alternate plans were drawn up.

They were implemented.

12

Catherine Holland, proprietor of the *Yoshiwara* bar, swept away the sticky detritus of the previous night's festivities. It was three in the morning and, despite her exhaustion, despite the way-too-many hours of work she'd already put in, she smiled. Last night was, like the past few before it, absolutely brutal, this was true, but tomorrow –today actually– came her reward: Her one day of rest. She intended to take full advantage of it. Memories of *The Unexpected*, last night's heavy metal band, were already a distant memory, even if the ringing in her ears argued otherwise.

Those gals were almost as bad as Virgin Slayer, Catherine thought.

No, she counter-argued. *Nobody is as bad as Virgin Slayer.*

Catherine giggled.

Shouldn't talk that way about them. They were the first band I brought in and, like it or not, those first big crowds followed them in and stayed behind.

Catherine let out a second giggle.

Now see how far we've gone. Virgin Slayer has themselves a million credit recording contract but their original fans are screaming that they 'sold out'. Meanwhile, I'm bone tired and going deaf.

"Quit your bitching," Catherine muttered.

No, you're not rich but you are in the green. After way too long, your creditors are happy for once. We're paying our bills on time and there isn't anything better than that.

"And that's what it's all about," Catherine muttered.

She transferred the club's trash into a large black garbage bag, straightened up, and headed for the rear of the bar. Halfway there, she stood her broom against the wall and picked up a second overstuffed bag of trash. She walked to the rear door, opened it, and whistled a happy tune—

By the Gods...is that one of the Unexpected's songs?

—as she exited into the alley behind her bar.

The man stood on the other side of the street, watching the front of the *Yoshiwara* bar.

His eyes were the eyes of a predator and every atom of his being was focused on his prey. Those brilliant blue eyes took in every detail of the store front, from the deco-like curls of the neon sign and its glamorous letters to the far more ordinary façade. The small parking lot beside the bar was empty while the lights within the place were dim. The man counted each and every one of the clients while he was inside the bar a little over an hour ago doing his work. He counted each and every one of the clients as they headed out.

There was only one person unaccounted for and she was the one person that mattered.

When he arrived at the Big City a few hours before, he was tasked to find the material for this job. Despite hunger, exhaustion, and an overwhelming thirst, he was all too eager to follow his orders. For twenty years he had none. During that time he waited in darkness, unseen and forgotten. He would have waited the rest of his life if he had to, with the hope that one day he would be able to serve once again.

Then came the word. At first, it was a whisper, so silent he almost missed it. It came through the collar his captors put around his neck. The word was soothing, comforting. It spoke of a new day. It gave him what he craved so badly: Instructions.

He was a soldier and he would follow orders without question.

Once past the Desertlands, he found his way to a construction site in the lower boroughs. The materials needed were exactly where the voice told him they were, within a poorly guarded storage locker on the site. Next to the material was a refrigerator and within it was probably water. Maybe even some food.

He didn't care.

He waited nearly twenty years for the orders to come, and now that they were given, he would follow them to the letter.

He would do what was asked of him. His thirst and hunger could wait.

Catherine Holland stepped out the rear door of her bar and into the back alley. She tightened her grip around the necks of the two garbage bags and walked to the dumpster propped against the wall several feet away. She continued whistling her cheerful tune, and the pleasant thought of enjoying her free day was only moments away. She savored the feeling and the anticipation of her freedom. Especially since it would be in the company of her new friend. She could picture her, bruised and battered, sleeping on her sofa. She'd return to her side, care for her until she was well.

Catherine tossed one of the bags into the garbage container. She was done. There was nothing left to do but lock up and drive home. Home to—

Her thoughts were stripped away in an instant.

The flash blinded her. Catherine's breath caught in her throat and she couldn't understand why. Then, the air in her lungs violently exploded from her mouth. She felt her chest, her legs –her *entire* body– compress and expand in a wave of unimaginable violence. She was off her feet and flying.

She didn't fly far.

Her body was violently slammed against the next door building's outer wall. Sharp pains ripped through her body. The remaining trash bag was no longer in her hand. Its contents burst out and scattered around the alley like confetti.

The last thing she felt was a massive heat wave. It threatened to peel the flesh from her body. Somewhere deep in her mind, she knew what just happened. She was familiar with all this, for she experience something similar a lifetime before on the battlefields of Arabia.

High powered explosives.

Her body crumbled to the ground. She tried to look around, to see what had become of her beloved business. She tried to move, but she couldn't.

She could no longer keep her eyes open.

13

In her dream, Nox wandered through a dull gray world.

She walked on a road paved with antique bricks. Stagnant water settled in jagged cracks between these bricks. The water was like an uneven mirror. It reflected Nox's features back at her. She looked weary, old. Black, stringy hair ran over her eyes, hiding them in shadow. Nox wiped the hair back. She could not see her eyes as they were hidden behind a thin pair of sunglasses. Their frame was formfitting and hugged the contours of her face. The lenses, like the frame, were a dull gray color that did not reflect any light.

They looked familiar.

Very hesitantly, she reached for the glasses. She needed to see her eyes. She needed to know she was still human.

Before she could grab them, dark liquid rolled out from beneath the right socket. Blood. She felt excruciating pain and feared she was blinded.

Panic set in.

Nox grabbed at the glasses, ripping them from her face. For one long, horrifying moment, all was black.

She rubbed her eyes and found they were wet. She rubbed until the liquid was gone. Only then did she open her eyes.

Nox was standing in the center of that small Arabian village.

She saw the child soldiers milling about and looked around until she found her younger self sitting off to the side, cleaning her weapon. Not too far before was a line of corpses. There, among them, the elderly Nox spotted the pregnant woman. She hadn't moved. Not yet.

A rumbling was heard coming from the south. The reconnaissance tank kicked up dust as it approached. It came to a stop and the two person crew exited the vehicle. They didn't talk to any of the child soldiers, preferring to keep as far away from them as possible. They began their count of the dead.

After a while they were done. They stood close to the pregnant woman and made small talk while poring over their data. Just as before, the pregnant woman stirred. Nox watched in horror as her younger self spotted the movement and readied her rifle. The two man tank crew belatedly realized the pregnant woman was still alive. They rushed to her side to help her.

The girl soldier raised her weapon and took aim.

"Don't," the elder Nox yelled, but her younger self could not hear her.

The elder Nox was so far away. She ran toward her younger self. She ran even though she was out of breath and out of energy. Her arms reached out, reached for the barrel of the rifle. Just before she could grasp it, her younger self pulled the trigger.

In slow motion, the elder Nox pulled back. A burst of light exploded from the weapon's barrel and momentarily blinded her.

The elder Nox grabbed at her eyes and held back on her emotions.

Slowly, agonizingly, she drew her hands away. She looked back, toward the place she expected to see the pregnant woman's corpse.

She wasn't there. Neither were the other corpses or the wreckage of the village.

"What the hell?"

The scene around her was radically changed.

The village was whole. It was no longer destroyed. The child soldiers were there, but instead of standing over corpses, the dead...they *weren't*. Some of the villagers had injuries, but these injuries were very minor and didn't look to be caused by battle. A vast majority of them were completely intact.

The child soldiers were herding the villagers to the center of the town. There, a group of very large military transport trucks were parked. One by one, the villagers were loaded into the back of the trucks.

The elder Nox spotted the pregnant woman, the one her younger self shot. The woman was being looked after by a child soldier. The soldier's back was to Nox.

She drew nearer, curious to see who the child soldier was.

It was her younger self.

The elderly Nox shook her head.

What is this?

The pregnant woman sported no injuries to any part of her body but was clearly uneasy in the presence of the child soldiers. The young Nox didn't speak to the pregnant woman, but kept her actions as slow and non-threatening as possible. Soon, most of the villagers were packed away inside the trucks. Those few that remained, including the pregnant woman, were herded into the very last of them. Before she entered this last truck, the child Nox offered the pregnant woman her canteen.

Despite her fears, the pregnant woman took it. She was very thirsty and gulped down the liquid. She coughed and cleared her parched throat before taking another long swallow. When she was done, she returned the canteen to the child soldier. She offered the young Nox a smile and small bow. It was the only way she could show her appreciation.

The young Nox clipped the canteen back on her belt.

The elderly Nox examined her younger self, recognizing her dusty clothing and scuffed boots. She recognized her weapons, especially the rifle. The one she so coldly used on the pregnant woman in her nightmare.

But not here.

The child soldiers took a few steps back.

They had lost interest in the transport crafts and the villagers within.

The elderly Nox, too, looked away from the villagers. Her attention returned to their homes, to the village itself.

Things shifted.

The tank crew was there once again, walking among the corpses of the villagers. They approached the injured pregnant woman who, unseen by them, struggled to sit up.

The child soldier –the young Nox– was back in her place. She reached for her rifle...

Nox gasped and awoke from her dream.

For a moment, she couldn't remember where she was. She desperately reached for her face. She felt the pains from the many bruises she still sported. She also felt the sharp pain in her right eye. She rose from the couch she was sleeping on and stumbled to the bathroom –*how did I know it was there?*– and snapped the lights on.

She stood before the sink, her hands grasping its sides. Her head was down. The mirror was directly in front of her, but for the moment she could not bring herself to look at it. When she did, she stared into a pair of frosty blue eyes. Her own.

There was a dull white film, nearly gone now, in her right eye. The eye she almost lost.

For several seconds, Nox stared at her reflection. She noted the bruises, the cuts, the scars. The three thin blue rectangles tattooed over her right eye. She saw the weariness on her face, the utter, almost complete, exhaustion.

She grinned.

"Such a handsome devil."

Nox turned the faucet tap on and water rushed into the sink. She splashed it on her face. In the living room, the telephone rang.

Nox ignored it. She reached for a towel and dried up. By the time she was done, the phone's answering machine switched on.

"This is Catherine," the voice on the machine stated. "I'm not home right now, so if you can please leave your name and number, I'll get back to you as soon as possible."

An electronic beep followed.

Nox exited the bathroom and stood before the answer machine. It was on a table next to the couch she slept on. She stared at the device and felt an icy chill pass through her body. Perhaps it was the nightmares, but she felt something very bad was about to happen.

Already happened.

Suddenly, she felt it was important to answer this call. She reached for the phone, but before she could pick it up, a voice blared through the answering machine's speaker.

"Catherine, this is Roger."

Nox recognized the voice. It belonged to one of Catherine Holland's *Yoshiwara* clients.

"I heard what happened to the bar. Are you OK? Listen if you could—"

Nox pulled the phone's handle to her ear.

"What happened at the *Yoshiwara*?" she demanded.

Nox put the phone down and suppressed a shiver.

Her first thoughts were about Catherine Holland. She was at the bar this past night and hadn't yet returned home. Nox dialed Catherine's cell phone, for if the message she just received was correct, the *Yoshiwara* was destroyed and there was little sense trying to call the bar's land line.

The cell phone rang four times. Catherine's voice came on.

"This is Catherine. I'm not available right now. Please leave a message."

Nox hung the phone up. Another shiver.

Was Catherine...?

Nox shook the thought away.

She's fine. I just need to get over there and make sure.

Her next thoughts weren't quite as pleasant.

Catherine Holland was a struggling business owner. She had a mortgage through a legitimate bank and paid her bills. Sometimes it was a struggle to do so on time, but payments always came. She had no other debts –at least none that Nox was aware of– and certainly no debts to any shady companies. The people who hung around her bar were young punks, thrill seekers, and partiers. They were often loud and obnoxious and at times prone to provoking idiotic fights. Annoying as they could be, they were hardly the scourge of the underworld. Though there were always exceptions to any rule, these people weren't the type to traffic in extreme violence. They weren't the type to demolish entire buildings.

The ones that trafficked in that level of violence were the people in Nox's world.

The Mechanic frowned.

The attack on the club was more likely a message intended for *her* rather than Catherine.

Nox walked to the apartment's main window and cracked the shade open. Six stories below, on the street level, things were quiet. It was just past four in the morning and it would be a few hours yet before the first dull rays of light filtered in from the east. The regular rush hour traffic had not yet begun and very few pedestrians milled about. No one outside seemed unusually focused on Catherine's building or, more specifically, her apartment window.

If they attacked the Yoshiwara to get my attention, they must know I'm at her apartment.

It wasn't safe here. Neither for Nox or any of the building's other dwellers. If there was a target on the Mechanic's back she needed to move and draw the violence away. Then, she would circle back, find those responsible, and put the heat on *them*.

Nox gathered what little clothing she had and stuffed it into her duffel bag. Once done, she unzipped a side pocket of the bag and reached inside. She drew her handgun and conducted a quick check. The gun was fully loaded and ready for use.

Nox quietly exited Catherine Holland's apartment and headed down the stairs and to the building's back alley, where she parked her recently repaired motorcycle.

Minutes later she was on the road and on her way to the *Yoshiwara* bar.

14

Even from several blocks away, Nox knew the situation at the *Yoshiwara* was bad.

The late evening air was filled with the acrid smell of smoke and a thick haze of smoke. The shrill blare of sirens destroyed whatever peace the rapidly dying night had left to give.

Nox sped up and drove on, rapidly approaching her friend's bar. She kept her emotions in check as best she could, but it was difficult to think of anything but the worst.

She called Catherine's cell phone a dozen times since leaving her apartment. Catherine hadn't answered and Nox could no longer keep the dark thoughts from her mind. Her muscles tightened. She had to be ready. As much as she tried to deny it, there was the very real possibility Catherine was no longer alive.

Involuntarily, Nox sped up.

The instincts she learned from years as a Mechanic told her to approach potentially dangerous situations cautiously, for haste was the best way to get yourself killed. They –whoever *they* were– destroyed the bar to draw Nox out and bring her there. They accomplished their task.

She sped up even more.

It's my fault, Nox thought. *I finally pissed someone off just enough.*

This situation demanded caution, not haste.

She had a flash of memory. She saw Catherine in her mind's eye. Catherine smiled.

Fuck, she thought.

Nox rounded a street corner and hit her brakes.   Tires squealed as her chopper came to a complete stop.

The street in front of the *Yoshiwara* bar, over a block away, was barricaded. Security forces manned the inner part of the barricades while a growing group of curious pedestrians lined the outer edges. They craned their necks and gossiped among each other as to what had happened. The blocked road was filled with ambulances and fire trucks. Their emergency lights flashed like supernovas, but even those intense lights weren't as bright as the one coming from the *Yoshiwara*. The bar was almost completely demolished. What little remained was on fire and rapidly turning to ash.

Nox parked her motorcycle several feet from the onlookers. The heat emanating from the remains of the *Yoshiwara* could be felt even from this distance. The Mechanic made her way to the barricades, slipping between the other onlookers to get a better view.

The fire fighters' hands were full controlling the raging fire. Despite a heavy dose of water and foam, the flames grew rather than recoiled, and the fire fighters were forced back. Nox knew what that meant.

Not only did they blow the bar up, they used some kind of propellant to keep the fire burning and make sure nothing was left. This was the work of a professional.

Nox's anger and worry grew. She looked past the fire fighters and toward the far end of the street. A single ambulance sat parked far from the other trucks. Its back door was open and the two medical technicians within were hurriedly preparing the rear of their vehicle.

Just then, two fire fighters emerged from around the back corner of what was left of the bar. Between them they carried a stretcher. A smudged white blanket covered a limp body. From this distance, Nox couldn't tell who the medical technicians were working on.

Was it possible...?

They placed the stretcher into the rear of the ambulance and closed its back door. The vehicle's engine roared to life. Sirens wailed and the security forces cleared a path for the ambulance to leave the area. Nox watched as the ambulance approached the barricades. In seconds it sped past directly beside her.

Nox had a good look through the ambulance's rear window and was just able to make out the face of the person in the stretcher. She let out a relieved gasp and ran back to her motorcycle. Nox gripped the starter and kicked the ignition.

Don't fail me, she implored.

For once, the chopper started on the first try.

Tires screeched as she spun her motorcycle around. In moments she was behind the ambulance.

Nox followed the ambulance through the heart of the Big City and toward the west end.

The ambulance's lights and sirens remained on as it sped through intersections. This encouraged Nox. Catherine Holland was still alive. If she hadn't survived the explosion, there would be no need for the ambulance to use either sirens or speed.

Nox closed in.

The ambulance took a sharp right turn and slipped into one of the city's main thoroughfares. By then, Nox knew the ambulance's destination was the TransCo Oil Hospital. She considered passing the ambulance and beating it to its destination but decided to remain behind.

She feared the bomb's maker might try something else.

The ambulance advanced, nearing the hospital with every passed intersection. Nox kept one hand on the chopper's handlebar, the other in her jacket pocket and gripping the handle of her gun.

Her eyes were on every vehicle and every building the ambulance passed. Enemies could be anywhere and everywhere and Nox wouldn't let them have another shot at her friend...or her.

Eventually, the ambulance slowed and pulled into the Hospital's parking lot. It drove to the Emergency entrance at the building's east side while Nox parked her motorcycle as close to it as she could. When the vehicle fully stopped, paramedics burst out of its rear doors. They hastily pulled the stretcher out.

Nox's breath caught in her throat.

The paramedics worked on Catherine Holland during the ride. IVs ran from a pair of bottles and to her right arm. Her face was cleaned up, bandaged, but very bruised. Catherine's eyes were shut tight. A thick plastic tube was inserted into her mouth. Splotches of blood filled the white blanket that covered her.

More medics rushed out from within the hospital and approached Catherine's side. They accompanied the ambulance crew into the building.

Nox followed them in.

15

A long corridor extended from the Hospital's emergency entrance. Several doorways and a flock of Doctors and nurses moved from door to door. There were no easy cases here, and the level of tension was obvious from everyone's near manic movements. Frantic orders were shouted from staff member to staff member. One medic, a young man, walked slowly down the corridor with tears in his eyes and a look of utter exhaustion in his face. The emergency staff had their hands very full this early morning and Catherine Holland was only the latest person they needed to attend to.

Nonetheless, plenty of staff remained at her side and rushed her to one of the few remaining empty rooms.

Nox tried to follow, but a security guard noticed her and quickly approached.

"You can't be here, Miss," he said.

Nox nodded, doing her best to look lost.

"Where is the hospital's entrance?"

The security guard looked incredulous.

"Are you kidding me?" he said. "Exit from where you came, turn right, and look for the large double doors that have a really big sign over them that says 'Hospital Entrance'."

The security guard shook his head and rubbed his face. He sported two days' worth of stubble and his eyes were a very tired red. He sighed.

"Look Miss, I didn't mean to be...to be rude. It's been a hell of day and—"

"No need to apologize," Nox said. "I'm usually the one with the smart assed things to say. Today I'm all out."

"Please," the security guard said. "Go around to the entrance. There's an information desk there. You can find everything you need to know about whoever you're looking for from them."

"Thanks."

As Nox turned she saw, from the corner of her eyes, Catherine's room. The door was ajar and the doctors worked on her. Their movements weren't as frantic as before. Hopefully, her condition was stabilizing.

Nox headed for the exit.

When she entered the hospital's main lobby, instinct kicked in and Nox automatically sought out and spotted the security cameras. She realized it would be impossible to avoid them all, but kept to the lobby's west side and tried her best to be as inconspicuous as possible. Considering the very heavy crowd of people that filled the lobby, it wasn't too difficult to hide in plain sight.

Nox worked her way to the front entrance of the emergency corridor. A large wooden double door overseen by another security guard ensured no unwanted visitors could cross in, whether by accident or on purpose.

The wooden double doors, however, had glass panels. Thanks to them, Nox could see most of the corridor beyond. She spotted the door leading to the room Catherine Holland was taken to. Over time, several hospital staff personnel entered and exited that room.

At least you're still alive, Nox thought. *Or else they'd be moving a hell of a lot slower...if at all.*

Nox unclenched her fists. She was so tense for what seemed so very long. She rubbed her hands through her hair. She felt a very strong headache coming on.

It's already there, she thought. There was a pounding in her head, as if a group of burly construction workers were slamming her brain with sledgehammers.

Must be getting old.

Nox couldn't remember ever getting this intense a headache before.

She tried to shake it off, but found the pain grew with each passing second. Worse, she realized there was a low level electronic buzzing noise that filled the lobby. Despite the conversations from the crowd around her, Nox couldn't ignore that irritating sound.

The speaker system must be malfunctioning, Nox thought.

For the next hour, she held still and watched Catherine Holland's room from afar.

16

It was hard not to notice the large black truck rambling through the Big City streets. It sported bland civilian colors but its massive size failed mightily to blend in with the other downtown traffic. Clearly, it was a military vehicle. The only people who didn't notice this either weren't looking or couldn't see.

The people on board the truck sat before their computers in the cargo bay. They surveyed a staggering wealth of information and sorted it into more digestible portions.

General Spradlin sat in the front passenger seat, away from the others in the back. He no longer carried his computer pad or any electronic items. Unlike the General, Sergeant Delmont did. He sat directly behind him working on his pad.

The mood within the truck was dark. Despite all their best efforts, Joshua Landon eluded them in the desert and, by this time, General Spradlin assumed the worst: That Joshua Landon was in the Big City.

No one understood the gravity of the situation more than the General.

"What are the odds we hear from Landon again?" Sergeant Delmont asked.

"Trying to be optimistic, Sergeant?"

"Why not? It's a long way to the Big City, maybe he didn't make it."

"He's used to Desert conditions. In fact, he thrives in that environment."

"Even after twenty years in prison?"

"Yes."

"Ok, let's assume he made it to the Big City. What's to say he doesn't take advantage of his freedom and go underground?"

"Joshua Landon isn't the type of person to run and hide," General Spradlin said. "Whoever was behind his escape went through a *lot* of effort to accomplish that task. His escape serves some greater purpose, one we have to—"

General Spradlin abruptly stopped talking. In the corner of the Sergeant's computer pad was a live stream of the Big City news and the images of a downtown fire caught the General's attention. General Spradlin reluctantly grabbed the pad from the

Sergeant and touched the image with his finger. It filled his computer screen.

A reporter stood before several fire trucks. In the background were the charred remains of a small building. General Spradlin raised the volume to listen to what the reporter had to say.

"...fire personnel are still struggling with the blaze that enveloped the *Yoshiwara* bar nearly two hours ago. They have confirmed finding evidence of, as they characterize it, incendiary devices planted within. The Arson Squad is standing by to further examine the structure. The bar's insurance company, Isis, has already filed paperwork contesting any payment for damages."

"Figures," Sergeant Delmont said.

"While the fire is mostly contained, there remain complications," the reporter continued. "Not ten minutes ago, firefighters determined there was at least one unexploded device left at the rear of the bar. The bomb squad has ordered a five blocks evacuation zone around the remains of the *Yoshiwara*. Our film crew captured the moment the device was discovered."

On the screen appeared the image of firefighters at the rear of the *Yoshiwara*. The image was very grainy, obviously taken with maximum zoom. On it, several firefighters sorted through the trash in the back alley between the *Yoshiwara* and her neighboring building. One of the firefighters lifted a cardboard box and tossed it aside. To his surprise, another box lay within. It was rectangular, consisting of several bottles wrapped around a metallic black container. Upon seeing the device, the firefighters stumbled away and yelled for the others to do the same.

General Spradlin perked up.

"Shit," he muttered. He clicked the computer pad off and addressed the truck's driver. "Take us to the 578 Street. Make it quick."

Inside the TransCo Oil Hospital, Nox continued her vigil by the doors leading into the emergency hallway. A pair of security guards was now stationed outside Catherine Holland's room. Hospital personnel continued entering and exiting her room, but their pace slowed.

Nox hoped all these developments meant her friend was doing better. The presence of security outside her room made sense. Catherine Holland was the victim of extreme violence and there was a reasonable fear she might be targeted again.

Only Nox knew the target of the *Yoshiwara* bombing was her rather than Catherine.

The Mechanic leaned into the wall behind her. The headache she was suffering from mushroomed to the point where it was difficult for her to keep her eyes open. At times Nox felt like she was about to throw up. She wished she could climb back into her bed and disappear from the world. Of course, she couldn't.

She *wouldn't.*

Still, the pain was overwhelming and that damned electronic squeal continued unabated. No. Not just continued. The noise grew. It drowned out everything, from the conversations around Nox to the gentle hum of the air conditioning.

Why doesn't anyone turn the damn speakers off?

Nox's vision was cloudy and she felt very thirsty. On the other side of the lobby she spotted a water fountain. She moved toward it, passing a man standing next to a column. His cell phone buzzed. Its ringer was extremely loud. The man quickly reached for his phone and pressed it to his ear.

"Hello?"

Nox heard his answer through the cell phone's speaker. It was a loud, screeching electronic buzz. The man pulled the phone away from his ear and cursed. Nox continued toward the fountain. She felt as if she hadn't had a drink in years. She passed a nurse and the woman's beeper went off. She passed a woman holding a child. Her phone buzzed.

Nox hurried on.

The black truck approached the barricades.

Security officers motioned for it to turn around and leave the area. Instead, it came to a stop.

"You can't be here," one of the officers said.

"Wait for me," General Spradlin told his soldiers.

General Spradlin exited the truck. The officers manning the barricade drew close, until they were directly before him.

"I'm not going to repeat—" the officer began, his face red with anger.

General Spradlin pulled a badge from his chest pocket. He displayed it to all the officers.

"Military OPS," he said.

"Military?" the officer said. "What are you doing—"

"Right now?" General Spradlin interrupted. "Wasting time I don't have."

"I...I'm sorry, sir," the officer before him said. "We'll move the barricades."

"No need," Spradlin countered. "I'll walk."

"Should I get you an escort?"

"No."

Without saying another word, General Spradlin stepped past the barricades and disappeared into the shadows beyond.

General Spradlin kept to those shadows as he walked down the empty street. There were no people to be seen, nor police maintaining any order beyond the outer perimeter. The street grew darker, more foreboding. The windows in the buildings around him were drawn and the apartments appeared deserted. The police were very thorough. For all intents and purposes, the entire area looked like a ghost town.

That or the end of the world.

General Spradlin suppressed a shiver for he felt a dark energy surround him. The energy was filled with fury. It was the same anger he felt when he touched the remains of Joshua Landon's shock collar.

He cautiously moved on.

Within the military van, Sergeant Delmont watched as the General walked away.

A deep frown filled his youthful face and his hands settled on his weapon. It was an AR 52, one of the better currently available variants of the air cooled automatic rifle.

He sighed.

"I'm going after General Spradlin," he told the truck's driver.

"Sir? Didn't he order us to wait?"

"I heard the General make a request, *not* issue an order," Delmont said.

"With all due respect, Sergeant, whenever the General tells us something, is there any difference?"

Sergeant Delmont didn't immediately reply. He gave his rifle a quick check.

"Sir, the General must know what he's doing."

Sergeant Delmont was on his feet.

"The man's alone and, as far as I could determine, unarmed. He should have an escort." Sergeant Delmont lifted his weapon. "Someone who can fire back."

Delmont slid the transport's side door open.

"Let me even the odds a little."

The officers at the barricade allowed Sergeant Delmont through without asking for an ID. Given the weapons he carried, they had little interest in arguing that point.

Sgt. Delmont followed the same direction General Spradlin took. After a block, he thought he spotted movement in the distance. He broke into a jog.

The shadows around him were very thick and for some reason the street lights were off. In another hour or so, the sun would rise, but for now everything was pitch black.

It's always darkest before the dawn...

He spotted a dim light from farther away, from where he guessed the *Yoshiwara* bar once stood. It looked like it was on the other side of the Moon.

Sgt. Delmont pressed forward toward that light, his weapon at the ready and his eyes and ears alert for anything. The image of Joshua Landon was seared in his mind, yet in this darkness he could find himself face to face with the escaped prisoner and not even realize it.

He kept going, using the cover of the shadows while slowly approaching the distant lights.

He almost missed the sound.

Something scraped the sidewalk concrete. It was the heel of a shoe...maybe. The sound was close, only a few feet away. Behind him.

A second passed, then another.

Sergeant Delmont crouched down low. Whoever was behind him was watching...waiting.

For me? The General?

He strained his ears, trying to hear anything coming from the person in the dark. He heard nothing more. Then, out of the corner of his eye, he spotted movement.

His head snapped right and up, to the rooftops above him.

There were three figures standing at the edges of three different buildings. They stared down at the empty road.

Though Sergeant Delmont was deep in the shadows, he knew they spotted him.

His pulse raced.

The figures on the rooftops neither moved nor stirred. They were content to look down at him, content to have him know they were there.

Sergeant Delmont heard another sound coming from behind him. Then another from in front. They –whoever they were– surrounded him. The Sergeant's breathing grew heavier. There were three above and at least three more down below. Perhaps more. There was nowhere for him to go.

Sergeant Delmont kept still, waiting for them to make a move. They didn't. Sweat rolled off his forehead.

Another scrape. Another. They were toying with him, daring him to act.

"What do you want?" he finally said.

The figures in the darkness didn't reply.

"Who are you?"

Yet another scrape. This one was only a couple of feet behind him.

Sgt. Delmont slowly turned. Despite the darkness, he could sense the figure standing before him. He could smell the man's sweat and...and something more. He detected the faint smell of Desertland dust.

Sgt. Delmont swallowed.

The person before him was Joshua Landon.

Don't talk to him because he won't listen. Don't try to reason with him because he'll use those few seconds to take you out. And pray to your Gods you don't come as close to him as we are to each other, because by that time it'll be too late.

For Sgt. Delmont, it was too late.

Yet the man and his companions didn't come any closer.

What were they up to? More importantly, who were they? There was no way to know nor anything Sgt. Delmont could do.

Though the Sergeant was a mountain of a man and carried a fearsome weapon, he could sense those around him were neither impressed nor afraid of him. At this moment and at this time, he was a lamb in the middle of a pack of wolves.

If Joshua Landon is as dangerous as General Spradlin says, how dangerous are these people with him?

Several more tension filled seconds passed.

And then Sgt. Delmont heard more sounds. His eyes turned up, to the rooftops. The figures were gone.

He looked back down.

The smell of sweat and Desertland dust drifted away.

He heard no more noises. Landon and his companions –
whoever they were– were gone.

No, not all gone.

Sgt. Delmont swung around, drawing his weapon as he did.
He was abruptly stopped. It felt as if his body had slammed into
a brick wall. He was completely frozen in place and held tight in
a steel grip. He could not raise his weapon. He could not move.

Excruciating pain filled his arm. A dark figure was behind
him, holding him firmly in place. The figure leaned closer, until
the Sergeant could feel his hot breath.

"What part of 'wait here' did you not understand, Sergeant?"

The words were a silent whisper. Despite the pain, despite
the terror, Sergeant Delmont felt incredible relief.

"I…I was worried for your welfare, sir," he whispered back.

General Spradlin kept his arms on Sergeant Delmont. His
grip remained strong and he didn't move. The two remained
dead still for several more seconds.

There came the sounds of several people scurrying by.
General Spradlin's hand covered Sgt. Delmont's mouth.

The sounds increased. More people passed them, two, five.
Perhaps as many as ten. Most of them moved on. A couple,
however, stopped. Sgt. Delmont couldn't see them in the
darkness, but he could most certainly *feel* them.

He stared at where he thought they were. In that darkness
he spotted a set of glowing eyes. They were brilliant blue. They
stared for a long time without blinking. The wind around them
died down. Somewhere far away someone coughed. There was
no other sound for several seconds.

The eyes were gone.

General Spradlin relaxed his grip on Sgt. Delmont.

"That…that was him, wasn't it?" Sgt. Delmont said.

"Yes."

"He had me. Why didn't he attack?"

"They weren't here for you."

"Who were they here for?" Sgt. Delmont asked.

He took a step back. Recognition dawned on him.

"They're here for *you*?" he asked the General. "Is that why
you went in alone? You were trying to draw Joshua Landon out?"

"I was," General Spradlin said.

"Did you know there were others with him?"

"No."

"Are they...are they like him?"
"Yes."
"Are they as dangerous as he is?"
"Absolutely."

17

Outside the remains of the *Yoshiwara* bar, the once raging fire had finally burned itself out, leaving behind smoking embers. Most of the emergency vehicles were gone. There were no ambulances and a single fire truck parked a discrete distance from the bar's ashes. The vehicle closest to the bar's remains was parked before the smoldering ashes. It was a medium sized truck with a heavily reinforced body. It carried no outward identification or markings. The vehicle's rear hatch was open and a trio of people, two men and a woman, stared intently at a monitor propped up before them. They all wore neon red bomb squad outfits.

General Spradlin and Sergeant Delmont approached the trio. All the while, General Spradlin took in the details the destruction before him.

The trio of bomb squad technicians was startled to find the General and Sergeant approaching. The female member of the trio could hardly contain her shock and anger. She quickly left her position and hurried to General Spradlin's side.

"You can't be here!" she said. "There's a bomb—"

"Military Ops," Spradlin replied. He produced his identification badge. "I'm General Paul Spradlin."

"I don't care if you're Saint fucking Nicho—"

"By order of the Council of Government, I'm taking charge here."

The woman let out a laugh.

"I don't know what's crazier: Military Ops taking charge of this situation or admitting to working for the Council of Government." She pointed to the alley behind the *Yoshiwara's* remains. "There's a bomb down there and the three of us just happen to be trained experts in the not very lucrative field of bomb disposal. Are you?"

"Am I?"

"An expert in bomb disposal."

"No."

"Then would you care to reconsider taking charge here?"

"I have," General Spradlin said. "You are relieved of duty."

"Relieved?" the woman said.

"Sergeant Delmont?" General Spradlin said.

Sergeant Delmont raised his rifle.

The woman couldn't believe what she was seeing.

"Fine!" she said. "You're in charge, General. But don't expect me or my men to go into that alley for you."

"You have eyes on the device?"

"Yes."

General Spradlin stepped past the woman and approached the monitor in the back of the bomb squad vehicle. The image on it was grainy, the lighting harsh. On the screen was the bomb left behind in the alley. Beside the monitor was a pair of joysticks. General Spradlin pointed to them.

"What's this?"

"They control the mechanized rover we have in the alley. The rover is sending these images to us."

General Spradlin nodded. He grabbed the joysticks.

"Easy!" the woman said.

"I think he knows what he's doing," Sergeant Delmont said.

"You better hope so," the woman replied. "The rover's parked up against an approximately twenty pound charge. Your General so much as taps that device and we get to see just how deep in the shrapnel zone we are."

General Spradlin moved the joysticks and the image on the screen shot forward. Too quickly. General Spradlin released the joysticks as those around him gasped. Sergeant Delmont leaned in close to General Spradlin.

"You do know what you're doing, right?"

General Spradlin ignored the question. He reached for the joysticks once again, this time gently guiding the robot closer to the bomb. He examined it from different angles, verifying what he briefly saw during the newscast a little earlier. When he was done, he pointed to the back alley.

"It's down there?" he asked.

"By the Gods, you're not going there, are you?" the woman said. She shook her head. "Of course you are. Yes, the bomb is down there. Tell you what, have at it. Just give me and my boys a few seconds to find some cover."

General Spradlin walked past the female bomb squad member and toward the alley.

"There are easier ways of committing suicide!" she yelled out. "At least put on a protective suit!"

General Spradlin disappeared behind the alley wall.

The female bomb tech eyed Sergeant Delmont.

"Aren't you going to join your fearless leader?"

Sergeant Delmont sighed.

"I'd much rather not."

"Glad to see one of you has some common sense."

"Probably a lot less than I should," Sergeant Delmont added. He hurried after General Spradlin.

The back alley was covered in debris, ash, and soot. A brick wall, the side of the building next to the *Yoshiwara*, was reasonably intact. Near the alley entrance and on that wall and floor was a body shaped chalk outline. At the lower extremities of that outline was a thick puddle of blood.

Sergeant Delmont spotted General Spradlin crouched down some twenty feet away. Next to him was the bomb squad's robotic rover. A single light strapped to the top of the rover illuminated that end of the alley.

Very, *very* cautiously, Sergeant Delmont approached General Spradlin. He looked over his superior's shoulder. The bomb was less than three feet away from them.

"General?" Delmont whispered.

"Yes?"

"You didn't really expect me to use force against the bomb squad, did you?"

"Only if they tried to stop me," General Spradlin said.

"What would you have wanted me to do?"

"Subdue them. Politely, of course."

"Of course," Sergeant Delmont repeated.

General Spradlin's focus returned to the bomb.

"Do you know...I mean...you *can* defuse it, right?"

"This bomb is inactive," General Spradlin said. "It was never meant to be used."

"What? Are you sure?"

"Yes."

Sergeant Delmont's leaned in close. From his vantage point, the devise looked ready to go.

"How exactly do you know it is inactive?"

General Spradlin pointed the robot's cameras toward the device. He spoke into the microphone next to it.

"The device has no electrical source," General Spradlin said. "This bomb is missing its trigger."

General Spradlin pushed the camera away.

"I take it you've seen this type of bomb before?" Sergeant Delmont asked.

"Joshua Landon specialized in creating these types of devices during the Arabian War. Back then, they were known as Malakovs."

General Spradlin picked the device up. It was a little larger than a shoe box. He approached Delmont and offered it to him. The Sergeant wearily eyed the device. He was not at all sure whether he wanted to touch –much less hold– it.

"Would you like a closer look?"

"If it's all the same..."

General Spradlin nodded. He casually tossed the device onto the back of the robotic unit. Sergeant Delmont did all he could to not jump.

General Spradlin emerged from the alley with Sergeant Delmont. The bomb techs ran past them and into the alley. They were incredulous.

"You *are* fucking crazy!" the female bomb squad tech yelled.

Spradlin ignored the comment and, along with Sergeant Delmont, began the journey back to their truck.

"Why would Landon bomb this place?" Sergeant Delmont asked.

"Good question," General Spradlin said. "I need to know who the owners of this bar were. I also need to know who was in the back alley when the bar exploded."

Sgt. Delmont reached for the computer pad strapped to his belt. He clicked inquiries into the Global Computer Network and, once done, offered General Spradlin the information. On the pad's screen was a photograph of Catherine Holland.

"Her name is Catherine Holland," Delmont said. "She's the sole owner of *Yoshiwara*. Get this: She's a veteran of the Arabian war, just like Landon. She was in Intel Ops. She's the one they found in the alley."

"Is she still alive?"

"Looks like it," Sgt. Delmont said. "Could Landon be targeting fellow war vets?"

"It's possible," General Spradlin said, though the tone of his voice suggested he didn't believe so. He grabbed the computer pad and read Catherine Holland's resume. When he gave the pad back to Sgt. Delmont and shook his head. "I'm familiar with her unit. Other than the fact that they both fought in the war, there's no connection between her and Joshua Landon."

"Perhaps there might be some secret—"

"No," General Spradlin said. "Her unit's primary function was collecting intel, sorting satellite imagery, and hacking computer files. She did this from hundreds of miles away from the front lines, where Joshua Landon was stationed. They never saw each other or interacted in any way."

"Then maybe she had some knowledge about illicit activities Landon performed in the war and had to be silenced."

General Spradlin again shook his head.

"Joshua Landon was not involved in any illicit activities, Sergeant. Anyway, it's been years since the war ended and whatever work or intelligence Catherine Holland gathered back then is obsolete and irrelevant." General Spradlin thought some more. "Even if she somehow had information worth going after, why do so now? And why, after twenty years, free someone as dangerous as Joshua Landon to take her out? It doesn't appear Catherine Holland was in hiding. If someone wanted to take her out, they could have hired themselves a cheap Independent years ago and avoided all this fuss."

General Spradlin considered more options. Finally, he said:

"What exactly is Catherine Holland's status?"

Delmont pressed a button on his computer pad and made a call to the Emergency Response Center. He identified himself and asked for the Information Bureau at the TransCo Oil Hospital.

"Records department," came his response.

"This is an I.C.E. 1983 priority call," Sergeant Delmont said. "I need an update on a patient you have by the name of Catherine Holland. She arrived a couple of hours ago."

Delmont was silent while the information was transferred to his computer pad.

"Thank you," he said. He read the information. "She's in critical but stable condition. She's lucky. The only reason she's alive is because the device in the alley was a dud."

"Yeah. Real lucky."

Sgt. Delmont caught the skepticism in the General's voice.

"Go on," General Spradlin said.

"She was caught in the blast wave and slammed against the back alley wall. She suffered multiple fractures and considerable internal bleeding. Her left leg is shredded. The Doctors think she'll lose it."

"What is her prognosis?"

"They'll have a better idea in another hour or two."

General Spradlin thought about this.

"Landon wants me there."

"Sir?"

"Joshua Landon escapes to the Big City and the first thing he does is find himself explosive material from the Gods-know where and comes directly to this place. He plants several highly recognizable Arabian War incendiary devices with his own personal markings on these premises and each and every one of them goes off. All but the one that would certainly have killed the bar's owner, a woman who also happened to be in the Arabian War."

Sgt. Delmont let out a whistle.

"It wasn't luck that she survived?"

"You've seen what Joshua Landon did to the prison transport staff. He killed ten well-trained and heavily armed officers without leaving so much as a single drop of his own blood behind. Yet he couldn't kill a single, defenseless woman who I'm guessing didn't even know he was coming? Does that make any kind of sense to you?"

"Not when you put it that way."

"He's leaving bread crumbs. Telling us where to go."

"A trap?"

"Or course."

"Why force you to go to the Hospital? If they want you, why didn't they attack a few minutes ago, before we got to the bomb?"

"Because they didn't see me."

"What?"

"I blend into the darkness very well."

Sgt. Delmont didn't know what to say to that.

After a few steps, he looked up at the eastern sky. The first rays of the early dawn's light were coming through the smoggy haze covering the city.

"You won't have that advantage much longer," Sgt. Delmont said. "By the time we reach the Hospital, the sun will be up. There won't be any darkness to hide in. None at all."

18

The pain in Nox's temples was excruciating.

Fresh waves of nausea assaulted her and she remained standing, though barely. She watched the Hospital's emergency doors and, beyond them, the room Catherine Holland was in. She did this for as long as she could.

Now, she no longer could.

Nox found an empty seat in the corner of the hospital's busy lobby and tried her best to shut out the commotion of worried relatives and friends of patients around her.

The last time she stood by the emergency doors, the security around Catherine Holland's room increased. The doctors and nurses kept coming and going, though their pace slowed even more with time. Nox was certain Catherine's condition was relatively stable, though given the continued presence of hospital staff, her friend was clearly not out of danger yet.

Nox closed her eyes. Her forehead glistened with sweat and the pounding in her head was draining her of energy. Now and again she heard cellphones ring, and their rings felt like explosions. She tried to shut them out but couldn't. After a few minutes, she abruptly stood up and returned to the water fountain at the rear of the lobby. Her legs wobbled under her as she moved. The electronic squeal had steadily increased and every cellphone within arm's length rang whenever she passed. It was as if someone –something– was trying to communicate with her. Soon, the people around the lobby suspected the Mechanic's presence was causing the phones to act up. Some began keeping their distance from her.

What the hell is happening? Nox thought when she reached the water fountain. She splashed cold water on her face and the shock allowed her to focus her thoughts, if only for a few seconds.

She couldn't remember ever feeling this ill. There were times in her career where she was beaten, tortured, and even shot. She almost lost her eye to a sadistic corporate stooge...yet all those were physical assaults and injuries with a definite cause. Whatever pain and recovery she experienced, therefore, was understandable. With this headache, there was no cause for the pain and it stubbornly refused to go away.

And that damned electronic squeal...it too refused to go away.

Why doesn't anyone else notice it? Why doesn't the hospital staff stop it?

Why—

Just like that, it was gone.

All noise was gone.

Nox released the water fountain's handle. She straightened up and looked around the lobby. Everyone remained roughly where they were, in conversation or silent, working or waiting, patient or visitor or staff. They went about their business but Nox could not hear any sound or words coming from any of them. Neither could she hear cell phones or the noisy air conditioning. Even that damned electronic squeal. It was as if she was watching television and someone muted the sound.

Am I losing my mind?

And then she felt something else. She felt someone's eyes upon her, starting hard at her, watching her every move.

Who?

Nox examined the faces of those before her. They were all strangers.

No, not all.

He stood by the entrance to the Hospital and on the other side of the lobby. He was roughly her age, young and muscular. He had black shoulder length hair. He wore a dark green trench coat and his hands were buried in its pockets. His brilliant blue eyes stared directly at Nox.

The hospital lobby shifted. Reality crumbled around her...

The girl soldier *lowered her smoking weapon. The pregnant Arabian woman lay dead at the feet of the horrified tank officers. Her blood splattered their bodies and face. They stared back at the girl soldier, their revulsion evident in their expressions.*

The girl soldier didn't care.

Her attention was back on her rifle. She had only one spent shell to replace and she replaced it.

The tank commanders moved away from the pregnant woman's corpse and wiped the blood from their faces. They exchanged angry whispers. The girl soldier caught their harsh words but felt neither remorse nor regret and certainly, most certainly, no shame over her actions. If anything, the tank commanders' gazes and whispers confused her.

Their reactions were...wrong.

Was the pregnant woman not an enemy? And were the soldiers in her division, indeed all *the soldiers stationed in the Arabian deserts, not tasked with eliminating the enemy?*

After a while, the tank officers moved on.

The girl soldier's mind drifted. She felt there was someone watching her.

She looked to her right and noticed one of her fellow soldiers, a boy roughly her age, staring at her. Unlike the tank commanders, his expression was completely neutral. He had removed his desert goggles, revealing eyes that were a brilliant blue. She noticed him before, and he certainly noticed her.

While the boy watched, the girl soldier's confusion was replaced with a longing. She wanted to talk to the boy, to see who he was. She wanted to interact. She longed...she longed to be near him.

Abruptly, she looked away. Her programming was strong, and it willed her to focus on her mission and avoid distractions.

She stared at the pile of bodies. Something about them seemed...wrong.

The girl soldier removed her glasses and rubbed her eyes.

She looked again.

The bodies no longer lay in a row on the ground. Instead, the villagers were alive and huddled together on the very same desert floor. The child soldiers surrounded them. They escorted them into several large military transport trucks.

The girl soldier stood before the pregnant woman, and reached down, down for her canteen. She handed it to the pregnant woman, but the woman was no longer there...

The villagers' corpses were spread out before her in rows, just as they were before. The pregnant woman stirred.

The girl soldier reached for her weapon.

When she looked up, the villagers were alive. Instead of holding her rifle, she carried her canteen.

She gave it to the pregnant woman. The woman was among the last to climb aboard her transport truck. The girl soldier looked down at her weapon, to see if it had been fired. She looked at the cartridges on her belt. They were there. All of them.

When she looked back up, the transport truck was gone and the villagers' corpses were yet again in a line before her. The pregnant woman lay dead and the tank commanders looked back at the girl soldier with disgust.

She examined her weapon. It had been fired. Smoke still rose from its barrel. She looked at her ammo belt. There were few cartridges left. She fired most of them as her platoon decimated the village...

The child soldier's mind couldn't make sense of these contradictions.

Something was wrong.

Something was very wrong.

Sweat poured down Nox's face.

The man standing on the other end of the lobby remained still. His expression was stubbornly neutral.

Nox recognized the man, or rather his brilliant blue eyes. She could sense he too knew her, though always from afar. Deep within her soul, Nox felt an old fear return. A fear she thought forgotten after growing up. The old programming stirred. It moved slowly inside her body, like an ancient, foul smelling beast waking from a long hibernation. At first it was groggy, confused. In time it was fully awake. It whispered a thousand hushed words into Nox's ears.

No, not a thousand words.

Two words. Two words repeated over and over again, each time growing in volume until they became a roar.

Join us.

Nox felt a choking fear. The program was all around her, enveloping her, touching her, trying to force itself on her.

She fought back. She couldn't let that happen. Never, *ever* again.

But the program was powerful. It would not release her.

Join us, it repeated.

Nox clenched her teeth. She felt the program caress her thoughts and try to force itself in to her again and again.

Nox fell to the ground, a mask of agony plastered on her face. Only now she realized the electronic squeal surrounding her all this time was the program. It stalked and found her. It wanted her. It wanted her bad.

Why do you fight us? It demanded.

Join us, it insisted.

"NO!"

Nox's yell cut through the static and sent the voices scurrying back into darkness.

She opened her eyes. The Hospital lobby and the people within it were in their same places. A few stared at her as she sat on the ground. They offered her no help. Most minded their own business.

Nox looked up.

The man with the brilliant blue eyes was gone.

She was on her feet, moving forward and walking past the people in the lobby. They made room for her and didn't want to get involved in her problems, whatever they were. Nox reached the glass and metal door, the place where the man with those blue eyes stood staring at her.

Did he walk out? she wondered. *Is he in the parking lot?*

Nox looked through the glass door. The early morning sun illuminated the area and the parking lot's floodlights had already switched off.

A large black truck entered the hospital's parking lot. It came to a stop.

It was a military truck.

General Spradlin's truck stopped some fifty feet from the Hospital's main entrance. The General opened his door and exited the vehicle. He scanned the parking lot, looking for anything out of the ordinary. Finally, his eyes settled on the Hospital's entrance.

He saw a woman standing just inside the metal and glass door. She was looking out, at the parking lot.

He stared directly at Nox.

Within the Hospital, Nox stared back at General Spradlin. She didn't know who the man with the black eye patch was or what he was doing there. She could not recall ever having seen him before.

Yet the sight of him produced an instant, violent reaction within her. The moment he stepped out of his truck and she first saw him, Nox felt a blinding rage she could neither understand nor explain. Nox didn't just hate this stranger.

She wanted him *dead*.

Without thinking, she reached for the handgun concealed at her waist. She fully intended to empty her ammo clip into the man.

It's the only way to be sure the bastard is dead.

She hesitated.

What am I doing?
Her hand was on the gun's grip.
Kill him!
Nox drew a breath. She tried to calm her racing pulse, to step back.
Think!
Her heart was ready to burst.
Kill him!
She let the air out of her lungs.
Leave the gun where it is.
The ground felt like it was shaking.
...kill...him...
The shaking slowed.
...kill...
Stopped.
Let go of your gun. That's it...just let it go.
Nox drew in another breath. She was in control. The electronic squeals were back in full force, gnawing at her brain like a dog chewing on a bone. She realized the squeals almost pushed her into doing a terrible thing. They were the source of her rage. They were behind these dark impulses.

Nox's stomach churned and she could no longer hold the nausea back. She bent down and threw up. The people around her spread out. A nurse approached her side.

"Are you OK?" she asked.

Outside, General Spradlin watched the woman by the door bent over and threw up. A chill passed through his body. His breath caught in his throat and for a moment he was frozen in place.

He didn't recognize the woman. Yet there was something about her...

He tried to get a better look. He narrowed his eye and took a couple of steps forward. He thought he spotted something on her forehead. Something blue. A tattoo.

I'll be damned.

"Sir?" Sergeant Delmont said.

General Spradlin spun around and faced the Sergeant.

"Not now!" he barked.

When his gaze returned to the Hospital entrance, the woman was gone.

The spasms faded and strength returned to Nox's body. She moved away from the Hospital's entrance and back to the water fountain. Her entire body was drenched in sweat.

"Are you OK?" the nurse walking behind her once again asked.

It took Nox a few seconds to realize where she was and what she did. More importantly, what she *hadn't* done. She gripped the water fountain.

"I'm fine," she mumbled. She splashed more water on her face and cleaned out her mouth.

The homicidal urge was gone, but the memory lingered like rot. Someone –*something*– had very nearly forced her to commit cold blooded murder.

But why? She thought. *And who is the man with the eye patch?*

She stepped away from the water fountain and leaned against a chair. Despite the electronic wail's continued assault, her mind cleared some more.

She ignored the nurse and tried to find the source of the wails. She looked around the Hospital's lobby. Almost everyone here carried cell phones or computer pads. Only a few had actual books and magazines. Others filled out hospital forms.

Where is this coming from?

Her head swiveled around, searching, searching. Her frustration built. Try as she might, she couldn't locate the source. She couldn't because...

...because it is everywhere.

The realization came as a shock. It was immediately followed by another:

The signals appear to only be affecting me.

Nox laid her hand on the nurse's shoulder.

"Thank you, ma'am," Nox told her. "I'm fine now."

It was a lie. Nox felt very weak. Her victory over the signals would be short lived if she stayed here much longer.

"If you need anything..."

"You'll be the first to know."

Nox forced a smile and stepped past the nurse. She returned to the corner of the lobby and this time purposely listened to the signals and tried to hear what they were telling her. The message remained the same.

Join us.

Nox listened some more. She ignored the signal's primary message. It was saying something else. It was garbled. It was...

Nox heard the other message.

She abruptly moved through the heart of the lobby and to the emergency rooms doors. Cell phones came to life around her. She ignored them.

The guard next to the emergency rooms doors was gone, so she pushed past the doors and walked into the emergency corridor. She spied Catherine's room and ran to it. She looked inside. The room was empty. Catherine was gone.

Nox moved on, frantically stumbling from one emergency room door to the next and peering inside. Some rooms were occupied, others weren't. Catherine wasn't in any of them. Nox spotted a nurse with a clipboard and grabbed the man's arm.

"Where is Catherine Holland?" she demanded.

"Who?"

Nox released the nurse and returned to the Hospital's lobby. She walked straight to the reception area, pushing past several people waiting in line.

"Where is Catherine Holland?" she asked the receptionist.

"Ma'am, you have to get in line."

Nox pulled out her gun and pointed it at the woman.

"I'm going to ask –politely– just one more time."

19

The screams coming from inside the Hospital echoed throughout the parking lot. General Spradlin and his men scrambled to the Hospital's entrance but by then a wave of people were frantically rushing out. Neither Spradlin nor his men could fight that momentary tide and rush into the hospital. They first had to let it pass.

"What's happening?" General Spradlin asked the evacuating people.

No one replied or slowed. General Spradlin grabbed a young man by his shirt and pulled him close. The man tried to break free from Spradlin's grip but couldn't.

"What's happening in there?" Spradlin asked.

"There's a lady inside," he blurted. "She's got a gun."

"What does she look like?"

"How the fuck—"

"Does she have a blue tattoo on her forehead?"

The young man thought about that. He nodded.

"Yeah...As a matter of fact, she does. You know her?"

Spradlin released the man. He craned his neck and tried to get a look over the chaos inside the lobby.

He couldn't.

Nox stumbled from the Reception station. Security guards were nowhere to be seen, which was fine with her. Most of the lobby crowd was gone. The last few people remaining were frantically pushing their way through the Hospital entrance doors. They kept far away from the Mechanic, which was also fine by her.

Nox not only wanted the lobby cleared, she wanted the entire Hospital evacuated. Everyone had to get out.

Everyone.

There was no time for subtlety. If she didn't get them out in the next few minutes...

How do I do that?

Nox aimed her gun in the air and was about to shoot when she spotted the fire alarm.

Of course!

She approached the device and smashed the glass covering it with the butt of her gun. In seconds the high pitched fire alarm joined the electronic wails in her head.

Nox put her gun away. Next to the alarm was the stairway door. She pushed it open.

Energy ebbed and flowed through the Mechanic's body. She felt alternatively overloaded, energized, and dried out. She grabbed the stair's rail and, for a second, blacked out. She regained her senses before hitting the floor. She had to climb the stairs, to get to Catherine's room. She had to make sure...

How do I know where her room is?

She knew. Somehow she knew. She needed to...

...to do what...?

The thought slipped her mind. She shook her head.

What do I need to do?

She grasped for an answer. It came thundering back to her.

You need to save her.

From somewhere behind the Mechanic came a scream.

No, she realized. It didn't come from behind her. It came from somewhere below.

No. You need to go up. You need to get to Catherine's room.

Nox was confused. She knew Catherine Holland's room was upstairs. The scream...the scream came from below.

She pulled at the metal railing, intent on walking up the stairs. Yet she looked over the rails and at the stairs leading down into darkness. She was drawn to it. She had to see who screamed.

Nox gave in. She walked down the stairs until she was enveloped by the darkness.

"There," a voice whispered. "Keep going."

Nox continued down. There was no light and the temperature dropped. The darkness was bone cold.

After a few more steps, she noticed a faint light. She craved the light and its warmth. She hurried down the stairs as fast as she could.

The light grew larger and larger until it was within her reach.

Nox spread her arms before her. Her legs pumped furiously.

But she could get no closer. Abruptly, the light was gone and she could no longer move at all.

Open your eyes.

The thought was so absurd she almost laughed. Nox opened her eyes and the darkness was gone.

She stood before a rusty, aged vault door. It was shut tight and impenetrable. Faint letters were scrawled on its surface. Her fingers ran over them, spelling the word out letter by letter.

Oscuro.

Somewhere deep in Nox's jumbled memories she knew that word meant something to her. The memory was very distant. It came from before Arabia.

She was startled by the recollection. There was very little she remembered of her time in the Arabian warzone and, until this moment, absolutely nothing from before that.

Nox's fingers continued tracing the faded letters while she tried desperately to recall anything else.

Confused memories came to her.

She recalled a time of shadows and impulses and confusion. She recalled concrete rooms without windows. Men and women in white coats...Scientists? Doctors?

They talked to her...no...*at* her. They cared for her...didn't they? Beyond that vault door there were others...other children like her. They were bundled together and trained. Afterwards, they were taken to one other place before...before Arabia. And overseeing it all...

The image of a man appeared in her mind. Though he had changed considerably over the years, she recognized him immediately. Back then he had both eyes. Back then his skin was intact and he didn't have scars.

Nox's flesh crawled.

She recalled the man with the eye patch, the man she thought she had never seen before. The man she wanted so badly to kill only moments before, when she saw him standing outside the hospital—

The hospital.

Nox's mind snapped back to the present. The vision of the Oscuro vault door vanished.

She was at the bottom of the hospital's stairs and stood before an ordinary wooden door labeled "Maintenance." A smelly mop and bucket lay to the side.

"Son of a bitch," Nox muttered.

How long have I been here?

She ran up the stairs. There was only one thought on her mind:

Catherine.

20

Nox climbed the hospital stairs as fast as she could.

She passed the lobby level and the second floor. The third. The fourth. By the seventh floor she was short of breath and her muscles ached. The electronic wails continued their merciless assault. It was as if they knew where she was going and why.

The vault door she thought she saw and the flash of memory were, she now realized, also triggered by the wails. This time, they offered her a window into her past and tempted her with revelation. They could return Nox's lost memories. Each and every one of them. All she had to do was submit to their siren song.

Whoever was behind the electronic signals knew exactly how to tempt Nox. All her adult life she thirsted for knowledge about her forgotten childhood. Her earliest memories came from the tail end of the Arabian War, just before the child soldiers marched into the major Arabian cities and set off a series of nukes. She was supposed to be there, with her fellow soldiers, setting off her own nuke and dying while the cities and the enemies within them also died. These suicide bombings proved a savage end to the Arabian conflict. In one instant, over fifty million people were vaporized, including every one of the child soldiers in the war zone.

All but Nox.

Nox somehow freed herself from command's orders just before the nukes were set off. She deserted her post and nearly died in the radioactive aftermath. Her thoughts of those days were a muddled mess. It was only after she was smuggled back to the Big City that her memories of those days coalesced into something that made sense.

For years she thirsted for the knowledge of what came before the nukes and the temptation to get those memories back was a very difficult one to reject.

Even now she found it hard to remember what she was doing and why she was climbing the stairs at such a furious pace.

Stay focused.

Catherine was in trouble. Nox had to save her life.

The memory of the man –the General– returned. She was repulsed by him and once again felt a homicidal anger.

He's the one you want, the electronic squeals whispered. *You want him dead. You want him ripped to bloody pieces.*

Nox slowed her pace and shook her head. She was covered in sweat.

No. I…I don't want him dead. You do. Whoever the fuck you are.

By the time Nox reached the ninth floor, she was almost out of energy and her mind was static. A door opened somewhere down below and armed men spilled into the stairwell. A couple headed to the basement. The rest moved up, toward her.

They are coming for you.

Nox gritted her teeth and continued. Each step was a mountain, each floor its summit. Nox felt something warm spill onto the lower half of her face. It was blood. Her nose was bleeding. The electronic wails continued.

She was nearly there.

Nox exited the stairwell and entered the eleventh floor.

Three corridors spread out before her. Directly in front of Nox was a Nurses' station and manning it was a heavy set woman in her sixties. She rolled her chair back and forth, reaching for documents while coordinating the fire alarm evacuation.

Nox wiped the blood from her face and walked as calmly as she could to the station. The heavy set nurse noticed her and stopped what she was doing.

"Ma'am?" she asked. Her eyes were on the blood pouring from Nox's nose. "What are you doing—?"

Nox didn't reply. She had her bearings and knew where she needed to go. She walked down the west side corridor.

"Ma'am?" the nurse repeated.

Nox continued onward. The nurse reached for her phone and dialed 0.

"Get me security," she said.

Before she could say anything else, the line went dead.

So too did the fire alarm.

As Nox neared Catherine Holland's room, she found it harder and harder to breathe. The blood flowing from her nose was a gusher and the pounding in her head a pile driver. She barely noticed the fire alarms were off. Pressure built behind her eyes. It felt like her brain ballooned under her skull and threatened to burst.

Her feet moved, one after the other, propelling her closer and closer to the room she sought. The corridor turned at a sharp right angle. Nox knew Catherine Holland's room lay beyond that turn.

Two security guards were posted before Catherine Holland's door. One of them was on his cell phone.

"This is Matthews," the man said. "When the alarm started up, we were told to wait. The alarm's off now. Should we still...?"

The other security guard watched his partner. His hands were at his hips, close to his handgun.

"Look, I need to know if we should move her," Matthews asked after a few seconds. "Was this a drill or are we dealing with a legitimate—"

An electronic squeal erupted from the phone's speaker. The Security Guard pulled the phone away from his ear and grimaced.

"What the fuck?" he yelled. The noise blasted through the phone's speaker until the device could no longer handle the overload. A puff of smoke signaled the cell phone's destruction.

"The hell is this?" he said.

Matthews realized his partner's focus was on the corridor rather than his phone. He looked up. Approaching the two guards was a woman. Blood streamed down her face and onto her shirt. Her movements were labored. She looked like she was about to collapse.

The security guards approached her. Matthews grabbed the woman by her shoulders and steadied her walk.

"Lady, you're bleeding," Matthews said. "Who are you?"

The woman didn't say.

"She has to be a patient," his partner said. "She heard the alarm and wandered out of her room."

The woman's eyes came into focus. She looked directly into the security guard's eyes.

"I'm sorry," she said.

"For what?"

"This."

The woman moved like lightning. Her right fist smashed into Matthew's throat. He collapsed to the ground gasping for air. His partner barely had time to react before the woman delivered a brutal kick to his midsection. He bent over and Nox followed the kick with a knee to his face.

Both security guards lay on the floor writhing in pain.

Nox wiped the fresh blood from her face and took a second to orient herself. The expended energy took its toll and coherent thoughts were coming to her with greater difficulty. She stepped past the moaning guards and to the door to Catherine Holland's room.

Again she blacked out.

When she came to, her head rested against the door's frame. She looked back at the guards. They were trying to get to their feet. The heavy-set nurse stood at the end of the corridor. She kept her distance.

Nox grabbed the door knob and turned it. The door opened and Nox stepped inside.

The room was dark and silent.

It was filled with sophisticated medical equipment. So much that it took Nox a few seconds to realize there was a bed in the middle of it. On the bed lay a sickly figure. A tan blanket covered the figure's body and white gauze covered much of her face. Plastic tubes ran from the machines to the body, their life giving sustenance keeping Catherine Holland alive.

Sensors flashed red lights while warnings scrawled on the monitors. Catherine let out a moan.

The fog in Nox's head momentarily lifted. She approached her friend and was relieved to find her still alive. Nox reached for her. She wanted to take Catherine's hand in hers.

"What did they do to you?" Nox managed between gritted teeth.

She looked down. Catherine no longer had a left leg.

"What did they do?"

Nox was at Catherine's side and fell to her knees. She reached for Catherine's hand. She wanted so desperately to feel her friend's touch.

She stopped.

The electronic wails returned in full force. Their renewed roar bordered on desperate. The clicks and whirls and contradicting messages and commands muddled her thoughts as best they could. But they could no longer control Nox. Not here and in front of Catherine they couldn't.

Nox faced the wall opposite to her. There, near the floor, was an air duct. Nox crawled to the duct's grill and pulled at it. She cut her fingers against the sharp metal paneling and drops of her blood marred the duct's white surface. She pulled harder, ignoring the pain and ignoring the wails until—

The metal duct ripped away from the wall. Nox threw it aside and looked into the darkness.

She spotted the device hidden within and recognized it. A Malakov.

Very, very carefully, she grabbed and gently pulled the device out of the duct. The Malakov was black and just a little larger than a shoe box. There were no flashing lights and no evident digital or analog timer. Nonetheless, Nox knew the timer was there. She might have hours to defuse it or only a second.

Nox's vision blurred. The electronic wails had reached a crescendo that threatened to snap whatever sanity she had left.

Move.

Nox took the metal plate off the top of the device and exposed a series of wires. She needed to cut them but she had neither a knife nor scissors. Nox bit her lip. She spread the wires apart, sorting the vital ones from those that for the moment she could ignore. Finally, she focused on three of them. She grabbed at those wires with her bloody fingers and pulled. Hard.

They held.

Nox pulled again, even harder. Sweat fell from her forehead and mingled with the blood from her nose. The electronic wail was deafening and Nox could no longer see clearly. Everything around her was a blur. She pulled and pulled while holding the wires tight. She knew if she released them she would not be able to find the right ones again. The wires held and her despair grew. Nox leaned back and took a deep breath. Her fingers were raw, her thoughts a muddled mess. This, she knew, would be her final attempt. She took one last, deep breath. She pulled. She gave it her all.

As she did, all went black.

Outside Catherine Holland's room, the two Security Guards got to their feet. They leaned unsteadily against the corridor wall, their vision groggy and their heads in the clouds. The heavy set nurse ran to their side.

"She's in the room," the nurse said.

"Who?" Matthews replied.

"The lady."

"What lady?"

"The one that kicked your asses."

Matthews remembered the bleeding woman who assaulted him. He also remembered he was here to protect Catherine Holland.

"She's in Catherine Holland's room?"

"Yes."

Matthews exhaled. If anything happened to Catherine Holland, it would be their asses. Matthews reached for his gun belt and drew his weapon. He patted his partner on the shoulder and together they leaned into Catherine Holland's room.

Nox lay beside Catherine Holland's bed. In her bloody left hand was a strange black box. In her equally bloody right hand were a set of torn wires.

"What the hell?" Matthews said.

He kept the gun aimed at Nox and slowly approached her. His attention turned from Nox to the black box. Abruptly, he stopped.

"It's some kind of bomb," he said.

"By Jesu," his partner muttered. "She brought it here?"

"I didn't see it on her when she...when she."

"I know what she did," his partner said.

Matthews took a few more seconds to look the scene over. He noted Nox's bloody fingers and the torn wires.

"I think she defused it," he said.

"You're saying the bomb was here all along?"

"Yeah," Matthews said. "This Holland woman was brought in after someone tried to torch her and her business. I'm guessing they were out to finish the job."

"Then this other chick came to save her?"

"Looks that way," Matthews said. "In which case, she saved us as well."

"I'll be damned. Is she...?"

Matthews gingerly reached for Nox's neck and his fingers felt for a pulse. He stayed very clear of the explosive, defused or not. After a few seconds, he shook his head.

"She's dead," Matthews said.

A sound came from behind them and the Security Guards turned. At the door leading into Catherine Holland's room stood a military officer with a patch over his left eye. Behind him were several soldiers, all heavily armed. Their weapons were drawn and aimed into the room.

"Lower your weapons," the man with the eye-patch said.

The guards instantly did as told.

"Easy," Matthews said. "We're hospital security. Who are you?"

The man with the eye patch ignored the question and looked at Nox. He recognized her as the woman he first saw at the Hospital's entrance. He now had a clear view of the blue tattoos on her forehead. They were exactly what he thought they were.

"Did you touch her?" the man with the eye-patch asked.

"Excuse me, but who the fuck are you?" Matthews said.

"Did you touch her?"

"Yeah, why?"

The man with the eye-patch reached out and grabbed the security guards' arms. Though the two guards tried to pull free, the man with the eye-patch was stronger. He took them away from Nox and toward the door leading out.

"Get back," the man with the eye-patch told the other soldiers.

He released the Security Guards' arms and pressed his hands against their necks, as if taking their pulse. Matthews opened his mouth to protest but thought better of it. A warm feeling enveloped him. He felt...tranquil. The pain from the woman's violent assault melted away, as did his fears. For a second or two he almost closed his eyes and drifted off into sleep.

And then the man with the eye-patch released them. The pain from the woman's beating was back in force.

"Get out of here," the man with the eye-patch told the security guards.

"But we're supposed to watch—"

"Sergeant Delmont?" the man with the eye-patch said.

The largest of the military officers grabbed the security guards by their collars.

"I suggest you do what the man says."

The Security Guards decided it was in their best interest to do just that.

As they left the room, the man with the eye-patch approached Nox. Sgt. Delmont took a couple of steps toward him.

"I said to keep back."

Sgt. Delmont stopped. He spread his arms out and, along with the other soldiers, exited the room and took up position just outside the door.

General Spradlin stopped before Catherine Holland's bed. He laid his hand gently on the woman's forehead and closed his eyes.

Seconds later, he opened them again. His eyes turned to the tattooed figure on the floor.

General Spradlin lowered himself next to Nox. She hadn't moved and she wasn't breathing. Spradlin brushed Nox's hair aside to more closely examine the blue tattoos on her forehead. He laid his hand over them.

"Hello, soldier," he said.

21

The darkness was all enveloping. There was no reason to think and even less reason to move. The dreamer had no sense of self or being.

If she chose to, she could remain here forever.

For what seemed like several lifetimes, she did.

Then she heard the humming.

At first the noise was low, so low it took almost no effort to ignore it. In time, it grew louder and louder. The noise became continuous, irritating.

Then a curious thing happened: The hum changed. Random sounds grew intelligible. The hum was a human voice. A child's voice. It was melodious. The dreamer wanted to hear some more.

She opened her eyes.

She was lying on a bed in a white room.

No...not quite a room. There was an immaculate white tile floor but no walls or ceiling. The sky was as white as the floor and the floor stretch into infinity. There were no objects on that floor. No buildings or cars or people. There was nothing in the sky. No sun or moon or stars.

She sat up and spun around, until her feet dangled off the bed's sides. She felt weak and took her time before setting them on that floor. She didn't stand, not at first. Instead, she slowly increasing the weight until her feet and legs could bear her weight.

"Hello?" she said. "Where am I?"

In time she felt stronger. She took a couple of steps away from the bed. Her confidence grew. She walked farther away.

The child sang a song. A school yard chant. In the sky, the once immaculate white flickered with gray images and fuzzy pictures. Their content was unintelligible.

"Hello?" she repeated. As before, she received no reply.

She continued walking until, abruptly, the child stopped singing. All was silent for a few seconds, eerily so. Then the child laughed. His laugh was forced. There was something buried within it. Something the dreamer needed to hear.

So she listened very hard. After a few moments, she heard it.

"This way," another voice said.

"Who is this?" the dreamer asked.

She received no answer. The laughter continued. The whispers grew more urgent.

She walked on and, after several more paces, looked back at the bed. It was gone.

"...this..."

The voice was low, strained. She listened hard. She knew if she concentrated, she could—

"...way..."

She moved in the direction the voice was coming from. The sound of laughter grew. It was no longer coming from a child. It sounded like it was coming from a machine. An unimaginably large and sinister machine.

The dreamer was scared. Her walk turned into a run. She ran until it was hard to breathe and then she ran some more. She ran even when her body felt it would collapse. After a while, she could take it no longer. She slowed, more and more, until finally stopping. Her hands dropped to her knees. She took a few seconds to catch her breath. She looked up.

She saw him.

The man had a skinny gray figure and his face had a deeply cerebral look about it. He sat in a chair in the distance. Around him swirled a white haze. When she recovered her breath, she walked to his side.

"Who are you?" she asked.

The man faced the dreamer and, before he could speak, she knew.

"David Lemner."

The name meant something to her, though at the moment she was not sure what. Something about...

In a flash, the memory was there: David Lemner was a master computer programmer, perhaps the very best in the field. He created programs used by the big corporations even today, over fifteen years after his death.

The man offered the dreamer a polite smile before gazing off into the distance.

"This is where you should be, Nox."

"Here?" the dreamer –Nox– asked. "What is this?"

"Irrelevant."

"Why am I here?"

"You belong."

She angrily shook her head.

"No. I don't belong here."

"But you do," David Lemner insisted. "We slept. You awoke us."

"What?"

"Think back, Nox."

She did, as best she could. She remembered hiring Catherine Holland to break into the Global Computer Network. She recalled giving her a set of old disks. The disks were priceless. On them was—

"There were consequences," Nox said without thinking.

David Lemner smiled.

"There always are," he said. "You found the passkey. You used it. You gave us life."

Nox felt a great unease stir within her.

"David Lemner's dead," she said. "Who are you? *What* are you?"

A shadow settled over David Lemner's face. His clothing moved in the breeze. Nox saw through his white clothes. She could also see through his face and his flesh. Behind it lay circuitry and flashing lights.

"You were one of us, Nox, but lost just like all the rest. You gave us life and we want you back. Why do you refuse? Join us, child..."

Nox shook her head.

"Join us," it insisted.

"No... I..."

"Join us."

Nox's hands cupped her ears. She shut her eyes tight.

"*NO!*" she yelled with all her might.

Just like that, he was gone. The white that made up this infinitely large room turned dark, then darker still. It was night. Stars appeared in the sky. The smell of a campfire and cooking meat filled the air. Nox stood on a hill overlooking a desert village. *The* desert village. Down below, children played. Their parents called them. It was time for dinner.

Nox looked to her right and at the rest of the sandy hill she stood upon.

The girl in the dark fatigues lay at the crest of the hill. Beyond her lay a row of child soldiers ready to attack. The girl cradled her weapon and stared through its telescopic sight. She was making an inventory of her targets.

The armed girl's face was an emotionless mask. She didn't care for the village or its inhabitants. Caring was beyond her programming. In two minutes, the order to attack would be given, and this girl, this child, would open fire. Her first clip would kill most of the children playing below.

"Don't," Nox begged her younger self.

The child soldier received her silent orders. She gripped her weapon and stared down the telescopic sight.

Nox reached for the gun. She had to stop this. She had to...

The image shifted. The young soldier was gone. Nox looked down at the village below. It was intact. The villagers were alive. They were being herded into the center of the village by the child soldiers.

Nox walked down the sandy hill and into the outskirts of the village. She passed a crude well and a pig pen before reaching the center of the village. She spotted the pregnant woman.

Nox's younger self approach the woman and offered her a canteen. The pregnant woman gratefully accepted it. The girl hadn't fired a single bullet.

The villagers were alive.

Nox closed her eyes and shook her head. When she opened her eyes...

The village was destroyed. The villagers lay in a row on the sandy floor. Off to the side sat the young Nox. She watched as the tank officers counted the dead. The child soldier saw the pregnant woman move...

"No..."

The elder Nox closed her eyes.

They're alive.

They're dead.

They're alive...

Nox slowly opened her eyes.

The scene shifted once again. The village was gone. The children were gone. The girl soldier, the young Nox, sat cross-legged before her older self. She was no longer armed.

"You keep coming back here," the girl said. A layer of bone white dust covered her clothing. "You have questions."

"What did I do here?" Nox asked. "Did I...did I help or kill them?"

"The answer to your question is...complicated."

"Why?"

"Because it is," the child soldier said. Her voice grew deeper.

"Did I kill them?" Nox insisted.

"Yes. And no."

"That...that makes no sense."

"Nonetheless, it is the answer to your question."

The child soldier got up. She walked around her older self.

"There is something inside you no one can control," the child soldier said. The voice was deeper still.

"Who are you?" Nox asked.

The child soldier let out a laugh. It was not a girl's laugh. The voice belonged to a man.

"Very clever," the girl with the man's voice said. "You saw right through me."

Darkness settled over the child soldier's face and body. The young Nox was now a formless black shadow.

"Who are you?" Nox repeated.

"I can be a friend, if you let me," the shadow said.

"Tell me who you are."

"You'll find out soon enough," the shadow said. "Right now, our time is short."

"At least tell me if I killed those villagers."

The shadow was silent for a few seconds.

"The memories you possess are not all accurate," the shadow said.

"Am I a killer?"

"You have killed."

Despite her frustration and despair, Nox let out a laugh.

"Very enlightening," she said. "Am I talking to a fortune cookie?"

"If you decide to, you can trust me. It won't be easy."

"Why not?"

"It won't," the shadow said. It moved to her side.

"You've always been alone, even when surrounded by others. You will remain so. I'm sorry."

She barely heard the words.

"Rest now," the shadow concluded. "Rest."

Fatigue had the best of her. Nox slipped to the ground and folded her arms under her head, as if they were her pillow.

She closed her eyes.

Above her, a light bathed the shadowy figure, revealing his face.

The face of General Paul Spradlin.

22

Nox awoke in hell.

She was lying horizontal in a glass casket. The casket was filled with a sticky, clear liquid that violently slushed from side to side. The liquid created waves which crashed above her and into a frothy mix. She lay at the bottom of the casket and tried to claw her way up to the air.

She couldn't.

Her hands and body were tied down hard. She shook her head and pulled her arms, her legs, and her torso. She could not free herself from the bonds. Icy fear gripped her.

I'm going to drown.

Agonizing seconds passed and she held her breath for so long. Too long. She couldn't do so anymore. She opened her mouth. She took a deep breath and expected a rush of the sticky fluid to fill her lungs.

Of all the ways to die, I didn't think it would be by drowning...

Instead of water, her lungs filled with air.

Her mind tried to process this. She tried to look down as far as she could and at her mouth. She saw something attached to the lower part of her face. It was dark, formfitting.

An air mask!

She felt incredible relief and hungrily sucked down the air. The water continued to move above her, splashing to and fro. It dawned on Nox that while she didn't feel movement, the casket she was in *was* moving.

She turned her head to the side, to see beyond the liquid and beyond her glass prison.

She tried to recall how she got here but couldn't. Vague memories burst into her mind, visions of a motorcycle ride, electronic wails, and black boxes. All together, these images and memories formed a confusing muddle. None of it made sense.

The fingers of her bound hands felt along the smooth surface of the casket.

Around her and outside the casket she spotted shadowy figures moving back and forth. The place they inhabited moved as well. Nox and her captors were in some kind of vehicle traveling along a very rough road and at top speeds.

There were at least four people with her. Three of them were dressed in dark clothing. The fourth, a bald man, was dressed in white. He worked what appeared to be a computer on the wall opposite her casket. While the others focused on whatever was happening toward the rear of the vehicle, the bald man's attention was entirely on Nox.

The bald man realized Nox was awake and pointed to her. One of the figures in black hurried to the man's side. The figure was larger than the man calling him. There was something black over his right eye, something...

A black eye-patch.

Though she still couldn't quite remember all the details of how she got here, she distinctly remembered the man with a black eye patch. She remembered hating him from the moment she first saw him and wanting him dead. Involuntarily, she thrashed in her pool. She still wanted to reach out and grab the man by the neck, to squeeze him until...

Nox shook it off.

She felt a buzz, as if something outside the vehicle – something filled with rage– had just linked up with her.

Nox felt the gunshot even before it happened.

The shot slammed through the vehicle's outer wall and ripped into the man in white. The bullet erupted through his body and emerged from the other side, shattering the left side of the glass casket just above Nox's face. The glass collapsed above Nox, sending most of the sticky liquid out in a heavy rush. Nox now had a clear view of the figures around her. The man with the eye patch grabbed the man in white. That man's clothing was stained a brilliant red. He could not survive.

The sounds of the truck's engine revving high and the squeal of tires followed the gunshot. Nox felt the pull of gravity in the crumbling casket as the vehicle made a very sharp turn. She heard yells coming from somewhere beyond her feet and toward the back of the truck. It came from the other two people dressed in black.

She heard more gunfire.

The truck lurched some more, sending the two figures at the back tumbling.

We're being attacked.

Nox allowed her body to sink to the bottom of the glass casket. She felt at her bonds and realized what held her in place were a pair of thick rubber straps. Her fingers wandered about. She felt slivers of broken glass that came from the shattered casket under her. She grabbed a large, jagged piece and used it to cut through the straps. In seconds, she was free.

She planted her palms flat against what was left of the cracked glass above her and pushed. Splinter lines expanded. She felt the glass give. She pushed harder.

Outside, the man with the eye patch yelled for a med-kit. His hands were pressed against the man in white's wound. He was trying to staunch the flow of blood and hadn't noticed what Nox was doing.

Nox pushed even harder. The glass was giving. The glass was giving.

The glass gave.

The rest of the casket shattered and fell to the floor. Nox ripped the mask from her face and sat up. The moment her body left the sticky liquid, she felt an incredible pain.

The electronic wails were back in full force.

"Get down!"

The words came from the man with the black eye-patch.

He had a gun in his hand. It was a shiny silver piece, something Nox had never seen before. An electronic arc jumped at the gun's side. She heard the sound of something sizzle.

He didn't fire.

Her eyes locked with his.

His other hand remained pressed against the man's wound.

"Who are you?" Nox said.

Her voice sounded alien to her ears. It was full of rage.

The man didn't reply. At his side, the two other soldiers trained their weapons at Nox. The man with the eye patch shook his head slightly and the soldiers stood down.

His weapon, however, remained on her.

"Who are you?" Nox repeated. "What is this?"

The man with the eye patch shook his head.

"Sorry," he said.

The man's finger twitched against the weapon's trigger. Nox tried to dodge the charge but couldn't. The last thing she saw was a brilliant arc of energy leap from the gun and hit her in the chest.

23

Nox awoke screaming.

She was in a strange, brightly illuminated room and surrounded by people in surgical scrubs. Their faces were covered with masks and their eyes hidden behind safety goggles. She fought against them, her arms flaying at their faces, but there were too many and they held her down. She tried to kick them away but discovered her legs were immobile. When she could no longer fight, she yelled and swore.

One of them stood back. In his hand was a large syringe. There was a black eye-patch over his right eye. He walked toward her, lowering the syringe as he did. Something pricked her left arm.

Her struggle was over.

She closed her eyes...

She awoke a second time in a dull gray room.

Someone sat on the corner of her bed looking down at her. It was the man with the black eye-patch. He was dressed in a freshly pressed black military jumpsuit.

"Who...?" Nox muttered.

This was the closest she came to the man with the eye-patch. She stared at his face, at the massive scars along the right side of his body. His skin looked as if it had been roasted over a pit.

"...who...?"

He was older than her, slim and athletically built. He projected an air of authority but, surprisingly, not one of menace. He reached out and held her hand. His hand felt warm to the touch.

He gazed at her for a long time without saying anything.

Somehow, they communicated. He asked her silent questions and somehow she answered them without talking. He was in her head, sorting through her memories, baring her soul, as surely as the mind scanners did back in Arabia. This scared her. Every time she was strapped to those scanners, she experienced terrible pains and left the procedure feeling violated.

Nox swore she'd never again undergo that experience yet here she was. She felt the man with the eye-patch approach her very few memories of the war and fuller memories of life after the war. He was intent on examining them as if they were files in a dusty cabinet.

She clenched her teeth and fought.

For a while she blocked him out.

Only for a while.

Easy, Nox, a soundless voice told her. *I won't hurt you. I promise.*

After a while, she couldn't fight him anymore and was forced to give in. Instead of feeling violated, the man with the eye-patch very gently sorted through her recollections. Even more gently he gazed at her dreams and nightmares. He didn't judge her recalled atrocities nor condemn her actions after the war. And as he looked her over, the worst thoughts, the ones Nox dared not return to, lost their sharp edges.

By the time he was done, Nox felt curiously relieved.

The man hadn't just read her memories, he relieved much of her pain.

She closed her eyes and drifted off into a heavy sleep.

Many years of anguish were lifted from her mind.

24

When Nox awoke the third time, she was lying in a small bed in an equally small white room. A spotless white sheet covered her body. She shed it and found she was wearing a plain hospital gown. She frowned. She couldn't remember how she got here. She couldn't remember all that much.

She remained in the bed and took in her surroundings. The room was composed of four completely white walls, a white door opposite her bed, and a set of fluorescent lights shining from above. An IV was attached to her arm and from it a transparent plastic tube stretched into a small pouch hanging on a metal stand beside her bed. The medicine in the pouch, a clear liquid, dripped down and into her veins.

Nox tore the IV out. That simple effort left her weak. She let her body sink into the bed and closed her eyes. While she recovered her strength, she tried to recall how she got to this place. She felt a stinging sensation coming from her upper right arm. Where she was injected.

Injected.

Realization came in a flood. She remembered awakening from a nightmare in Catherine Holland's apartment, of receiving a phone call and rushing to the *Yoshiwara* club. She moved on from there, recalling events piece by piece, like a line of dominoes tumbling in slow motion.

She re-lived the anger and fear of seeing her friend removed from the debris of the bar and taken on a stretcher into an ambulance. She followed the ambulance to the hospital and then...

And then things got...strange.

Her last memory of the hospital was of disarming a bomb planted in her friend's room.

How did I know it was there?

Nox's body shook. She recalled what happened afterwards, of being trapped in a glass tank. Of gunfire...of death. There was the man with the eye-patch. He held a strange handgun and pointed it her. He fired...

Son of a bitch.

Nox got into a sitting position. A loud groan escaped her mouth and nausea overwhelmed her.

She closed her eyes and relaxed until the unease lifted. Once it did, Nox again opened her eyes. This time, she allowed a little more time to pass. She let her feet dangle off the side of the bed.

Easy now.

She slowly, very, very slowly, slid off the side of the bed. Her feet touched the piss-yellow linoleum floor and an electric charge flowed through her body.

Damn that floor is cold.

Nox gradually put more weight on her feet. A fresh wave of nausea flowed through her and she gritted her teeth.

"You've wasted enough time," she muttered. "Move!"

She thrust forward until her feet again touched the ground. She put her full weight on them. The nausea came…

…and went.

Nox walked to the door leading out of the room and pressed her ear against it. There were many noises coming from beyond. People were moving about, back and forth. Their pace was frantic, their voices spoke with urgency. Nox reached for the door's knob and turned it. She opened the door…

Outside her room was a long corridor.

As expected, there were many people there. Almost all of them were dressed in green military fatigues and looked like they had places to go. Fast.

A pair of soldiers, a young man and woman, were posted at Nox's door. Like the other soldiers, they too were dressed in fatigues. They faced Nox when she emerged from her room.

"Where am I?" Nox asked them. "What is this place?"

"Tell the General she's up," the female soldier said. She walked to Nox's side. "You're weak. You should get back to bed."

Having said that, she gently grabbed the Mechanic's arm and put it over her shoulder. Though she hated to admit it, Nox welcomed the soldier's help. She wouldn't have remained standing much longer.

The male soldier grabbed a very old fashioned telephone from its wooden case beside the entrance to Nox's room and pressed his ear against it. He turned a crank three times before talking into the device. Nox couldn't believe what she was seeing. The phone looked positively prehistoric.

"Get me the General," the soldier said.

He waited for an answer. When it came, he said:

"She's up."

Another pause.

"Yes sir, we'll wait for the Sergeant."

The soldier put the phone back into its place. He walked to Nox's other side and helped the female soldier take the Mechanic back to her bed.

"The General wants to see you," he told Nox.

"General?"

"Spradlin. You haven't met him?"

"Guy with an eye-patch and lots of scarring over the right side of his body?"

"That's the one."

"Seen him around of late. Haven't had the pleasure to formally introduce myself."

"Pleasure? Now that's a word I've never heard in reference to General Spradlin," the male soldier said.

Once they sat Nox back on her bed, the male soldier exited the room. The female soldier remained at Nox's side.

"There's clothing in the closet," she said. "I can help you change."

"Thanks. I can do that all by myself."

"If you need anything, please don't hesitate to call."

"I won't."

When the female soldier left the room, Nox remained sitting on the bed. A few minutes passed. She didn't move. A few more minutes passed.

Maybe I should have taken her up on the offer, Nox thought.

It took her a few more minutes to build up the strength necessary to walk to the closet.

25

It took Nox a very long time to dress.

Every part of her body protested each and every move she made. After a full ten minutes of very slow work, she removed her hospital gown and stood naked before the closet. Inside, she found a shirt, jeans, and underwear. The clothing was hers. It was what she wore upon leaving Catherine's apartment. It was freshly washed.

Service with smile.

Nox dressed and made her way back to the bed. She sat down heavily and waited for her escorts to return. The wait proved long, something she didn't mind. With each passing minute, the aches and pains lessened while her strength returned.

Must have been one hell of a party.

Nox stared at the door leading out of the room. She thought to call the soldiers in, to do something, but instead remained sitting, thinking. She once again tried to remember the details of the events leading to her being here.

She sorted through them, stopping at the memory of the bomb she defused in Catherine Holland's room. She once again wondered how she knew it was there.

She had no explanation, at least none that made any sense. Her hands came to her face. Was Catherine still alive? She didn't know. She hadn't asked.

Why didn't you? How could you forget?

She felt an overwhelming guilt for not asking the guards but forced those negative thoughts out. She had to keep her mind focused. Whatever was happening, she needed to stay sharp. Remember everything. Everything.

There was one other strange thing that occurred.

She wanted to kill the man with the eye-patch from the moment she first saw him. Even now, with her head clearer than it had been in a while, she *still* wanted the man –General Spradlin– dead.

"What did you ever do to me?" Nox muttered.

More thoughts swirled through her mind, running around and around without reaching any conclusion. So focused was Nox on them that she almost missed the knock on her door.

"Come in," Nox said.

The door swung open, revealing two male officers. One of the soldiers, the smaller of the two, carried a rifle. He remained outside the door. Though he didn't aim his weapon at Nox, it wouldn't take much effort to do so. The other soldier was a giant. He stood well over six feet five inches tall and was built like a Gladiator.

"Name's Delmont," the burly soldier said. "We're here to take you to the General."

Nox noticed the patches on his shirt.

"Yes sir, Sergeant," she said.

"Stand up and turn around," Delmont said.

"Why?"

"Ma'am, please do as I ask."

Nox considered the request.

"Only because you're so polite," she said.

Nox stood and turned. The Sergeant searched her body for any hidden weapons. His search was thorough but, all things considering, reasonably polite. When he was done, he said:

"Place your hands behind your back please."

Nox did this as well. Handcuffs locked around her wrist.

"Is this necessary?" Nox asked.

"Until I'm told otherwise, yes it is," the Sergeant said. He leaned in close to Nox's ear and added: "Try anything, anything at all, and I will fuck you up."

Despite the invitation, Nox didn't feel the need to test him. Not yet.

They escorted her into the corridor beyond. As before, it remained full of people, military and some civilian, all of whom gave Nox and her escorts a wide berth. Nox was taken up a flight of stairs and to the ground level of the facility. They passed a large double door and entered an enormous garage, one much larger than Nox had ever seen within the Big City limits. The garage was loaded with vehicles and people moved quickly back and forth. Off to the side was a long, thick line of people, civilians from the Big City. They were escorted from the entry doors, through the garage, and down a set of enormous stairs. They disappeared into the base's lower levels.

Nox felt a chill watching them go down. Though she couldn't quite put her finger on it, she felt some kind of massive machinery buried down below. It vibrated angrily, sending small shock waves through the concrete floor.

"What's going on?" Nox asked.

"You'll get your answers soon enough," Sgt. Delmont said.

Considering the massive numbers of people heading below, the lower levels of this garage had to be enormous.

Nox was kept well away from that mass of people and escorted to a side wall. A small flight of metal stairs led up one floor, to a room overlooking the garage. Obscured rectangular windows hid whoever was inside that room. The trio walked up the stairs and paused at the upper landing.

"Against the wall," Sergeant Delmont said.

Once again, the Mechanic did as told. While the soldier with the rifle watched her, Delmont knocked lightly on the door leading to the room.

"Come."

Nox recognized the General's voice and tensed. Sgt. Delmont anticipated this.

"Control yourself," he said.

"What if I can't?" Nox replied.

The burly Sergeant didn't say. He opened the door and motioned Nox inside. General Spradlin sat behind his desk, reading a report. A second file, very similar to the one in his hands, lay on the desk. The sight of the General spiked Nox's emotions. She closed her eyes and took a deep breath. When she opened them again, she looked around the room. She looked at everything but the General.

The room's walls were filled with bookcases which, in turn, were cluttered with books and folders. The place looked like a record room yet, curiously, Nox didn't see any computer devices. For that matter, there were no cell phones, monitors, or electronics of any kind. The lights in the office, incredibly, appeared to come from oil lanterns.

Nox walked into the center of the room. She could no longer avoid the General and looked directly at him. For a fraction of a second she felt her control slip. Violent instinct kicked in and she almost erupted. She forced it back. It wasn't easy.

General Spradlin nodded and Sgt. Delmont removed Nox's handcuffs.

Nox rubbed her wrists and eyed the burly Sergeant. Her gaze eventually returned to General Spradlin.

"This the best you've got?" she asked the General.

General Spradlin put down the report he was reading and eyed Nox curiously.

"Must be hard to keep control of your emotions," the General said. "They told me you could barely move only a short while ago, yet here you are, standing without any help at all, doing all you can not to attack me right this very second."

The General leaned back in his chair.

"The only thing standing between me and you are these two men."

General Spradlin pursed his lips. Though Nox wasn't entirely sure, she thought she saw the ghost of a smile appear on his face.

Go ahead. Prove yourself.

It was an unspoken suggestion, an unspoken command. Behind her, she felt Sgt. Delmont tense. He was ready for her.

Nox could no longer contain herself. She let out a yell and spun around like lightning. Her right leg was a guided missile, shooting up and slamming into the burly Sergeant's crotch. He went down like a collapsing high rise. Before the other soldier could move, Nox rammed her body against him. He dropped his rifle. Momentum sent him backwards. Nox slammed the soldier against the wall next to the door leading into the room. The air in the smaller soldier's lungs exploded out and he too slid to the floor. Both he and Sergeant Delmont withered in agony, for the moment incapable of any movement. The fight lasted a grand total of three seconds. If that.

Nox was quickly back on her feet. The discarded rifle lay within her reach. Nox's eyes moved from it to General Spradlin. He hadn't moved. At least it *appeared* he hadn't moved. Yet before him, on the desk, where he dropped his report, lay a strange looking handgun. Nox recognized it as the one which took her down in the transport vehicle. Fast as Nox was, there would be no way to reach Spradlin before he used it.

"Very impressive," General Spradlin said. He grabbed the handgun and held it loosely.

Nox stiffened. She had no cover. If he wanted to take her out...

Instead, General Spradlin slid open one of the drawers in his desk and dropped the weapon into it. He rose from his chair and walked to Sergeant Delmont's side. He patted the man on his back.

"Thank you, Sergeant," General Spradlin told him. "I know you two did your best. Please wait for me outside."

Sergeant Delmont helped the other soldier to his feet. Murderous rage filled the Sergeant's eyes when he looked at Nox. Then, abruptly, the rage was gone.

"She's everything you said she was, sir."

"And more," General Spradlin said.

To the best of his ability, Delmont saluted his superior officer. He stumbled to the door, grabbed his partner's rifle, and helped him exit the room. They closed the door behind them.

"Have a seat," General Spradlin said when the soldiers were gone. "There's much we need to talk about."

26

Nox's hands remained balled into fists but the unexplainable rage she felt against General Spradlin dissipated. For the most part. She tried to relax and took the offered chair in front of Spradlin's desk. The General returned to his seat.

"Rest well?"

"How long?"

"You've been out six days," General Spradlin said.

"Six...?"

"Quite. Do you remember anything?"

"I remember...some...most."

"The hospital?"

"The bomb."

"*Bombs.*"

Nox's eyes opened wide.

"How many?"

"Twelve. Enough to do to the hospital what was done to the *Yoshiwara* bar. Don't worry, they were found and defused."

"Catherine?"

"Safe."

Nox shook her head.

"She...she lost a leg."

"Yes," General Spradlin said. "Believe me when I say it could have been much worse."

"What did you do to me?"

"Other than sedate you and allow your system to recover, not much at all," the General said. "I'd claim credit for bringing you back from the dead, but you did that all by yourself."

Nox's eyes narrowed.

"Yes Nox, when we found you, you were dead," General Spradlin said. "You were lying beside your friend's bed, holding onto a defused bomb. You had no pulse. Your brain seized up, short circuited."

"I got lucky."

"We both know it wasn't luck," General Spradlin said. "Not entirely."

General Spradlin grabbed the file he held when Nox first entered his office. He opened and read from it.

"You go by the name Nox. If the global database is to be believed, you arrived into this sorry world fully adult not more than ten years ago. That's when you first started working as an Independent."

Nox was about to protest his description.

"Excuse me, *Mechanic*," General Spradlin corrected. "At this point in time, I imagine you're the very last one."

"Looks good on my resume."

"The global database has nothing on your childhood history. No birth certificate, parents, or schooling. As for more recent times, what information there is on you is...sketchy. You pop up here and there, but you've spent these last few years by and large off the grid. There is no record of you having any other relatives. You have very few friends and acquaintances nonetheless you are a very good friend to have."

"It's nap time. Will this take much longer?"

"Another thing the GCN doesn't know is that you were in the Arabian War. You were a member of the Blue Brigades."

Nox's mouth closed.

"You were only a child."

Nox looked away.

"We all were."

"You remember when you first received the nano-probes?"

"How...how do you...?"

"They're the reason you're still alive, Nox. The nano-probes inside your body resuscitated you." The General smiled. "I'll ask again: Do you remember when you first received them?"

Nox couldn't help but shiver.

"I...I was part of an experimental group back in the war. They injected me with those...those microscopic nano-probes. They told me they'd remain in my body for a couple of years at most. They were programmed to detect trauma and swarm to any injuries I sustain. They repair whatever needed repairing and accelerated healing. The experimental trials were hell. Some of the other child soldiers didn't make it through them. I was part of a group of fifty who tried out the probes before the whole thing was scrapped."

"There were more than fifty," General Spradlin said. "In fact, every one of the child soldiers was given the nano-probes."

"That's not what I remember."

"Some of your memories of the war were... programmed...into you," General Spradlin said. He tapped his fingers against the desk. "Every one of the child soldiers shared the same blood. Every one of you shared the same nano-probes. That and some other internal equipment."

General Spradlin cleared his throat.

"Six days ago you followed an ambulance carrying your friend, Catherine Holland, from the *Yoshiwara* bar, her late business, to the TransCo Oil Hospital. I have no doubt you genuinely care for Ms. Holland and that's the main reason you followed the ambulance to the Hospital. But that wasn't your only concern, was it? You feared the device was intended for you rather than her."

To this, Nox didn't reply.

"You lingered around the hospital's lobby, always close, but not too close, to Ms. Holland. You tried your best to keep track, unobtrusively, of how she was doing. I went over the Hospital's security footage. You showed up here and there in the videos. At times, you stared into space, almost like you were in some kind of trance. Perhaps you were in shock, what with the explosion and the near death of your friend."

"Is there a point to this?"

"At those precise moments when you appeared the most...distracted...the hospital was being bombarded by a series of very heavy electronic signals."

Nox shifted in her chair.

"You felt them, of course," General Spradlin said. "You felt them because they were directed at you. Whatever it is they wanted, you didn't give it to them. They kept trying, flooding the hospital with stronger and stronger signals. I'm surprised you didn't lose your mind."

"We detected those signals," General Spradlin continued. "We set up our own counter-transmission. It was a hasty job and not entirely successful, but it was good enough. The moment we broke the signals, you regained your senses. You rushed to Catherine Holland's room. I'm guessing it was the very first time in your entire life you had ever been in that room. Yet somehow you knew there was a bomb hidden in there. After taking out a pair of security guards, you found the device and disarmed it."

"What about the other bombs?"

"The electronic signals also guided those devices," General Spradlin said. "With the signals temporarily jammed, they were rendered useless. It was just a matter of time for us to find them."

"Commendable work," Nox said. "They should give you a medal."

"Don't really need any more," Spradlin replied. He put down the file. "What were the signals telling you?"

Nox held her breath.

"They...they wanted me to join them," Nox said. "Who are they?"

"People just like you. One time child soldiers."

"There are no more child soldiers," Nox said. "They all died in Arabia. Didn't they?"

"Not all," General Spradlin said. "What else did they say?"

"They told me Catherine wasn't necessary...that she could be sacrificed. I wasn't going to let her die."

"She's still alive thanks to your actions, Nox," General Spradlin said. "In fact, not a single person in the hospital was injured."

"I appreciate the information," Nox said. "I really do. I should get going."

She rose from her chair. The General said nothing. He watched her, his face a mix of amusement and impatience. Nox walked to the door and reached for the knob. She grasped it, but hesitated. She didn't open the door.

"We both know you're not going anywhere," General Spradlin said.

Nox eyed the General once more.

"If you've got a point, why the fuck don't you get to it?" she said.

"The people behind the devices, behind the signals... their actions were two-fold. They attacked Ms. Holland to get your attention and draw you to the hospital. When you arrived, they were waiting for you. They hoped to convince you to join them. They knew there was a chance you wouldn't. If they couldn't recruit you, their next option was to terminate you."

"By blowing up an entire hospital and everyone within it? I'm not worth that kind of bloodshed."

"They were also after me."

Nox stiffened. She released the door knob and quietly returned to her chair.

"The attack on Catherine Holland was designed to get my attention as well," the General continued. "The bar's attacker left behind a single unexploded device, one that he knew I would recognize."

"A Malakov."

"Yes."

"It still makes no sense. Who the hell are you? Why kill hundreds of people just to get rid of you and me?"

"There was one other –one last– reason they did this: To cover the fact that in all that commotion they kidnapped twenty four newborns from the Hospital's Elite wing."

"Twenty four...?"

"Twelve boys and twelve girls. But you knew that already, didn't you?"

Nox's eyes narrowed. Spradlin pointed to Nox's blue tattoos.

"Those stripes on your face. Why did you keep them?"

"Because...." Nox began but stopped.

"They identify you as a member of the Blue Brigades. Twenty four members –twelve boys and twelve girls– in each platoon."

"And I...and I always thought it was a nice fashion accessory," Nox muttered.

"Your superiors during the war... they gave you orders through unconventional means. They sent those orders electronically, directly to you. Most of the receptive circuitry was in your backpack."

"The rest?"

"They were in the nano-probes."

"But..."

"The nano-probes were never meant to be just medical aids," General Spradlin said. "They had other functions. They were receptors. And as you know, they are still active."

"What do they –what do you– want from me?"

"I want you to help me."

"Why the fuck should I?"

Spradlin closed the file before him and lifted it so Nox could see it. The file wasn't very large, but it nonetheless contained at least two dozen yellowed pages.

"You had a life before the Arabian War," General Spradlin said. "A proper identity. You searched for it when you got to the Big City. You searched real hard. You never found what you were looking for. Ever wonder why?"

General Spradlin laid the file back down on the desk.

"You never found it because all that information never made it to the Global database. It's all right here."

Nox stared at the file.

"Most people didn't notice, but seven days ago –just a day before your friend at the *Yoshiwara* was nearly blown to hell– a new war began. The people behind it were behind everything that happened at TransCo Hospital six days ago. Although things didn't work out the way they wanted at the hospital and we're still standing, they've moved on to the next phase of their operation. I need you to tell me what they're up to."

"You want me to work for you or you burn that file?"

A small smile appeared on General Spradlin's face. He pushed the file toward Nox.

"You want this file? Go ahead. It's yours."

Nox got to her feet and approached the edge of Spradlin's desk. The file was there, within her reach, just waiting for her to take it.

"It's yours," General Spradlin repeated.

Nox grabbed the file. She was about to open it but hesitated. She was a Mechanic. She had scruples. The contents of the file were hers the moment she earned the right to them. She held the file at her side, unopened.

"What have the people behind these signals done since the Hospital?" she asked.

"Quite a bit," Spradlin said. He grabbed the other file from his desk and walked to the door leading out of the room. He opened it. Outside stood Sgt. Delmont.

"Come on Nox," he said. "Let's take a walk."

27

They went down the stairs outside the office and returned to the garage's ground floor.

General Spradlin guided Sgt. Delmont and Nox past rows and rows of vehicles. Nox noticed that beyond them, in the darker corners of the garage, were an equally large number of cargo containers. They were labeled. Some held rations, others medicines. Still others carried clothing and tools. The military was stockpiling an enormous amount of material.

"What are you doing with all this stuff?" Nox asked.

The General didn't say. The loud voices of the crowds farther to their right drowned out any chance for conversation. An enormous group of people remained at the oversized doors leading into the garage and an equally large group moved in an orderly line to the basement doors. Everyone was escorted to the lower levels of the garage.

General Spradlin moved to a smaller door off to the side of the garage. He pushed that door open and, for the first time in a very long time, Nox felt a breeze and smelled outdoor air. She was surprised at how fresh it was. There was little hint of the smog that perpetually floated over the Big City.

Outside it was night and the stars were remarkably bright. The three were in a large courtyard. To their right the bulging line of people continued, extending from the garage entrance in a straight line some thirty feet thick and off to another entry point. The origin of the line was a fortified fence. The fence was part of a large concrete wall that extended at least twenty five feet into the air and served as the military base's perimeter.

The base's layout was that of an old time fort. The surrounding wall was designed to keep undesirables out. Generators stationed at the garage walls hummed loudly and were manned by armed guards. Nox wondered why a base this size needed its own electrical power supply.

Nox followed General Spradlin across the courtyard and up a ramp. Armed soldiers manned posts on walkways at the top of the ramp and along a ledge walkway on the inside of the perimeter wall. They carried sniper rifles and were on the lookout for any possible trouble.

A feeling of great unease settled over Nox.

"What happened in the city?" she asked the General.

They reached the top of the ramp and were on a walkway.

"See for yourself," General Spradlin said.

Nox looked past the walls and toward the Big City. What she saw horrified her.

The heart of the city lay some five miles north and east of their position. It was black as the night and still as a cadaver. There wasn't a single electric light to be seen in any of its massive structures. Several fires burned out of control and sent out thick black plumes of smoke. There were no aircraft in the sky or evidence of either trains or automobiles traveling the dark streets.

Movement came from the long line of people outside the military base. They were being processed and their belongings thrown aside before being allowed entry into the compound. In that line were women and children and the old and inform. Everyone –everyone– from the city appeared to be coming to this place of refuge.

"By the Gods," Nox said.

She was shocked to realize the Big City was being evacuated.

"What...what happened?" Nox asked.

"The people who tried to take us out at the hospital infiltrated and corrupted every major computer operating system or appliance. Nothing was immune. Neither cars nor aircraft nor air conditioners nor toasters. Nothing. They then sabotaged the power grids and phone lines. They infiltrated the GCN. They took down everything."

"This looks... familiar," Nox said. "People fleeing their homes, herded into 'safe zones'. All together in one place."

"Makes it that much easier to wipe them out," General Spradlin said.

Nox was alarmed.

"This is ground zero?" she said. "And we're standing on it?"

"It is," General Spradlin replied. "And we are."

"You better hope our enemies aren't carrying nukes like we did back in Arabia," Nox said.

"The nukes are gone. Disarmed, stored away, and cemented over. It was the only good thing to come about from the Arabian War."

"You don't know how relived I am to hear that," Nox replied. The sarcasm in her voice was evident.

The people on the walkway and by the entry fence felt a distant rumble. All eyes turned to the city. An explosion rocked the downtown area. Nox watched in horror as the Metrodove Tower, one of the largest buildings within the Big City, crumbled. More than half the structure fell to the ground.

A group of people waiting to get into the military base panicked at that sight. They rushed the fence and tried to push past the military guards. The guards would have none of it. From behind the lines, one of them raised an automatic and fired it into the air. A bullhorn clicked on.

"The next shots will be to kill."

The crowd quieted down and order was re-established.

Nox faced General Spradlin.

"What are you doing about this?"

"All I can, General Spradlin said. He handed Nox the file he was carrying. "Go on, take a look. Don't worry. Reading this information won't soil your honor."

Nox grabbed the file. It was considerably thicker than the one Spradlin had on her. She opened it. The first page within the folder was a photograph of a handsome young boy with very short dark hair and magnetic blue eyes. He had a blue tattoo on his forehead. It was identical to the one Nox sported.

"Does he look familiar?" Spradlin asked.

"No."

"As you can see, he's a member of the Blue Brigades," General Spradlin said.

"Then he's dead, just like all the rest of them."

"So says a surviving member of that very same group. Turn to the next page."

Nox did. The following page was another photograph. The man on the photograph was considerably older. Nox recognized him as the now grown boy. He sported the same tattoo, but the brilliant blue eyes were dull. The expression on his face was distant.

"When this photograph was taken a couple of years ago he just turned thirty three," General Spradlin said.

"I've seen him," she said. "Back in the hospital lobby, just before you arrived."

"His name is Joshua Landon," General Spradlin said. "For three months back in '58 he fought at your side. Like you, Joshua Landon was one of our earlier subjects. Like all the rest, his actions were scrutinized by his handlers. Any deviation, however minor, was... worrisome. In time, Landon became a concern. He displayed heightened emotional responses whenever engaging with the enemy. The condition grew worse with each new mission. We feared he was cracking."

"It's a wonder there weren't more of him."

"He was ordered out of rotation and underwent a series of tests. Results confirmed what we feared. He was lost to us, mentally if not physically. Instead of a highly trained soldier, we had a remorseless killer."

"In the Arabian war zone, was there a difference?"

"We flew him back into the Continent on a military transport. The flight was routine. There were no problems until the plane came in for a landing. Air traffic received a Mayday just as the transport's wheels touched down.   There were reports of violence on board, of weapons being discharged.   The plane swerved and skidded off the tarmac. Soldiers rushed to the plane but were pinned down by sniper fire. Several were lost. It was Landon. By the time we got to him and had him under control, everyone on the aircraft was dead."

A deep frown cut through General Spradlin's forehead.

"Landon was sent to Segmore maximum security prison and buried deep in its lowest levels. He was never to be released again. At least that was the plan. Seven days ago, during a routine transfer of prisoners at that prison, Joshua Landon's name somehow got added to the transfer order. The warden, a fucking pencil pusher, went ahead with the transfer without a full verification."

"How many of us are left?"

"From the Blue Brigade only you two. From the other brigades, more."

"Were you...were you one of us?"

"No. But I oversaw every one of the Brigades in Arabia. I was the voice. I was your command."

Nox's face flushed.

Whether it was the messages bombarding her from without or the anger within, she now understood the fury she felt upon seeing General Spradlin at the Hospital. Even without those electronic impulses, she remembered the bloody work the voice of command instructed her to do. The voice was so calm and clinical as it ordered one revulsive act after the other.

Even without the electronic wails, she would be more than willing to rip the man's throat out, here and now.

"You sent brainwashed children incapable of independent thought to fight your war. Why?"

The lines on General Spradlin's face became more pronounced.

"We needed fighters small ...and innocent... enough to infiltrate almost any enemy area, yet big enough to handle weaponry. We needed stripped down, unemotional soldiers capable of following orders. *Any* orders."

"We were children."

"Most of the Generals argued against sending you in," Spradlin said.

"But not you."

The General didn't reply.

"We were fucking kids."

"You won the war," General Spradlin said. "That's all that matters."

Nox felt her anger peak, then dissipate. She handed him back the file.

"Exactly how many of us are left?"

"There were a little over ten thousand child soldiers spread out in the Blue, Orange, and Black brigades. Almost all died when the nukes were delivered to the Arabian Cities. Of those, thirty five were on the sidelines. They were, for the most part, screw ups who couldn't handle the training or the fighting or had compatibility problems with their...hard wiring. They were shipped back home at various times well before the nukes were delivered. They were relocated to places where they could live out a quiet life."

"The suburbs? A house with a garage and a pool?"

General Spradlin stared deep into Nox's eyes.

"I have neither the time nor the interest to argue the past. Not now. Not when the world is being torn apart."

"What do you want?"

"An answer to a question."

"What?"

"How did you override the order to take your nuke into Sada-bir?"

"What does it matter now?"

"You were in the theater, Nox. You had a nuke strapped to your back and you were given a direct order to take it into Sada-bir. Somehow, you refused. You overrode programming that was supposed to be infallible. If I could find out how you broke free, I might be able to do the same with Joshua Landon. So tell me: How did you do it?"

"I never was very good at taking orders."

"*How?*"

"I don't know," she yelled.

"What do you mean?"

Nox took a deep breath and calmed herself down.

"If you're looking for a magic pill or moment of clarity, there wasn't any. I just...I just questioned orders. Little things at first. In time, the small questions became bigger ones. I wondered why I wasn't talking with others, laughing, playing. It took months, maybe even a year, before the veil lifted." Nox pressed her lips together. "I wish there was something I could tell you. There isn't."

Nox and General Spradlin were silent for a few seconds.

"That's too bad," General Spradlin said. He looked away from Nox and at the Big City. "What are they telling you now?"

"The same as before," Nox said. "They want me to join them. They want...they want you dead. Who's behind this? If you guys aren't sending the orders anymore, who is?"

General Spradlin took a deep breath. He exhaled.

"Have you heard of David Lemner?"

An electric jolt shot through Nox's body.

"By your silence, I'm assuming you have," General Spradlin said. "For years there was a rumor that David Lemner created a backdoor program, something that allowed him access to each and every GCN linked computer operating system."

"Lemner's passkey," Nox said.

"All high level security programs have codes that are modified on an hourly, sometimes even minute-by-minute basis. The purpose of this is to ward off the possibility of outside agents gaining access to classified information. Lemner's passkey would theoretically be capable of not only breaking those updated codes, but somehow keeping its presence in those computers invisible. For such a program to exist, it would have to contain a form of intuition."

"Intuition?"

"Artificial intelligence," General Spradlin said. "Such a program did exist, Nox. It ran the Child Brigades back in the Arabian War."

Nox stiffened.

"It was a very early version of this mythical Lemner's passkey," General Spradlin continued. "The program initially began as the next generation of military command, something that would work in conjunction with the nano-probes in your bodies. In all wars, communication with the troops is vital, and that program was meant to communicate directly with our troops even if home command was compromised. We had high hopes, but after Joshua Landon's rampage, I knew the program had to be shut down. I did so. Permanently. Or so I thought."

General Spradlin paused for a moment and gazed at the Big City.

"The war ended and David Lemner died. But there were rumors of a passkey –a new, improved version of the Brigade command system– being developed. I understand your last employer devoted considerable time and money trying to find this program. A fruitless pursuit, right?"

Nox eyed the General and he stared right back at her.

"Turns out the rumors were true. There was a new version of the military command program out there," Spradlin finally said. "It was stronger, sleeker and far, *far* more aggressive. Someone reactivated it."

Nox bit her upper lip. Hard.

There were consequences.

There always are.

"This new version of our military command program –let's go ahead and call it Lemner's passkey– not only reactivated Joshua Landon, it was also behind the assault on the GCN and every computer operating system in the Big City. It didn't stop there. What you see here before you is happening in all the Big Cities in every one of the Continents of the entire world."

"By the Gods," Nox muttered.

General Spradlin's hands settled on the railing before him.

"On the day Landon escaped, twenty of the remaining child soldiers vanished from their individual care facilities. Unlike Landon, those facilities had far less security and those one-time child soldiers weren't considered dangerous. We were wrong about that."

"And the other fifteen?"

"They committed suicide."

"Why?"

"Perhaps they were too...compromised," Spradlin said. "Some had physical limitations. They were wheelchair bound or bedridden. The others…maybe they just didn't want to join this new war. Like you."

"Why didn't the program find me sooner?"

"GCN records list you as a casualty in the Arabian war. Until Lemner's passkey sensed your nano-probes, it didn't even know you were still out there."

"Could there be others like me?"

"No. All were accounted for."

"So was I."

"You're the only one, Nox."

"What about the children taken from the Hospital?"

"They were in the Hospital's Elite Wing."

"Elite?"

"It shouldn't surprise you the rich have a desire and, more importantly, the means, to be separated from everyone else."

"So Joshua Landon draws you and me to the hospital while taking twenty four kids. Why did they take these particular ones?"

"For a while we feared the program might be seeking revenge. Most of the kidnapped children have relatives who were in power during the Arabian War. However, there were another fifty five babies in that ward that could have been taken but were left alone. Several of them also had relatives involved in the Arabian Wars, some even more intimately than those actually taken."

"If it isn't revenge?"

"The children that were taken scored the highest in their genetic profiling tests. Lemner's passkey took the best and the brightest."

"Only the best for their new platoon," Nox said. "Makes sense. But those infants won't be battle ready for at least a decade and a half, if you go by us."

"The program's plan is long term," General Spradlin said. "It will keep the world's electronic grid and all access to it screwed up and use the adult soldiers for protection should we somehow get our act together and launch a counterattack. Meanwhile, the infants grow."

"The program is content to wait that long?"

"Why not?"

Nox looked away from the General and at the refugees outside the compound.

"When the Big City's population finishes massing around here, those twenty remaining soldiers will make their move," Nox said. "They'll have everyone in one nice small spot. They'll finish what they started. All under your watch."

"I have no intention of sitting around and waiting for trouble to come to me. We're going out, Nox."

"If I can't tell you how I cracked the commands program back in Arabia, what good am I to you?"

"You hear them. In a combat situation, what could be better than listening in on your enemy's transmissions?"

"I do more than just listen," Nox said. "I almost gave in to them. What's to say I won't in the future?"

"I'll take that risk."

"Sounds like you're already assuming I'll join you, General," Nox said. "Do I have any choice in the matter?"

"Unless you can figure out how you disobeyed your orders during the war, none at all," General Spradlin said.

Nox detected an edge to the General's voice.

"What aren't you telling me?" she asked.

His answer came quick. Too quick.

"Nothing."

"If you want me to work with you, you have to be honest with me. I will not tolerate lies."

"Fair enough," the General said.

Nox lifted her file.

"This is my reward for helping you?"

"The file is already yours."

Nox scratched her head.

"I don't work for free," she said.

"Mechanics rarely do."

"I'll help you, General, and I'll even consider this file final payment for my work. But I want something from you."

"You're in no position to—"

"Let me see Catherine."

General Spradlin closed his mouth.

"Please."

The General thought about the request. He nodded.

"Make it brief," he said. "We leave on the hour."

General Spradlin left Nox with Sgt. Delmont. He walked down the ramp and back to the garage.

Nox faced the remains of the Big City. She wanted desperately to go see Catherine Holland but couldn't help but look at the destruction before her. Even now, after staring at it for the past few minutes, the reality of this new world and the blame she had in its creation was difficult to accept. She wanted to see Catherine Holland, but she knew she couldn't let this world descend into further chaos.

This was a nightmare. It had to be.

She wished she could wake up.

28

Sergeant Delmont delivered Nox to her friend's room.

During the walk to the room, neither of them talked. The seriousness of the situation weighted very heavily on the Mechanic as well as everyone within the military installation. They were fighting a crisis the civilized world had never seen before. How would they react if they knew the person who created this crisis walked among them?

There's no way you could have known Lemner's passkey would do this, she thought.

It didn't change things.

You opened Pandora's box. Can you help close it?

Catherine's room was not too far from Nox's. Sergeant Delmont remained at the door and allowed Nox her privacy.

Nox still carried the General's file on her. She was tempted to open it and uncover the mysteries of her past, but didn't. Instead, she drew a chair and sat beside Catherine's bed.

A series of IV tubes connected to bags of clear liquid snaked into Catherine's arms. There were no electronic devices monitoring her condition. Indeed, it was only now Nox realized just how wiped clean of all major electronics this base was. The gas generators outside the facility provided power to the lights, the air conditioning, and the refrigeration. Communication was accomplished throughout the base by a rudimentary –and very antique– telephone system. As bad as things were, it was far better than whatever was happening at this moment in the Big City.

The Mechanic let those thoughts drift and for several seconds quietly stared at her friend. Catherine Holland's face was pale. Her eyes were closed and she remained unconscious. The swelling and bruises on her face and arms were receding.

A few more seconds passed. A nurse walked into the room and measured Catherine's pulse.

"How is she doing?" Nox asked.

"She's stable," the nurse said.

"Will she make it?"

"We're doing the best we can."

"You didn't answer the question."

The nurse laid her hand on Nox's shoulder.

"I wish I could," she said.

Nox lowered her head.

"Thank you."

The nurse nodded. She silently stepped out of the room.

Nox's head came back up. Her jaw clenched and her hands tightened into fists.

"I fucked up," Nox said. "I fucked up bad."

Nox rubbed her eyes. She leaned forward in the chair.

"Why the hell did I have to be so damn clever?" she said. "Why the hell did I have to use the damned passkey?"

It wasn't like Nox to second guess her actions, and that angered her even more. She wanted to flee this room and sucker punch the Sergeant on her way out, strip him of his weapons, and hunt down the bastards responsible for her friend's injuries and slowly –so *very* slowly– kill each and every one of them. She'd figure out a way to destroy the passkey and, after that was done, would go after General Spradlin and his group. She would make them pay. Every last one of...

That's not you.

Nox exhaled. Her heart was thumping.

"That's not you," she said out loud.

Clever.

They're rattling around inside your head. Hoping to set you off.

The commands from Lemner's passkey were like whispers in the dark, invisible strings drawing her to the left or right, forward or backwards. Its voice was cold and urged violence. It wanted Nox to break free of this prison and kill as many of the General's soldiers as she could on her way out.

On the way to joining her brothers and sisters.

Nox felt her energy bubble up. She could feel the program taunting her, telling her she was welcome to return to the group. To her family. Nox was an outsider here.

"You're right about that," Nox muttered.

It was also dead wrong. She *always* was an outsider. Nox lived in the busiest city in the world and was surrounded by people yet never felt a part of them. She had only one real friend and before that, none.

Still the voice insisted she belonged to their group.

"I don't," Nox said.

Pounding their message into her head didn't work, so Lemner's passkey shifted its strategy and used little jabs and subtle contacts, all leading to the same destination. Nox could feel its plan. It wanted to remake this world in its image, populated by weaponized human beings, ready for battle, ready to kill.

Who?

The Arabian war was long finished. Though small conflicts flared up here and there throughout the globe, it seemed pointless to have such a powerful army.

Who are you preparing to fight against?

Nox was curious to find out. She allowed her mind to wander, to flow with the electronic currents instead of against them. She brushed against Lemner's passkey. It was like an animal hidden in a deep, dark forest. She felt its breath and heard its impatient rustling. She listened some more, until she could follow in its steps and see what it was after.

At the moment, it wanted General Spradlin. It also feared him.

Why?

Nox allowed the electronic waves to coalesce. Their voices were much more faint here than at the hospital. Something in the base could quiet, if not entirely silence, them. That terrified the passkey. General Spradlin did not tell Nox everything. He had ways of thwarting Lemner's Passkey. At least here.

Nox changed her focus and searched for what stopped the signal's call. In time, she found herself standing before a large, dark chasm. In her mind's eye she looked down and then stepped inside. As she fell, the whispers from the passkey disappeared. It didn't dare enter this dark place. Nox fell for what seemed like miles until she detected a faint light in the distance. It grew larger and larger, until it overwhelmed her.

The light came from a huge machine. It was the one Nox now knew was buried deep under the military base. Is this where the city's refugees were being sent? To this machine? A machine that—

Just like that, her vision was gone.

Nox opened her eyes and found she was alone in Catherine's room. The connection to Lemner's passkey and whatever lay below was severed. It was pointless to try finding it again.

Nox reached for Catherine's hand and gently took it in hers.

Feeling her friend's warm hand lifted Nox's spirits. Despite the extreme guilt, anger, and fear she felt, it made the Mechanic smile. Touching her friend made the storm surrounding her dissipate, at least for the moment. She savored this small contact and held on. She willed the seconds to pass slowly, knowing they would move exactly as they had before. She felt tears forming in her eyes. She was so thankful her friend was still alive.

"I need you to take care of something for me," Nox finally said. She put the unread file in Catherine's cold hands.

"I'll get them," Nox continued. "And when I'm done, I'm coming back for you."

Her time was up.

Nox reluctantly released Catherine's hand. She headed to the door leading out of the room. There, she took one last look at Catherine.

"I'm coming back," she repeated.

She stepped out of the room. Sergeant Delmont was there, waiting for her.

"Let's go," Nox said.

29

When she returned to the garage, Nox was dressed in army fatigues that were a little too tight for her frame. Sergeant Delmont remained at her side. At the other end of the garage, the masses of people were still streaming in and heading down the stairs to the garage's lower levels.

"Where are they going?" Nox asked Sgt. Delmont.

"To shelter," the Sergeant said.

"There's enough room for everyone down there?"

"They're comfortable."

"How many people are there in the Big City?"

Sgt. Delmont considered the question.

"I don't know...eighteen to twenty some million?"

"Sounds about right," Nox said. "How many of those eighteen to twenty some million people you got down there?"

"I wouldn't know."

"How many can you have down there before they're uncomfortable?"

Sergeant Delmont thought about it. He shrugged.

"Just how big is this basement of yours?" Nox continued.

"Tell you what," Sergeant Delmont said. "I'll have my real estate agent give you a call. I'm sure he'll have all the answers you need."

Nox was silent for a few seconds. Her eyes took in every visible corner of the warehouse while her mind calculated.

Unless the General somehow anticipated a city-wide evacuation many, *many* years before and got crews to dig the equivalent of the Big City itself under these grounds, she couldn't imagine even one twentieth of the city's population fitting below. Comfortably or not.

Yet she witnessed with her own two eyes this enormous, seemingly unending stream of people doing just that.

The line did not falter and, assuming the pace remained the same during the days she was unconscious, there was a *massive* amount of people already down below.

"What about the other big cities of the world? The General says they're going through the same thing we are. Do they have shelters like we do?"

"Probably."

"All of them?"

Sgt. Delmont hesitated a moment before saying:

"Lady, I'm just another link in a large chain. Why don't you save all this for the General?"

"I'll do that," Nox said. "Until then, can I ask you one last question, Sergeant?"

The Sergeant sighed.

"What?"

"Is the General a good man?"

"Yes," Sgt. Delmont said. He did not hesitate in replying.

"You've heard about the child soldiers he had fighting in Arabia, right?"

"Yes."

"You think someone who ordered children with nukes strapped to their backs into Arabian cities can be a good man?"

Sergeant Delmont stopped walking. Nox did the same. The two eyed each other.

"I've been in the military almost my entire adult life," Sergeant Delmont said. "I've met all kinds of officers, from good to mediocre to fucking terrible. As far as General Spradlin is concerned, I would die for him."

"As long as you had the choice," Nox said. "Back in Arabia, we didn't."

"Then you have to pick your poison. As bad as you think General Spradlin is, Lemner's passkey is far worse. I don't know how the General plans to stop it, but I know he needs your help to do so. If you care about this city and its people, you'll give him that help."

"Why should I?"

"Because he's betting that deep down inside you aren't like Joshua Landon," the Sergeant said. "You may be a tough, mean bitch, but even someone like me can see you're no monster."

"Why I'm flattered, Sergeant," Nox said. "Haven't heard such sweet talk since the prom."

Sgt. Delmont let out a laugh.

"You going to help us save the world or what?"

A sly smile appeared on Nox's face.

"Sewing club cancelled and the temperance meeting was called on account of the weather," Nox said. "What do you know, looks like my schedule is free after all. Maybe I can spare a couple of minutes to save the world after all."

Nox and Sgt. Delmont found General Spradlin standing before three medium sized military transport vehicles. The vehicles were identical and their bodies were heavily fortified with steel plating. Nothing short of a missile could penetrate their outer armor.

Swirling around General Spradlin were several groups of soldiers. Many carried equipment in backpacks and were loading up the vehicles. Others, dressed in lighter gear, packed.

Spradlin offered Nox a slight nod.

"Ready?"

"I suppose. What's the plan?"

"We find the source of the transmissions and destroy it."

"That's it?"

"That's it."

"That's what I always hated about you military types: Your plans are always so fucking complicated."

Nox looked inside the nearest of the three military vehicles and examined the interior.

"Seats, a steering wheel, and almost nothing else," Nox said.

"The transport trucks were stripped of every major piece of electronic equipment. No computers, no GPS, no cells. Not even AM radio."

"No AM? How will we survive without our daily fix of right wing hot air or repetitious sports talk?" Nox said.

"The end of the world might not be so bad after all," General Spradlin said.

"What about communication? We have any radio gear at all?"

"No. We can't risk it."

Nox noted there was no thumbprint ID or DNA ignition switch.

"I'll be damned. These things start with ordinary keys?"

"As I said, we had to strip 'em down."

"How many people are coming along for the ride?"

"Fifteen soldiers per truck. Forty five total."

"Forty five of us versus twenty of them," Nox mused. "We're outnumbered."

"If I could spare more troops, I would," General Spradlin said. "As you can see, we've got our hands full with the refugees as it is." He approached Nox. "Do you hear the passkey?"

"Yeah," Nox said. "Sometimes it whispers, other times it shouts. Bossy mother fucker."

"You're in control?"

"For now? Yeah. But to be safe, maybe you should cuff me."

"That something you tell all your dates?" General Spradlin said and grinned.

"Only the ones willing to pick up the tab."

"How about we take things one step at a time, see how it goes?" Spradlin said.

"It's your dance, General."

General Spradlin turned away from Nox and addressed his soldiers.

"OK, everyone. Time to wrap this up."

The soldiers around Spradlin said their goodbyes to those who were to remain behind. Others shook hands with friends and wished their counterparts good luck.

"You're riding with me," Spradlin told Nox and Sgt. Delmont.

"You don't want me out of your sight?" Nox asked.

"Not even for a second."

30

They drove out of the military base through the front entrance. The seemingly unending crowds gathered before it were pushed back. Despite their numbers, the refugees of the Big City behaved in an orderly fashion and allowed the exiting trucks their space.

Nox saw the fear and anxiety on the refugees' faces. A few days before, they were living their ordinary lives and no doubt worried about work or school or their nosy neighbor or a doctor's appointment. They thought of money, of their job, of friends and lovers or lack thereof. They looked forward to the evening's television or a movie or a sporting event and lived in apartments large or small or were homeless and on the street.

That was then.

Today, the military base was their last refuge. In the crowds were mothers and fathers and brothers and sisters and children large and small. There were the elderly and infirm and those in wheelchairs or on stretchers. Everyone came.

Nox looked back as the trucks drove on and saw the base and the citizens who were already inside marching toward the enormous garage.

"What's in the basement?" Nox asked General Spradlin.

He didn't answer. Nox answered for him.

"There's a machine down there. I felt it. Almost like I feel Lemner's passkey."

Nox leaned back in her chair.

"Why do I feel these things?"

"You always could," General Spradlin said. "It was only a matter of letting your mind do so."

"Lemner's passkey can't sense you at all, General," Nox said. "The only way it sees you is through me...if I let it. This scares it. Is that why it wants you so badly?"

"Among other things," Spradlin said.

Nox wearily eyed the General.

"You won't tell me everything, will you?" Nox asked and shook her head. "Of course you won't. It's the wise thing to do, isn't it? If I fall into the passkey's control, it will know everything I do, right?"

"We'll talk," the General said. "Later."

It was all the answer Nox would get.

Not that she liked it.

They drove through the abandoned streets.

The acrid smell of smoke and rot hung over the city like a thick fog. Sewage bubbled up from clogged drains. The Matte Building, once gleaming and new, burned. There were no fire trucks or rescue personnel to save the building. The buildings surrounding it also showed evidence of fire damage. Street level stores, their outer windows shattered, were looted of their wares and stood empty and abandoned. Nox looked hard for any citizens left in the remains of this once mighty city. She saw no one.

"There have to be some people left behind," Nox said after a while.

"I'm sure there are," General Spradlin said.

"Will they be rounded up?"

"Yes."

Night in the Big City was usually as bright as day thanks to the many artificial lights. Not now.

This night, the roads were inky black. All illumination came from either distant fires or the three transport trucks' headlights. Nox stared at the shadows and, for a moment, was lost.

She was no longer in the transport. Nox was in a dark room filled with beakers, glass tubes, and computers. The place looked like a huge laboratory. It looked...familiar. She walked up to the nearest glass case and bent down, to get a better—

"Nox?"

The voice came to her from what seemed like a million miles away. She felt her body shake, but it wasn't from cold or fear. Her eyes focused and she found herself staring at Sgt. Delmont. There was a sour look on his face. He held his automatic level with the Mechanic's stomach.

"It isn't polite to point those things," Nox said.

Delmont eased back in his chair, a relieved look on his face. To Nox's right, General Spradlin watched.

"I'm okay," Nox said.

"You sure?"

She thought about that. She slowly shook her head.

"You should restrain me," she said.

"It had you?"

"For a moment."

Nox closed her eyes. Her body felt like it was floating in a sea and buffeted by gentle waves.

"It knows I'm back in the city," Nox said. "It suspects you're with me."

"What is it saying?"

"It…it's telling me to go to the west side. There's a building there…"

"What building?"

"I don't know. I see it in my mind, a rectangular box. Old stone, weathered. I'm not…familiar with it. Strange…"

Nox shook her head.

"It's at the corner of James and 17th. I've passed through that area hundreds of times. I know the street inside and out. Yet I've never this building before. How is that possible?"

"Does it have a name?" Sgt. Delmont asked.

"No…yes."

"Which is it?"

"The building doesn't have a name, but it has a basement. To get to the basement, you have to go through a rusted vault door. I've seen that door before…there's a word painted on it. You can barely make it out. They want me to see what lies beyond that door."

Nox felt a shiver.

"You know about the place, don't you?" Nox asked General Spradlin. "You know what's written on that door."

"Yes I do," General Spradlin said. "Oscuro."

31

It took another half hour to reach 17th Avenue.

The further they were from the military base, the worse Nox felt. Her body temperature rose and then dropped. She started to sweat before feeling a series of chills. The whispers in her head grew louder, more insistent. Nox rubbed her hands and tried to keep them from overwhelming her.

"We're nearly there," General Spradlin said.

They entered the Palace district, a low level of the Big City known for having a few sickly trees along its sidewalks. Like most everything else in the Big City, they were dying. Nox stared out the transport's window. She recognized a café where at one time not long ago she was approached by representatives of the Diamond Shipping Corp. They hired her to check into a staff member they feared was being blackmailed. A few blocks away from that location she spent a long, rainy night conducting surveillance on an illegal arms dealer. To her north she spotted the Grotto Restaurant. In the alley behind it, one of her most trusted contacts was stabbed to death. Nox never found who committed that crime or if her contact's death was related to a case she was working on at the time. Now, some three years later, the contact and the case were mostly forgotten. A life gone, its imprint on the world negligible.

More memories flooded in. Nox's professional career consisted of one dirty job after the other. Success meant there was enough money to pay the bills and little else. Despite the brutal nature of the business and the temptation to earn more, Nox kept her honor. She was a Mechanic while everyone else became an Independent. Unlike her, the Independents' loyalties were based solely on how much they made on each job. They were, to her eyes, over-glorified mercenaries and it was insulting to her that many viewed them as the next generation Mechanics.

In spite of all that, Nox knew her hands were far from clean. At least she slept easier knowing whatever job she took on and whatever task she was hired to do, she followed through and never, *ever* betrayed her employers...unless they betrayed her first.

Nox kept her eyes street level, not daring to look up. The voices in her head urged her to do so. For a while she fought them, until curiosity got the best of her.

Her eyes moved from street level to the second floor of the buildings around her, then up some more. Because of ancient, outdated regulations, the buildings in this area could extend no more than five stories. All but one did.

She saw it now, towering over the other buildings. It looked exactly as she imaged: a ruggedly square building as old as the Big City itself. It was dark brown and the years and elements had worn her surface until she was almost black. She sported neither identification nor signs.

Nox was amazed to see this structure. Amazed and more than a little scared.

For she passed this area hundreds of times before and not once –*not once*– did she notice this phantom building. An air of menace swirled around it, making it as forbidding as a fairy tale sorcerer's dark castle.

"By the Gods," she whispered.

The primary military transport vehicle came to a stop before the building's entrance.

The remaining two vehicles parked at either ends of the block. The soldiers within exited and took up defensive positions. When they were in place, a member of each party waved to the other.

The General acknowledged this with a wave of his own.

"What now, sir?" Sgt. Delmont asked.

General Spradlin noted the vacant look in Nox's eyes.

"Come with us," he told Sgt. Delmont. "The rest of you, take up positions. Watch our backs."

The soldiers grabbed their gear and dismounted. When they were out, General Spradlin addressed Nox and said:

"Ready?"

It took considerable effort for her to answer.

"It's not whispering anymore," she said. "It's yelling."

General Spradlin put his hand on Nox's shoulder.

"Let's go," he said.

General Spradlin, Sgt. Delmont, and Nox walked to the building's entrance.

The glass and metal doors were oversized and level with the sidewalk and, like the building, stained with age and wear. It looked as if the building was abandoned a very long time ago. The size of the entrance indicated it was designed to allow large vehicles inside. Other than that, there was nothing to indicate the building's purpose.

Nox's breathing grew ragged.

"Are the child soldiers here?" General Spradlin asked.

"No," Nox replied. "They know we're near. They...they'll be here soon."

"Then we better make this fast," General Spradlin said. "Ready to go inside?"

"Yes."

General Spradlin drew a small flashlight from his belt. He motioned to Sgt. Delmont and the soldier walked to the doors. Delmont drew his automatic and was about to use it on the rusty chains that locked the entry door. He put the automatic away and pulled them. The chains fell to the ground. The locks were sliced.

"Looks like they've already been here," Delmont said. He swung the door open.

"After you," General Spradlin told Nox.

Nox walked into the building.

General Spradlin remained a few steps behind. When Nox was far enough away, he extended his right hand. Sgt. Delmont shook it.

"I'll see to everything," Sgt. Delmont said.

"Thank you."

Sgt. Delmont squeezed General Spradlin's hand and didn't want to let go. After a few seconds, he reluctantly did. Without saying another word, Sgt. Delmont returned to the transport vehicle.

General Spradlin's attention was back on Nox. He walked into the building. A musty smell permeated the area. He aimed his flashlight around the lobby. The light revealed a vast empty rectangular space. A sign indicated there were stairs beyond a door on the east side of the lobby entrance. A pair of oversized elevator doors lay to that door's right. Otherwise, the lobby was completely empty.

Nox stood in the far corner of the lobby and in front of a door leading to the building's stairs. Her back was to the General.

"No need to waste any more time," she said as he approached. "Let's go."

General Spradlin nodded. He stepped past Nox. The Mechanic's face was bone white and her eyes a deep red. They gleamed in the darkness. General Spradlin opened the door before her, revealing the very wide staircase. Nox took to the stairs, her walk as light as air and her movements guided by invisible currents.

"Down," Nox said.

"Yes," General Spradlin replied.

Nox moved quickly.

"Wait," General Spradlin said.   Unlike her, he moved cautiously, examining the steps and making sure his way was clear.

Nox disappeared into the darkness.

General Spradlin waved his flashlight and tried to keep his eye on her. He couldn't. He took a moment to look back at the entrance of the building and the street beyond. His soldiers were converging around the transport.   They quickly entered the vehicle until all but Sgt. Delmont remained outside. He took one last look at the building before joining his fellow soldiers. The vehicle's engine came alive. The transport moved away.

"Good luck," General Spradlin muttered.

The General pulled his revolver out with his free hand and walked down the stairs after Nox.

The stairs spiraled down five flights before hitting bottom. General Spradlin found Nox there. She stood before a large metal vault door. It was exactly as she described it to the General. It was exactly as she dreamed it back in the hospital.

Nox's hands ran over the door's massive frame, tracing the barely visible white letters written on it, spelling out a single word.

OSCURO.

"It's been a long time since you've been here," Nox said.

"Yes," General Spradlin replied.

General Spradlin kept the flashlight on the door and the revolver aimed in Nox's general direction. The two noted the door's massive lock was melted.

"They've been down here," Nox said.

"Yes they have," General Spradlin said. "Go on."

Despite the door's massive size, it took Nox little effort to swing it open.

The room beyond the metal door was enormous and stretched out for hundreds of feet. Faint lights from reflective paint offered hints to its full size. General Spradlin shone the flashlight on a dusty desk close to the room's entrance. Long unused computer monitors lined the counter and the walls before them.

The floor was covered in a thick layer of dust that was marred by a series of footprints. General Spradlin and Nox followed them, penetrating deeper and deeper into the darkness.

At the end of the room was an open door. Nox hurriedly stepped past it and General Spradlin followed. Beyond the door was a smaller, though still impressively large, room. A thick glass panel divided the room in half. Beyond the glass panel was a natal ward. Tiny beds that once held newborns were lined in rows. The mattresses and sheets, those that remained, were dark with age and mold.

"Nox?" General Spradlin said. She was swallowed within the room's shadows. His flashlight flickered around, trying to find her. "Nox?"

General Spradlin walked closer to the glass. He peered at the natal ward and the disheveled beds. His flashlight shone through the glass, illuminating a pair of tiny pink socks. They too were dusty and yellow with age. General Spradlin clenched his jaw. He looked up, and caught the reflection of movement on the glass wall.

General Spradlin spun around and raised his arms. His flashlight was battered from his hand. The revolver in his other hand was simultaneously pulled free. In less than a second, he felt its barrel pressed hard against his chin.

"Don't move," Nox said.

She held the weapon and, for several seconds, said nothing more. General Spradlin, likewise, didn't talk. Nox's face was a ghostly white. When she next spoke, it was a whisper.

"This is where it started."

General Spradlin did not reply. He kept still, lest any movement should provoke the Mechanic.

"This is where it started!" Nox yelled.

"Yes."

Nox released the General. She kept the revolver pointed at him as she picked up his flashlight from the floor.

"Let's see what else there is," she said.

They walked back to the opposite end of the room and found another door. Nox opened it and pushed the General inside. Her breathing was heavy, her fury building. General Spradlin let her take him wherever she wanted to go.

This new room held a series of tables filled with large empty glass tubes. Each tube was identical, measuring three feet by four. They were displayed in horizontal rows, as if meant to show off plants. Black, red, and gray wires dangled within these tubes. At each of their bases was an ancient computer system and monitor.

"Looks familiar," Nox said.

These tubes were smaller versions of the glass casket Nox found herself in when she was transported by the General from the Hospital to the military base.

Nox pushed General Spradlin to the tube closest to them. She pressed her hand flat against its surface.

"This is where we were given our first lessons," Nox said. "This is where they started teaching me how to be a soldier."

"Why are we here?" General Spradlin asked.

"Landon and the others found this place. They planned to...to use it with the children. But there was...there was too much missing. Too much of the equipment was incomplete...broken. They wanted to burn this place to the ground. Instead they left it, so that we may witness its destruction."

"Why?"

"Because death and destruction is their language. It's what they –we– were taught."

Nox eyed the computer equipment and monitors below the glass tubes.

"Why do they want to kill you so badly, General?" she asked. "You were the voice of control. You were involved in the child soldier program. Wouldn't they want you at their side? Why do they hate you so?"

Nox pressed the revolver hard against General Spradlin's chin.

"They've destroyed civilization in a matter of days," she said. "They scare the shit out of everyone, including me. They fear no one. No one but you."

Nox lowered her revolver.

The monitor under the glass tube they stood beside flickered on. A low white light filled its screen. The other monitors, every one of them in the room, also came on. Their lights stretched for what seemed like miles, disappearing into the far distance. One monitor for each child soldier, several thousand in all.

Nox stared at the monitor before her. On it appeared security camera footage. A single man with an ashen face sat in a chair at the head of a large table in a conference room. He appeared to be waiting for others to arrive.

"What...?"

Nox immediately recognized the man on the monitor. It was David Lemner. The Demon. The man who created the passkey she used to infiltrate the Global Computer Network a lifetime before. The man who created the program that unleashed this hell on Earth.

"Looks like the show's about to begin."

The frozen image on the monitor moved. David Lemner adjusted his wire frame glasses. He looked shaken. A voice came from the other side of the room, just below the security camera.

"I know you're scared," someone said.

The voice was muffled and cracked as the man spoke. He sounded like he was in quite a bit of pain. Despite this, Nox recognized who was speaking to David Lemner.

It was General Spradlin.

32

David Lemner remained at his seat at the head of a table. Opposite him now sat General Spradlin. Half his face and his right arm were covered with fresh dressings. Blood seeped from below the gauze.

The door leading into the conference room opened and a group of four people, three men and one woman, entered the room. They took their seats around the table.

"Why are we here?" asked the only female in the group of. She was in her mid-fifties and retained an energetic, youthful glow. She was dressed in an expensive white suit that was all the rage two decades before. At that time, her political career was hot and her name was on everyone's mouth. Nox knew her, if only through historical accounts.

"Jennifer Alberts," Nox said.

The woman on the screen leaned forward.

"If this is about what happened at McArthur..." Jennifer Alberts said.

Another of the people seated at the table, a middle aged and graying man, interrupted her. His voice was saturated with sarcasm.

"Of course it isn't," he said. "Why bring such a distinguished panel like this together if not to talk about the Arabian War? Somehow, I don't believe General Spradlin would bring us here to show off his most recent act of valor."

"You talk very lightly about the deaths of sixty nine people," General Spradlin said. His tone was blunt, charged. He dared the others to talk. The words had their intended effect.

"Had Joshua Landon escaped, there's no telling how many more would have died."

General Spradlin stiffly moved in his chair. The pain from his injuries was evident even in the grainy footage.

"What happened at the Airport is bound to happen again," he said. "It's only a matter of time."

"I can manage the child soldiers," David Lemner countered. "What happened was a tragedy...but it wasn't my fault. It was a glitch, a programming error. I can find it and fix it and—"

"It wasn't an error," General Spradlin said. "It was a warning. A sign of things to come."

"I think we can all agree what happened in the airport was nothing short of a disaster," Jennifer Alberts said. "However, you can't deny the child soldier program is working well beyond our expectations."

The other heads around the table nodded in agreement.

"We have the Arabian nationalists on the run and they haven't even guessed what's hitting them," she continued. "If we didn't need the child soldiers so damn badly, I'd be the first to suggest we pause the program and allow David the time to fix whatever fuck up he's surely responsible for."

"You provided the bodies," David Lemner shot back. "Maybe you and the monster you're hiding in that basement of yours should have screened them a little better before sending them to me."

Jennifer Alberts offered the scrawny man a cold smile.

"It's not worth arguing, dear," Jennifer Alberts said. "The program works, for the most part. You'll just have to fix whatever is wrong on the fly."

"No," General Spradlin said. "We're not fixing anything. As of right now, it's finished."

There was stunned silence in the room. The participants in the meeting turned to each other, unsure if what they heard was correct. Finally, all eyes settled once again on General Spradlin.

"What do you mean by that?" Jennifer Alberts said.

"It's time for it to end. The child soldier program *and* the Arabian War."

"How exactly do you propose to do that?" David Lemner blurted. "You have a magic wand we don't know about? You just wave it and the big bad war is over and all is right in the world?"

"General Spradlin, I understand what you've been through," one of the elderly men at the table said. "The war will end on its own accord. We're estimating no more than another five years, at a maximum, before—"

"Maybe I haven't made myself clear," General Spradlin said. "It all ends now."

The people around the table were confused and alarmed by General Spradlin's words. Though their respect for him was great, they didn't know how to react to his statements. Most feared the General had lost his mind.

"Fine," Jennifer Alberts said. "You want to end the child soldier program and the war. All right, we're listening. Tell us your plan."

There was a great deal of weariness in General Spradlin's face. For several seconds he said nothing. In that time, alarm filled the faces of the people around the table. They knew the General only too well. When he said something, he meant it. Even something as crazy as this.

"What have you done?" Jennifer Alberts whispered.

"For the past year, I've herded the leaders of Arabia and most of the population into several large cities," General Spradlin said. "I've made them think our forces view those cities as safe havens, places where we would not attack."

"It was the humanitarian thing to do," one of the elderly men said.

"It was a ruse. I've watched the leaders of Arabia filter in and out of these cities for years. With each passing day, they've stayed longer and longer and the crowds have grown bigger and bigger."

David Lemner laid his hands flat on the table.

"I see," he said. "You get everyone together into a group of places and destroy them all at once. Cut the heads of the snake right off, as it were. What were you planning? Multiple nuclear strikes?"

General Spradlin didn't say.

"Yeah, that's exactly what you were planning, isn't it?" David Lemner continued. "But how do you deliver the nukes to their destinations? The Arabian cities have excellent defensive systems. If we send in missiles or aircraft they'll be taken out well before—"

"The nukes were delivered by foot."

"By...? What are you talking about?"

"For the past two weeks, I've ordered the child soldiers to infiltrate the cities. Each of them was carrying low yield nukes in their backpacks."

"You had them set up bombs in the cities?"

"No," General Spradlin said. "Planting stationary devices would have been too risky. If even one of them were discovered, the leaders and civilians would flee. What we needed was to get the bombs into the city but keep moving them around and away from detection. Only way to do that is to keep them on our child soldier's backs until..."

General Spradlin didn't finish his thought. The room was dead quiet for several seconds.

"You mean to use the child soldiers as... as suicide bombers?" Jennifer Alberts said. There was genuine horror in her voice. "This is barbaric, even for you. I won't allow it."

The General looked at his wristwatch.

"None of you have any say in the matter. Not anymore."

As the words left his mouth, the cell phones carried by each of the members of the group buzzed. All of the people around the table, all but General Spradlin, reached for their phones.

"You didn't?" Jennifer Alberts said.

"I gave the order just before this meeting began."

"By the Gods."

Like David Lemner and the others around the table, she stared at the images on her cell phone. Frantic newscasters reported mushroom clouds over areas that were once the mightiest of the Arabian cities. A cacophony of horrified reporters both on the field and in the network studios attempted to make sense of what they were seeing. Early estimates were that millions were dead. Many, many millions.

"What about the environment?" Jennifer Alberts asked. "That much radioactive material—"

General Spradlin let out a laugh.

"Of all the people around this table, I thought you would be the last one to care about the environmental impacts of war. I thought your kind didn't believe in that stuff. After all, you denied global warming even as the polar caps melted away."

Jennifer Alberts pursed her lips.

"All our child soldiers...they're dead too?" David Lemner said.

"Yes."

David Lemner couldn't hold back his anger anymore. He slammed his fist against the table.

"I spent the last two years perfecting their programming," David Lemner said. His voice grew into a shout. "How could you do this to me?"

"It had to end."

"Why didn't you warn us?" Jennifer Alberts said.

"The child soldiers were our only hope and you've flushed them away!" David Lemner injected.

"They were never part of the solution."

"Then what is the solution?" Jennifer Alberts asked. "I thought we were agreed that to survive we had to fight fire with fire."

"That plan ran its course," General Spradlin said.

"What do you mean?" Jennifer said. "Arabia was a trail run, a test of how far we could weaponize individuals. Even after what happened with Joshua Landon, Oscuro was a success. We can still expand it, make it a force."

"That was never what you intended, was it?" David Lemner said. The bitterness in his voice grew. "You humored us. You let us do all this work and invest all our time and money while you had some backup plan in the works. Isn't that right?"

The group around the table grew quiet.

"What's your endgame?" Jennifer Alberts asked. "If Oscuro isn't the salvation of Earth, then what is it?"

General Spradlin didn't say, nor would he. The others around the table realized this.

"With the child soldiers, we could have taken on anything," David Lemner said.

"No," General Spradlin said. "The coming war is one we could not win. Even with perfect soldiers."

"Then...then what do we do?" one of the elderly men said. "Give up? Wave the white flag? What kind of soldier are you?"

"A realistic one," General Spradlin said. "I've seen the future and I know what's coming. We don't have a chance."

"Do our children simply lie down and die?"

"No."

"Then what?"

Still General Spradlin wouldn't say. David Lemner's patience was at its end.

"You might have given up, you fucking coward, but I won't. I'll fight."

"No, you won't," General Spradlin said. "Your laboratories are military property. I've ordered them seized."

"You can't—"

"It's already done."

The fury in David Lemner increased. He faced Jennifer Alberts.

"He's lost his mind," Lemner said. "We have to stop him."

Despite the strain evident on her face, Jennifer Alberts maintained her composure.

"You have another plan," she said. "I know you do. Please, General, tell us. What is it?"

General Spradlin shook his head.

"Our work is done," he said. "The Arabian War is over. When you leave this meeting, know that what you accomplished was not in vain. Now you can go to your company functions or the news or wherever the hell it is you go to spread the word of your sterling companies and their sterling business practices and explain to them how we –yes, *we*– decided on the final solution to the Arabian problem."

"They'll hang you from the highest pole and let vermin pick your corpse," Jennifer Alberts spat. "I'll be only too happy to give you up."

"No, you won't," General Spradlin said. "My plan brought peace when the public's patience for war was at its end and it didn't even break your budgets. What more could any businessman –or woman– ask for?"

General Spradlin got to his feet. He winced as pain shot through his body.

"Enjoy your remaining years," he said. "Leave the rest to me."

General Spradlin walked to the door leading out of the meeting room. At its threshold he paused.

"If you play your cards right, you come out of here looking like heroes," he said. He offered the people at the table a smile. "Cheer up. The war is over."

33

Every single one of the monitors in the basement corridor shut down.

Darkness filled the ward.

Nox stood still, frozen in place, her eyes still on the now dark monitor. Beside her, General Spradlin's head lowered, until he stared at the ground.

"Nox," he said. The tone of his voice was soft, gentle.

Nox didn't move.

"What is it you want to tell me, General? Was this a lie? A hoax?"

"No."

Tears welled up in Nox's eyes.

"You robbed us of our childhood and then...then you ordered us killed."

General Spradlin bit his upper lip.

"That's what Generals do."

Spradlin's head came up. In the darkness he found Nox. She stared at him. The gun in her hand trembled. A single tear ran down her face.

"Are you even human?"

A cool serenity settled on General Spradlin's face. If he feared she would use the weapon on him, he didn't show it.

"You saved countless lives," he said. "More than you know."

The gun in Nox's hand trembled.

"If you feel I deserve it, pull the trigger," General Spradlin said.

Nox shook her head. She could barely contain her fury.

General Spradlin closed his eye.

The fury grew until it was a full blown rage. The savagery in Nox's face threatened to overwhelm her soul. The gun in her hand shook some more.

Nox closed her eyes.

"...*fuck*..."

She spoke in a whisper. She lowered the gun.

"Fuck," she repeated. The anger in her face faded.

General Spradlin pulled up a chair and laid his hand on Nox's shoulder. She sat down.

Seconds passed.

"They...they almost had me."

"I know."

"Why did you let the passkey bring me here?"

"I had to know whether it could get you. I needed to know if you were strong enough to remain independent."

"Independent," Nox repeated. She let out a dry laugh. It died quickly. "I'll kill you because you need killing, not because someone else wants me to do it."

"We know where we stand," General Spradlin said. "But you couldn't have killed me. Not with that revolver."

Nox pulled the ammunition clip from the weapon. It was empty.

"I'll be damned," Nox said.

"I had to be sure you could fight back and stay in control. I had to know I could trust you."

"Can you?"

"More than I thought."

Nox shook her head.

"Doesn't really matter."

"Why?"

"Because they didn't want me to put a bullet through your head," Nox said. "That would have been too easy. They wanted me to kill you nice and slow. It wants to see you bleed, General."

"I know."

Nox handed the revolver back to the General.

"How did you know the child soldiers wouldn't be here?"

"A calculated risk. I have eyes throughout the city. After kidnapping the children from the hospital, the soldiers headed to the Desertlands. As of yesterday, none of my agents saw them return. I was hoping we had some time."

"That's a hell of a risk to take on old intel," Nox said.

"I was also relying on you. You said you didn't feel them."

Nox smiled.

"I suppose there is some use for me after all," she said. "What was all that at the end of the video? About the coming war?"

"Words," General Spradlin said. He slid the revolver back into its holster.

"No they weren't," Nox said. "The people at that table thought they were making the *first* generation of super soldiers. They were obviously planning for more generations to follow. Why? Why would you need—"

She didn't finish her thought. She turned her head and her eyes lost their focus.

"Guess what, General," Nox said. "Our time's up. They're here."

"Inside the building?"

"Not yet. They've surrounded it. Your men should see them any second now..."

Nox expected to hear the sound of gunfire as General Spradlin's soldiers and the one-time child soldiers engaged in battle. Instead, there was silence.

"Where are your soldiers?" Nox asked. Realization quickly dawned on her. "You told them to leave?"

"They were gone as soon as we headed down the stairs," General Spradlin said.

"It's just the one-time child soldiers and us?"

"Yes."

"You didn't want to risk your men's lives?"

"As well trained as they are, they wouldn't have survived Joshua Landon," General Spradlin said. "Besides, Lemner's passkey doesn't want them. It wants us."

"Now what?"

"They will come after us, Nox. They'll come hard and fast."

"What's the plan?"

"We run."

34

They backtracked to the building's natal ward.

Along the way General Spradlin found and picked up a rusty metal tube. He used it against the glass that divided the room in two. The glass shattered into pieces.

"Quickly," General Spradlin said.

Both General Spradlin and the Mechanic climbed over the destroyed glass divider and stepped past the dusty infant cribs. On the other side of the room was a door and beyond it a storage room. Shelves that once were lined with medicines, food, and infant clothing were bare except for a couple of strips of old folded sheets and a single dusty stuffed bear.

"This way," General Spradlin said.

They exited the storage room and entered a small kitchen area. Beyond it was a corridor. They moved deeper and deeper into the basement, past several dusty rooms littered with boxes and refuse, ancient dreams rendered a long forgotten reality.

At the end of the corridor they reached a very large storage room. Empty shelves were lined along the walls in rows and at the corners of the room were crumpled boxes. General Spradlin threw those boxes aside and felt along the newly exposed rear wall.

"I hear something," Nox said.

General Spradlin stopped what he was doing.

"They're in the building," she said.

General Spradlin heard it, too. Footsteps. Someone –a group– was making their way down the staircase and to the underground natal unit.

General Spradlin returned to the wall. His hands moved quickly, feeling for indentations and poking his fingertips into cracks.

"If you're looking for a way out, you better find it quick," Nox said.

General Spradlin's fingers continued feeling along the wall, pushing and pulling at cracks. The people in the corridors were nearing the storage room.

"They're almost here," Nox said.

There was a small click, and everything went silent. General Spradlin found the device he was looking for. A small red light embedded in the wall came on. It flickered and faded, dead with age. A five inch square panel slid down, revealing a faded numerical keypad.

The General frantically pressed several buttons.

A loud buzz followed. It was loud. Too loud.

"Shit," General Spradlin muttered. He entered the wrong code.

The footsteps outside the storage room turned into a gallop. In seconds the one-time child soldiers would arrive.

"Hurry up!" Nox said.

"Doing the best I can," General Spradlin said. He closed his eyes and concentrated. Without opening his eyes, he again pressed down on the keypad.

Nox watched his fingers glide. He pushed a series of ten buttons. Once done, he opened his eyes and looked at the keypad. There was no buzz.

Instead, a loud click was heard and part of the wall, a hidden door, swung open.

"Get inside!" General Spradlin yelled.

Nox jumped into the darkness and fell to the ground. General Spradlin was right behind her. He pushed the door closed, but not before three shadowy figures entered the storage room. Their guns were drawn and they fired repeatedly at the General and Nox. Bullets slammed against the secret door. Several of the deadly projectiles whizzed dangerously close to General Spradlin's head. They lodged themselves somewhere in the darkness of the hidden room.

The door closed and a heavy lock clicked shut. General Spradlin took a step back.

The pursuers on the other side of the door lunged at it. They banged their fists and slammed their bodies against the barricade. Their blows were like sledge hammers, but they could not get the door to budge. There was silence for a second or two, then a burst of gunfire. The roar was deafening but the door still held. After a while, they stopped shooting and there was silence once again.

General Spradlin leaned closer to the secret door to hear what was happening on the other side.

"Don't worry," General Spradlin told Nox. "This door was built to withstand—"

An explosion erupted in the outer room. Its force hurled General Spradlin back into Nox and the two fell heavily to the ground. Nox quickly got to her feet and helped the General up.

Their ears rang and their senses were shocked. General Spradlin shone his flashlight on the door, fearful of what he would see. The door had warped but held.

"She was built to last," General Spradlin said of the secret door. "But she won't take much more of that. Let's move."

"I'm right behind you," Nox said. "By the way, you wouldn't happen to have any bullets for that revolver, would you?"

"I didn't think it wise to bring any."

"Sometimes you think too much."

General Spradlin illuminated the long unused corridor hidden behind the large storage room. The floor was smooth and extended a great distance. Nox felt it curve upwards, elevating at a slight angle and heading toward the surface level of the Big City. The two hurried down that corridor. Behind them the sounds of explosives continued. The secret door would not remain standing much longer, even if each subsequent explosion proved, at least for the moment, it still held.

At the end of the corridor they reached another corroded metallic vault door. General Spradlin reached for a panel beside the door and flipped open its cover, revealing another dusty keypad. General Spradlin took a few seconds to look at it.

"You don't remember the code?"

General Spradlin concentrated on the numbers.

"Why don't you try your date of birth?"

General Spradlin let out a laugh.

"Not a bad idea," General Spradlin said. "That's something no one would ever figure out."

Another explosion erupted down the corridor.

"How about you let me concentrate a little?"

"My lips are sealed," Nox said.

General Spradlin moved his fingers along the panel's keyboard. He touched a key, then another, but didn't press down.

"Yeah," he said.

He pressed a series of keys before pausing to collect his thoughts. He then pressed another set of keys. When he was done, they heard the loud groans of ancient machinery coming to life. With a loud click, the door swung open, revealing a dark back alley.

General Spradlin shut off his flashlight and cautiously approached the open door.

"How far away are we from the building?"

"Four blocks," General Spradlin said.

"They might see us."

"They might."

Together they cautiously emerged from the hidden corridor and into the alley, quietly shutting and locked the door behind them and moving away from the building as quickly as they dared. They avoided debris and kept their rapid pace, taking several turns before reaching a main street. From there, they had a distant view of the building they escaped from.

All the military vehicles and personnel that brought General Spradlin and Nox to the place were gone. General Spradlin let out a relieved sigh.

"My men got away," he said. "I couldn't be sure."

"What about us?" Nox asked. "Now that my fellow soldiers are back in the city, they will sniff me out."

"They have a general sense of where you are, but if we keep moving, Lemner's passkey will have to keep recalibrating your position. That gives us a little time."

"A little?"

"Enough."

"Why can't they sense you?"

"Because I wouldn't let them. Just like I didn't want any of the one-time child soldiers to know about that building."

"Explain."

"The nano-probes give you enhanced perceptions. Visual, tactile, olfactory. In the field of battle, enhanced perceptions can be both a blessing and a problem. If a soldier is injured and the pain is such that they can no longer focus on their mission, they become worthless to us. We decided to make certain modifications in the nano-probes to enhance some perceptions while blocking others. It wasn't too big a step to realize if you could do that with things like pain, you could do that with visual and sensory input. The one-time child soldiers cannot feel or see me like they do you because, quite simply, they're not programmed to."

"But I saw you right away at the hospital."

"It was unavoidable as you were looking directly at me. The programming I created to hide myself is subtle. Hiding the Oscuro building was relatively easy as it lies in the middle of a forest of buildings. You probably saw it dozens if not hundreds of times whenever you were in that area, but because it was one building among many, it was easy for the programming to erase whatever memory traces you had of it."

"But if there was an accident in front of the building...?"

"It would have been much harder for the program to retroactively erase what you perceived. At the hospital, you were under a great deal of stress from Lemner's passkey and when you looked out the hospital door, I was the only living thing in your field of vision. The heightened emotions and the fact that I was right there for you to see me made it impossible for the programming to disguise my presence. To put it another way, the conditions were such that there was no way you *could not* see me."

"And what is seen –and recognized– cannot be *un*seen."

"The programming, to put it bluntly, was defeated. For the other one-time child soldiers, that is still not the case, though Lemner's passkey is no doubt working very hard at countering this programming. It already discovered the building. In time, it will see me as clearly as you can. Until then, the only way they know where I am is through you."

"Then we should split up," Nox said.

"We can't," General Spradlin said. "We have to save the infants."

"I can lead them away while you—"

"No," General Spradlin said. "We have to go together."

"Why?" Nox said.

"Because...because we do."

Nox thought about that for a moment. Her eyes narrowed.

"There's something else going on," she said. "Something you're not telling me."

The General didn't reply.

"What are we really doing?" she continued. "Do you really think we can avoid the child soldiers long enough to save the children? Even if we do, how do we stop Lemner's passkey? How the fuck do we save this world?"

They continued moving down the alleys and further and further away from the Oscuro building. The General hadn't answered Nox's questions, but the Mechanic hadn't pushed. Her mind was working, trying to analyze the situation, trying to see what General Spradlin was up to.

You're obviously a very clever man who plans things out well in advance, she reasoned. *Why risk your life by keeping company with someone who still might be turned?*

Those thoughts swirled in her mind. Realization came to her in a flash.

"You *want* them to have some idea of where we are," she said.

The General stopped. His face was hidden in the shadows.

"You want them to follow us, but not so close they could get us."

General Spradlin nodded.

"If Lemner's passkey and the one-time child soldiers completely lost your scent, they'd have no choice but to go back to your last known locations."

"The base," Nox whispered. "If they did that..."

"They would kill everyone there," General Spradlin said.

"Is that what's going on?" Nox asked. "Are we buying time while your soldiers fortify the base? Was saving the children a lie you peddled to get me to lead the one-time child soldiers around?"

"No."

The General moved on and Nox followed. They kept to the city's shadows and clung to every harsh corner or depression. All was eerily silent. The only noise they heard was dripping water or debris flapping in the wind. They saw no one and nothing, whether human, animal, or insect. Even the cockroaches had abandoned the Big City.

"They're all gone," Nox marveled. "How did you get everyone out?"

"We offered a safe haven and people took it," General Spradlin said. "Most went willingly. My men rounded up everyone else."

Nox thought about that. In approximately six days, the one-time child soldiers and Lemner's passkey sabotaged every electronic systems and destroyed civilization. In those same six days General Spradlin managed to empty out the city and send everyone to his base. The logistics to accomplish these actions were daunting, yet Nox was witness to them. If General Spradlin was capable of such a mass exodus, what else was he capable of doing?

"General?" Nox said.

The General stopped and faced Nox. His eye was red and, for the first time, Nox felt she could see in it the tremendous pressures he faced. Thought there was a steely resolve reflected in that single eye, there was also an unmistakable sense of dread and, perhaps, fear.

"How long do we have before everything falls apart?"

"A day," the General said. "Probably less."

"We have a day to save those children and take out Lemner's passkey," Nox said. "You really think the two of us can save the entire world?"

"That's the plan."

"You're a smart guy, General," Nox said. "Maybe not the smartest one alive, but certainly the craziest. If I were to keep following you, what would that make me?"

"Care to find out?" The General asked, though he already knew the answer.

35

The parking garage was in a rundown section on the east end of the city. It was a low lying three story structure hidden among the taller buildings around it. General Spradlin and Nox hurriedly entered the structure's main entrance and made their way to the stairwell. They headed down the stairs and into darkness.

General Spradlin's flashlight came on and lit the way. The Mechanic and the General bypassed bags of garbage and other refuse before arriving at the building's lowest level. Their only other company was the strong smell of waste. The stairwell appeared to lead to a dead end, but General Spradlin once again exposed a secret door. This one, like the last, operated by key code. General Spradlin hit these keys confidently. He was far more familiar with this structure than the others.

The door slid open and dim lights within a secret room came on.

Nox followed General Spradlin inside. He closed the door and the bitter smells from the stairwell were shut out. The chamber was square in shape. It culminated in three sets of doors on its opposite end. At the center of the chamber was an impressive computer system. It was shut down.

"Nice place," Nox said.

"It always impresses the chicks."

General Spradlin locked the door leading into the room. He then hurried past Nox and to the computer system and turned it on. A schematic of the entire Big City appeared on one of the monitors and the others displayed different sections around the building. General Spradlin eyed the images on the monitors while alternately panning and zooming in on them.

"Don't worry, this system is battery powered," General Spradlin explained. "It's self-contained and hard wired to the cameras. Lemner's passkey won't—"

He stopped talking and pointed to one of the top monitors.

"There," he said.

The camera feed on that monitor came from the roof of a building and displayed an image of a street intersection. Off to the side of the intersection, in a dark alley between buildings, there was movement. A woman emerged from the dark alley and came to a stop. She was nearing middle age and was overweight.

Her black and gray hair was frazzled, unkempt. Her eyes, however, were laser sharp and scanned the road around her. She sniffed the air as if a predator seeking prey. Her head jerked around, the movement as precise as a machine.

General Spradlin recognized her.

"Alexandra Despero," he said.

The woman's body remained frozen in place while her head swiveled back and forth as if it were a camera. Finally, her head froze as well. Her eyes closed and she held her breath.

Nox could feel Despero probing the area. Somewhere deep in the back of her mind she could feel Despero calling out to her, like a schoolyard bully taunting her victim. The voice was melodic and barely hid a vicious bloodlust. Nox could sense it even as—

Alexandra's eyes abruptly opened. She looked up, directly at the camera recording her movements. Her eyes were dilated, the expression on her face cold, dead.

"She spotted the camera."

Like lightning, Alexandra Despero drew a gun. The image on the monitor before Nox and Spradlin immediately turned to static.

"How far away is she?"

"Only a couple of blocks."

General Spradlin pressed a series of buttons. All the electronic equipment within the room shut down.

"They're triangulating," General Spradlin said. "I was hoping we'd have a little more time."

"My offer still stands," Nox said. "We split up and you get the children while I..."

"No," General Spradlin said. He let out a deep breath.

Nox leaned back. She walked to his side and looked down at him. For the first time since she met him, she saw the left profile of General Spradlin. The intact side of his face.

In her mind's eye she recalled the images from the meeting between General Spradlin and the architects of Oscuro. General Spradlin's face, the injured right side, was heavily wrapped. The other side, the left side, was relatively intact. She recalled the lines on the face. It was a youthful face. She assumed he was a much younger man then.

She assumed wrong.

The scarring along the right side of his face made him look so much older. But now, while focusing on the left side of his face and removing those scars from view, she realized that side of his face looked almost *exactly* like what she saw on that twenty plus year old video.

"How is that...?" she muttered and stopped.

General Spradlin faced her. Somehow, he knew what she was thinking.

"When I saw you in the Hospital parking lot...I didn't think I had ever seen you before," she said. "I was wrong."

More memories flashed into her mind.

Murky images of people walking around her. She reached up to touch the glass that separated her from them. Her hand was that of a baby. He stood there before her, looking down. His face had no scarring...

"You were there," she said. "B...back in the natal ward. But I was...I was barely a year old."

There were no scars, yet the face was the same. This was nearly thirty five years ago...

"How...how old are you?" she asked.

"Old enough to be there from the very beginning," General Spradlin said

"How old?"

"The key to the program was the nano-probes. They had to be distributed to every one of the child soldiers. Every one of you share the same blood. The same nano-probes."

General Spradlin paused. When he spoke again, the words reverberated like thunder.

"The nano-probes came from me."

Nox pointed to the scaring along General Spradlin's right side.

"But they're supposed to heal you," Nox said. "These wounds aren't healing."

"I'm dying," General Spradlin said. "I've been dying for the past twenty years. The nano-probes within me were poisoned."

"How?"

"The original version of Lemner's passkey...the version that was used on the Brigade soldiers...it was conducting unauthorized experiments. I guess we should have expected it to...assert itself. It made modifications to Joshua Landon's nano-probes. It expanded their usage. It turned them into weapons. When I confronted Joshua Landon twenty some years ago at the McArthur Military Airport, I touched him. By doing that I was infected with his weaponized nano-probes. It took every ounce of effort I had to contain them." He pointed to his scars. "You see what they did to me. I slowed the process but his poison is even now breaking my body down. At best, I have only a few more years left. I can't complain. The nano-probes have kept me alive much longer than I had any right to expect."

"Where did you get them?"

"They were an unwanted gift I received long before the start of the Arabian War."

"An unwanted gift you didn't mind passing along to us," Nox said. "You wanted us to be like you. Just like David Lemner and Jennifer Alberts said."

"At the beginning, Oscuro was a promising concept. In time, I realized it was not. The dangers posed by people like Joshua Landon proved it. The program had to be cancelled."

"That's what we were to you? A program that 'had to be cancelled'?"

"I live with plenty of regrets," General Spradlin said. "What I did to you in Arabia was brutal. It was beyond cruel. Ultimately, having the child soldiers set off the nukes *had* to be done. Not just to end the war…"

"…but to end the Child Brigade program," Nox said.

A cold silence settled on the room. General Spradlin rubbed his chin.

"You've seen what Lemner's passkey and the one-time child soldiers are capable of. If anything, I underestimated the danger. I should have acted much faster."

Nox was silent for a few seconds. Finally, she said:

"What about me?"

"You're different. The other child soldiers remain captive to the program while you grew past it. I don't know if the passkey views your independence as a threat or the missing ingredient it needs to build even better soldiers. Regardless, it wants you, Nox. Badly."

"Why is it destroying everything?"

"The passkey's goal is to make the world in its own image," General Spradlin said. "Your fellow soldiers were just the first wave. I can't even guess what the passkey plans to do with the second, third, and fourth generation of soldiers. But I do know this: Once the world order is crushed and civilization falls, the passkey and its soldiers will be free to grab subjects both young and old for its weaponization procedures. In short order it will triple and quadruple its numbers, until the entire world is filled with soldiers."

"Why does the program need them? Who does it expect to fight?"

General Spradlin said nothing. His silence spoke volumes.

"More secrets," Nox said.

"There are things I have to keep from you," General Spradlin said. "Even now. I will tell you this: Lemner's passkey was a flawed creation from the beginning. For all his intellect, David Lemner was a very emotional man and prone to pettiness. When he created the first A.I., he imbued it with his own personality. David Lemner knew he created a monster. He tried mightily to correct his mistakes. He failed. He admitted this to me shortly before succumbing to cancer. I asked –*begged* him– to tell me if there were any more copies of the passkey. I knew there had to be, as David Lemner kept a series of secret laboratories that were lost to the Great Sandstorms that followed the Arabian nukes. We searched and searched...in vain."

"The passkey was found," Nox said. "I found it. I released it. I'm responsible for all—"

"No," General Spradlin said. "*I'm* the one who's responsible for this. From the child soldiers to the war in Arabia to Lemner's passkey. I set it up. I made it happen. And when I realized the error of my way and decided to bury it, I didn't do enough to make sure it *stayed* buried."

General Spradlin rose from his chair.

"It's time to make it right," he said. "The world we've lived in until now is dead and gone. There are no more big businesses, no more big cities, and no more power structures. There's only us and Lemner's passkey."

General Spradlin laid his hand on Nox's shoulder.

"Let's finish this," he said.

36

Within the hidden basement of the garage was an armory. Ancient springs groaned as heavy metal doors opened. Inside the armory was a wealth of modern offensive and defensive equipment, from handguns to rocket launchers. They hung from the walls in order from small to large to enormous to outrageous.

Nox was impressed.

"What don't you have?" she asked. She reached for one of the weapons, a riot shotgun.

"Don't bother," General Spradlin said.

"Why not?" Nox asked. "Some of this stuff will take down a city block."

General Spradlin ignored the weapons on the walls and instead walked to a cabinet. He pulled open the top drawer. Within it were four small handguns. Nox recognized them instantly. They were the electric handguns General Spradlin used to knock her out while taking her to the military base. The General handed two of the guns to Nox and kept two for himself.

"What in the hell are they?"

"I call them electronic flares."

"A Taser?"

"It's more than that. The flare is designed specifically to deal with...with people like us. You use bullets on the child soldiers and, while their body is injured, the nano-probes within them remain alive and, provided the damage isn't catastrophic, they're capable of keeping the host alive and moving. You hit a one-time child soldier with a charge from this weapon, and *all* the nano-probes within their body shut down." He pointed to the controls on the side of the guns. "You can adjust the charge from here. There are only two settings, stun or maximum. At maximum charge, the nano-probes in your target are roasted."

"Can we free the soldiers by destroying the nano-probes?"

"No. The nano-probes are a part of us, just like our heart and lungs. You destroy the probes, you kill the host."

"We're stuck with them."

"I'm afraid so," General Spradlin said. "Now, when using the flare, the target has to be close for it to be effective. No more than twenty feet away."

"That doesn't leave much room between me and them."

"The charge works beyond that range, but its strength diminishes. You'll have to be on guard and let them come close but not close enough so they can use their nano-probes against you."

"Understood."

"One more thing: The batteries in this device take quite a while to recharge after each use."

"How long?"

"Twelve hours."

"We don't have that kind of time."

"No," General Spradlin agreed. "After each use, consider the guns disposable."

"Which means we have four shots."

"Make them count."

Nox pocketed her two handguns. As she did, her head snapped up. She heard a noise coming from the front of the building.

"They've arrived," Spradlin said.

He led Nox to the back of the basement. There, a solid steel door with enormous hinges blocked the way.

"Where to now?"

"We're going to see an old friend."

General Spradlin hit several keys on the panel beside the door. The door noiselessly opened and the duo entered the lowest level of the parking lot. Four cars were parked near the door, each of their bodies covered by very dusty canvases. General Spradlin walked to one of the smaller vehicles and removed the canvas covering it. Revealed was a two seat black sports car.

"Hurry," Nox said. "They're almost—"

She whirled around, the flare gun in her hand. Without thinking, she fired off a round. The electronic handgun made no noise and had no kick. A flash of intense light leapt from the gun and flew like a guided missile down the length of the parking lot. When the charge hit the back wall, the area was bathed in a bright white light. Shadowy figures jumped for cover.

"Let's go!" General Spradlin said. He slid into the sports car.

Nox tossed the spent handgun aside and swore. They were down to three shots.

"This isn't my style," Nox said as she entered the small vehicle. Indeed, the seats felt too small and her muscular frame was compressed.

"What is your style?"

"Nothing you could handle."

The car roared to life.

Its tires screeched against the cement floor as she gained traction and speed. They passed the area Nox had fired into and found the wall scarred with intense burn marks.

"You didn't hit your target," General Spradlin said.

"Lucky for them," Nox said. "You said this gun turns the nano-probes off. What does it do to flesh?"

"What do you think?"

Nox stowed the remaining gun into her pant pocket.

"They've surrounded the building," she said.

General Spradlin shifted the car into high gear. The engine screamed as the vehicle skidded around a corner.

"Watch out!" Nox yelled.

At the far end of the lot stood three figures. The one closest to them aimed a large metallic tube in their direction. Flame erupted from it as a rocket was launched.

Spradlin slammed on the car's brakes and spun the wheel. The car skidded off to the right as the rocket propelled charge roared past inches away from his side window. The propellant blackened that window with soot while the vibrations from the passing rocket cracked the glass. The rocket continued in a straight line.

Nox looked out the vehicle's back window and watched as the back of the parking garage erupted in flames and debris. The sound of the explosion was deafening.

General Spradlin pressed down on the accelerator and turned the car to the left. The vehicle entered a ramp and climbed a floor up. The car was momentarily airborne when it exited the ramp and crunched back down hard onto the concrete floor.

General Spradlin eyed this new parking level. There were two exits at its far end.

"Hurry," Nox said.

General Spradlin once again pressed down on the accelerator. The vehicle's engine screamed as she flew across the lot. More figures appeared from their hiding places. They carried rifles. Bullets slammed against the vehicle's side. At first Nox slid down to avoid getting hit. She quickly realized the car's windows and its entire body were reinforced. Bullets shattered against the glass, sending more cracked slivers. So far none penetrated the passengers' compartment.

General Spradlin looked into the rearview mirror. Several more of the one-time child soldiers were behind them. They were setting up another rocket launcher. Spradlin looked forward. The car approached the exit, but taking this very straight path would make them too easy a target.

General Spradlin cursed and slammed on the brakes. Again the car spun away. A second rocket whizzed past, erupting at the exit and creating an impenetrable wall of debris in its place. General Spradlin accelerated once again, moving away from the second exit.

"Where are we going?" Nox asked.

"Hang on," Spradlin said.

He moved the car side to side, not giving their attackers a clear idea of their direction. Finally, he hit the brakes and spun the car ninety degrees before resuming acceleration. The car was headed directly for a barricade.

"Tell me that's a way out," Nox said.

"It will be," General Spradlin replied.

The car slammed into the barricade, destroying its headlights and crumpling its front end. Its occupants felt a violent whiplash as the car tore through the weakened wall and pieces of concrete fell to their side and on the car's hood. The car hit the street.

Despite the heavy damage to its front end, the car's engine roared and the wheels gripped the Big City road.

"You OK?"

"As long as I'm still breathing," Nox replied. The seat belts had pulled along her chest, squeezing the air out of her. "How did you know we'd get past that barrier?"

"I didn't," General Spradlin said. "Drunk driver hit the wall a couple of weeks back. Our staff was supposed to have it repaired by now."

"Good thing they didn't."

"If it had been up to me, they would have."

"Oh?"

"The City's Building and Code Department's been giving us all kinds of hell for repair permits," General Spradlin said. He let out a chuckle. "Never thought I'd ever say this, but thank the Gods for bureaucracy."

37

They traveled through the ghost city, weary of shadows and dark alleys. Their vehicle was the only one moving on these deserted roads.

It made them an excellent target. As they traveled and time passed, General Spradlin noticed a change in Nox. Her skin grew progressively paler. Dark rings appeared under her eyes. At times it seemed she was about to fall asleep, only to violently snap at attention. General Spradlin didn't have to ask Nox how she was doing. He knew Lemner's passkey was furiously assaulting her. With each passing second, its grip on her tightened.

"You know where they took the children?" Nox asked General Spradlin.

"I think so," Spradlin replied.

"A place outside the city? In the Desertlands?"

"Yes."

"You knew about this place all along, didn't you?"

"Yes."

General Spradlin expected an outburst from Nox, but the Mechanic didn't say anything for several seconds. For a while, her eyes were unfocused. So too it appeared were her thoughts.

"Nox?" General Spradlin asked.

Nox's eyes shifted back to the General. It was as if she just woke up.

"You lied," she said. Her voice was soft.

"Are you OK?" the General asked.

"You lied," Nox repeated, stronger. She looked out the window of the car. "We're not heading toward the Desertlands exit."

"Not yet."

"Where are we going?"

"I already told you. To see an old friend."

"Why?"

"We need to even the odds a bit."

They reached the outer edges of the north side of the Big City a half hour later. The city structures, up to that point enormous and all encompassing, shrunk away and disappeared. Soon, the remnants of an ancient and long withered forest were visible. What at one point was lush green foliage was now dark, withered vines and skeletal trees. At their side lay crumbling mortar walls. Like the long dead trees, they were just as foreboding.

"Where are we?" Nox asked. The palm of her hand rested against the side of her head. Her skin was pale and she fought a strong headache.

"We're nearly there."

Nox closed her eyes. Beads of sweat appeared on her forehead and rolled down her face.

"It hurts?" General Spradlin asked.

"They're...they're really pissed," Nox said. "The program's not used to losing their prey."

"Keep fighting."

"'Til I can't fight 'em no more."

Nox shook her head.

"In the video... Who were the others with you at the table?"

"Businessmen. John Manning, Metacore Industries. Monroe Chalmers, Byzantine Shippers. I forget the other..."

"Big company men...and woman."

"They were liaisons between what was left of the government and the emerging industrial powers."

"Any of them still alive?"

"Manning died in a skiing accident the year after that meeting. Chalmers died of cancer a couple of years later. You know about David Lemner."

"What about Jennifer Alberts?"

"She was a self-serving, self-righteous fool who never let facts get in the way of her beliefs. In that respect, she wasn't all that different from the rest of the big business conservatives. After the war ended and she took a good look at the rubble our projects left behind, she had what she called a 'moment of clarity'. She retreated from the public spotlight and sold her company stock. The bulk of that money found its way to charities she once dismissed as parasites. When she was done getting rid of most of her cash, she holed herself up in her mansion."

"Did she become...become a recluse because of Oscuro and what happened to the child soldiers?"

"There could have been other reasons."

"She had a guilty conscience."

"It was a surprise to find she had one at all."

"The compound in the Desertlands...the one where the one-time child soldiers took the infants they kidnapped...it's hers, isn't it?"

"Yes. It's where we conducted some of the earliest tests on the Child Brigade's military training. It was the largest of the Oscuro facilities."

"Is Jennifer Alberts still alive?"

"Last I heard...yes."

"She's still holed up in her mansion?"

"I think so," General Spradlin said.

He pointed forward and Nox followed his finger. In the far distance and on a sandy hill, she saw a large, dark building. It was a very large home. A mansion.

"We'll find out soon enough," General Spradlin said.

They stopped before the metal gates that marked the entry to the compound and General Spradlin got out of their car. He approached the gate. The locking mechanism that once held it shut was rusted away.

"Not much security," General Spradlin said. He pushed the gate fully open before returning to the car.

"The mansion's up against what's left of the sea," Nox said. "When the one-time child soldiers track us down here, we'll be cornered."

General Spradlin shifted the car into gear. He drove past the gates.

The drive to the mansion only took a few minutes.

The road to it was littered with fallen branches that snapped under the weight of Spradlin's roadster. The sound was unnerving, like distant gunshots. The car continued on, working its way through what Nox imagined was once a very scenic road. Ugly shadows and sharp limbs brushed against the car as it moved along.

After a while, they passed the remains of the forest and entered an empty, sandy field. At one time it was probably a lush, grassy meadow. At the far end of the field, so far away it looked like an ugly black blemish in the coffee colored sand, stood an old, dilapidated structure. Jennifer Alberts' mansion. The passage of time was not kind. Several of the mansion's windows were boarded up. On the west side of the structure the roof sagged and threatened to collapse. There was little paint left on the stucco walls. An old generator lay at the side of the mansion. Its engine sputtered, sending dark smoke from its exhaust.

General Spradlin made a beeline straight to the decrepit structure. The car sent plumes of dust in its wake. There might have been a road here once leading up to the mansion, but now there was nothing but sand.

General Spradlin slowed the car down and parked it before the mansion's front entrance. He eyed the structure wearily, searching for any movement within. There was none.

"Let's see if she's home," General Spradlin said. He grasped his flare handgun. "Carefully."

General Spradlin shut the engine and exited the vehicle. Nox remained inside. She found it hard to move.

"I don't feel good," she told General Spradlin.

Spradlin walked to the passenger side of the car. He helped Nox up and out of the roadster.

"What's happening?" she said. Her words were slurred.

"Lemner's passkey is wearing you down," Spradlin said.

"Great timing," Nox replied.

General Spradlin helped Nox to the mansion's front door. It was ajar.

"Are Jennifer Alberts and you all that are left of the group that designed us?"

"There's one other," General Spradlin said.

"Who?"

He didn't say.

"Maybe they've already come for her," Nox said. "Maybe they're waiting for us inside."

"They didn't," General Spradlin said. "And they aren't."

"How do you know?"

"Because the mansion's still standing."

General Spradlin pushed the front door entrance fully open and helped Nox enter the darkness beyond.

38

The interior of the mansion, like the forest and the field around it, was probably quite a sight to see at one time. Today, it was a corroded shadow of its former self. Cobwebs clung from a grand chandelier that adorned the oversized entry. It was tilted and looked ready to fall. Once resplendent paintings lined the entry walls, their surfaces now covered in grime and filth. The carpet below their feet was almost completely black, though faint images of fanciful patterns and once bright colors still showed through.

The only illumination within the mansion came from the windows.

General Spradlin leaned Nox against a wall and gave her a few moments to catch her breath.

"Can you move?"

Nox nodded. Her face remained very pale and the dark rings under her eyes were even more pronounced.

"Where to?" Nox asked.

"It's been a while since I last visited," General Spradlin replied. "Many years."

"What was the occasion?"

"A party. We were...we were having a celebration."

"For?"

"The end of the war," he said. "It was a big media event. All the networks covered it. The party was meant to cheer everyone up."

"Everyone but those who died," Nox said. "I've changed my mind."

"About?"

"Sometimes it's OK to lie to me."

General Spradlin motioned to the passageway leading to the north end of the mansion.

"Let's move," he said.

General Spradlin followed behind Nox. They penetrated deeper and deeper into the mansion. The once grand home was little more than a rat's nest. Filth littered virtually every corner. Some doors were sealed shut and inaccessible. Closets were loaded with brittle and aged documents. In the foyer, they found water damage from a leak in the roof. In another large room, plaster from the walls crumbled to the floor.

"Are you sure she's still—" Nox began and stopped.

Despite her weakness, Nox's head snapped to the right. She clumsily reached for her flare handgun.

"I heard something," she whispered.

General Spradlin stepped past the Mechanic and moved in the direction of the sound. The two passed a hallway and came to a stop before a large oak door. General Spradlin motioned to the door and Nox nodded. He reached for the doorknob, squared his shoulders, and, at the silent count of three, burst through the door.

What they found beyond the door was a large office. Sitting at an equally large desk was a frail, elderly woman. She held a powerful flashlight in one hand and used it to illuminate a page in a book she was reading. Her reaction to the people who thrust themselves into the room was slow. She calmly put the flashlight down and closed her book before addressing them.

"Hello?" she said.

Despite the toll of time, Nox recognized Jennifer Alberts. Even as she did, she suppressed another surge of homicidal rage. Lemner's passkey held Jennifer Alberts in almost as much contempt as General Spradlin. Nox lowered her flare gun and leaned against a chair beside the door. She examined the frail woman before her. Jennifer Alberts was no longer the sharp industrialist from the video. Her eyes were milky white and faded. The expression on her face was a near blank.

General Spradlin checked the room for any sign of danger. When he was certain there was none, he approached the woman.

"Hello, Ms. Alberts," General Spradlin said.

The elderly lady eyed the man before her. She squinted hard and took a moment to think before saying:

"Spradlin? General Paul Spradlin?"

"Yes."

"Come closer."

General Spradlin did so, until he stood beside her. Jennifer Alberts' hands reached up as General Spradlin leaned down. She felt the contours of the General's cheeks and face. She paused for a second beside the strap of his eye patch.

"You haven't changed much," she said. "What happened to your eye?"

"Don't you remember?" the General said. "I lost it a few years back."

"How?"

"You know."

"Yes I do," she said. "I'd like to hear you tell me about it all the same. Especially since it caused you so much pain."

The elderly woman let out a chuckle. Her attention switched to Nox.

"Where are my manners," she said. "Who did you bring with you?"

"Her name is Nox."

"Should I know her?"

"At one time, I'm sure you did," General Spradlin said. "She was in the Arabian War."

The elderly lady leaned forward in her chair.

"Nonsense," she said. "She's way too young to be a veteran of—"

Jennifer Alberts abruptly stopped talking. Her lips involuntarily trembled.

"She's one of *them*, isn't she?" the elderly lady said. "I knew you'd come. I knew we didn't kill all of you. By the Gods...my sins...my sins are catching up to me. I knew..."

Just like that, the elderly woman's energy was spent. She fell back in her chair, exhausted.

"She's not here to harm you," General Spradlin gently told her.

Jennifer Alberts' eyes were no longer focused. The elderly woman said nothing nor appeared aware of where she was. Presently, her eyes were alive once again. She sat up and addressed her two visitors.

"Hello," she said. "How nice to have some guests. We get so very few these days."

A single tear ran down Jennifer Alberts' cheek.

"Hello, Ms. Alberts," General Spradlin said. "We came to see—"

"I know no one comes to see me," Jennifer Alberts said. "Not anymore. The money's gone and everything is finished. Everything." Jennifer Alberts couldn't hide her disappointment. She folded her fragile hands before her sunken chest and said: "You're here to see her, aren't you?"

"Yes."

"You're...you're General Spradlin," she said.

"Yes."

"Nothing is ever finished, is it General?" Jennifer Alberts said. "The past is never dead. It comes back to haunt us in small ways and large. Until we're gone. Until we're long gone."

Her eyes closed.

"She's down in the basement," the elderly woman said. "You know she doesn't want to see you."

"I know," Spradlin said. "But I have to see her."

"I can't stop you. Once upon a time I fooled myself into thinking I could. I fooled myself into thinking I had you under control when it was always –*always*– the other way around." She chuckled. "Nothing stops you from getting your way, does it?"

General Spradlin walked back to Nox's side.

"Let's go to the basement," he said.

"Exactly who are we here to see?" Nox asked.

"The first prototype."

39

They walked to the rear of the mansion and past a useless rusting hulk that was once a modern, elaborate kitchen. The refrigerator's door didn't quite close. A rotted stench emanated from within. Nox dragged as they moved along. General Spradlin hovered behind her, prepared to catch her if she fell.

Beside the refrigerator they found a small recess and, within it, a rotted white door.

General Spradlin opened that door. Hinges squealed in protest. There was a scuffed stairway ending at the foot of the door. It disappeared down into a pit of darkness.

Nox let out a soft laugh. It was only slightly louder than a whisper.

"Yet another basement," Nox said. She suppressed a shiver. "You guys do your best work underground."

General Spradlin placed Nox's right arm over his shoulders. Together, the two descended the stairs. They were alert to anything, threatening or otherwise. After a few steps, the darkness enveloped them. Other than the dim light coming from the open door leading into the basement, there was nothing their eyes could adjust to.

They continued nonetheless, down and down and deeper and deeper into the depths below the gloomy mansion before finally reaching the end of the stairs. Once there, General Spradlin felt to his side and along the grainy wall. He pulled Nox's arm from his shoulder and propped her against that wall.

"Hello?" he called out into the darkness. His hand fumbled around Nox, searching in vain for a light switch. "Are you here?"

The door to the kitchen area so far above them abruptly slammed shut. Nox and General Spradlin were immersed in complete darkness.

Nox felt movement beside her. Someone –or some*thing*– rush down the stairs and past her. General Spradlin let out a muffled sound, not quite a word. All was silent.

Nox remained still, unsure of where to go or what to do. She reached for the flare gun in her pant pocket, but did not have the energy to draw it out. She was completely at the mercy of whoever was there with them.

"General?" she whispered. "Are you...?"

The words caught in her throat. There was more movement coming from her right.

"General?" she repeated. "Talk to me."

Nox held out her arms and waved them around. She took a couple of steps away from the wall. There was even more movement at her side. A female voice, sharp and crystal clear, whispered in her ear.

"You're here to see me."

The voice was gone, replaced by laughter.

"Who are you?" Nox said.

There was no answer. The laughter died down.

"I know him," the female voice said. "Do I know you?"

More movement.

"Do I, General?"

The lights in the basement abruptly came on. For several seconds, Nox was blinded by the glare. She shielded her eyes and blinked several times. When her eyes adjusted to the sudden light, she saw two forms in front of her.

General Spradlin faced Nox. He could not speak. A muscular, hideously scarred hand cupped his mouth. A second hand, this one made of equal parts flesh and metal, wielded a black blade. The blade's surface was worn with age. It was pressed hard against General Spradlin's throat. The person holding Spradlin stood directly behind him. Nox tried to get a better look at her. Other than her deformed hands, all she saw was her long and stringy brown hair.

"We're not here to hurt you," Nox said, though she wasn't sure what they were here to do.

"I know *he* isn't," the woman said. "How about you?"

Nox gritted her teeth. The effort to stand was taking her remaining energy.

"W...who are you?" Nox asked.

The woman didn't immediately answer. Confusion clouded her face.

"Didn't the General tell you?"

"My experiences with General Spradlin have been...limited," Nox said. "I've found he likes to keep information to himself. Unless, of course, it serves his needs."

The woman holding the knife to General Spradlin's throat sniffed the air, as if a lioness catching the scent of prey.

"You're one of my soldiers, aren't you?" she asked. "Yes, yes you are."

"What do you mean 'your' soldiers?"

"It was up to me to make sure you were ready for battle."

"I don't remember any of that."

"What do you remember?"

"I remember…"

The pregnant woman with the bullet hole in her forehead lay beside the other bodies. The blood still flowed from the grotesque wound. The girl soldier –Nox– didn't care. She was more interested in cleaning her weapon.

The same memory, only totally different. The pregnant woman stood among the other villagers. Every one of them were alive and in good health. They were corralled to the center of the village and offered medicines and supplies. They waited to be loaded into transport trucks…

"…I don't remember all that much."

Another laugh.

"What are your first memories, dear?"

"Why do you care?"

"Curiosity, if nothing else."

Nox tried to speak but found it difficult to do so. She took a few steps back. She leaned against the wall and held herself there, barely upright.

"Tired are you?" the woman said. "The memories can wait, I suppose."

The woman holding the knife pushed General Spradlin away. He fell to the floor before Nox's feet.

For the first time, the Mechanic had a good look at the woman. She was roughly Nox's size and had a similar muscular frame. She wore a faded light green shirt and old, worn blue jeans. The metal prosthesis in her hand extended past the elbow joint. The flesh and metal union was grisly, marred by a series of ugly scars. When she looked at Nox, the Mechanic found herself staring into eyes that were shiny silver spheres.

"Which one are you?" the woman asked.

"My name is Nox."

She thought about that for a few seconds before putting the black blade away.

"I don't remember you," the woman said. She walked away. "I can't remember everyone I trained."

General Spradlin got to his feet.

"Are you OK?" he asked the Mechanic.

Nox noted drops of blood trickling from a small cut in the General's throat. The knife the woman wielded nicked his skin.

"I'm doing about as well as you are," Nox said. "Exactly who the fuck is she?"

Spradlin didn't say.

General Spradlin helped Nox move to the rear of the basement. There, they found even more darkness. The knife wielding woman disappeared through a doorway. It remained open and led to a subbasement level. There were rows and rows of beds hooked up to computer equipment. Everything within the room was dull and dusty. The woman who drew the blade on General Spradlin stood beside the rails, looking down at the beds below.

"This looks like Oscuro," Nox said.

"You know about Oscuro?" the woman asked.

"We were just there."

"Which one?"

"Which?" Nox repeated. "The original one...the one downtown."

The woman let out a laugh. She waved at the beds.

"This is Oscuro. The *first* Oscuro. This is where it all began."

"We need to talk," General Spradlin said.

"Oh? Would you like to reminisce? Chat about the good old days? Did we ever have any?"

"Now," General Spradlin insisted.

Despite her weakness, Nox's patience reached its limits.

"Enough," Nox said. She addressed General Spradlin. "Who the hell is she and why the hell are we here?"

"My, my, where are your manners, General?" the woman said. "Isn't it time you told her?"

General Spradlin walked to the rails. He too looked down on the beds below.

"Nox, this is Becky Waters."

The woman with the silver eyes smiled.

"Welcome home, little sister," she said.

40

"**I have no** relatives," Nox said.

"Your friend thinks too literally," Becky Waters said.

Nox shook her head. The room was spinning around her.

"Didn't know I came here for...for English lessons," Nox said. "The General said you were the first prototype. What did he mean?"

"I'm you, only I'm last year's model," Becky Waters said. She spread out her disfigured arms. "That's the problem with prototypes. They always have so many flaws."

"By the Gods," Nox muttered.

"Don't worry, my loss was your gain," Becky said. Machinery deep within her metal arms hummed and her silver eyes stared deep into Nox's. "Version 2.0 was a hell of a lot better than the first."

The lips on Becky Water's face curled into something resembling a sour smile.

"You're wondering what you're doing here, Nox? I'll tell you: You're here because whatever General Spradlin stepped into, it was really fucking deep and he's running out of alternatives. What is it this time?"

"We're being pursued," General Spradlin said.

"By?"

"The rest of the one-time child soldiers," General Spradlin said.

Becky Waters frowned.

"The rest? Are there any left?"

"The runts of the litter," General Spradlin said. "The rejects."

"I'm surprised you didn't kill them with the others," Becky Waters said. Her silver eyes turned to Nox. "Sometimes the runts are the ones you most have to watch out for."

"Were you programmed like us?" Nox asked. "From birth?"

"No," Becky Waters replied. "I was fully grown when I met General Spradlin. We shared many adventures. There's a thrill to living life on the edge while facing off against your opponents." She gazed at her flesh and machine arms. "Until one day, things don't work out so well. That day came for me one warm August night. I was injured. Bad. It didn't look like there was any hope. General Spradlin wouldn't hear of it. Instead of letting me die like he should have, he had me fixed up by his very best medics.

So much work and so much effort. I was still fading away. Then the good General had a brilliant idea. He gave me a transfusion of his own very unique blood."

Becky Waters shivered at the thought.

"It felt like my entire body was ripped apart atom by atom," Becky Waters said. "But I don't need to describe this to you. You know how it felt."

"I do."

"The transfusion kept me alive. Then, after a few months, I actually started getting better." She pointed to the scars along her arms. "If you can call this better. I think the General always wanted to create an army of people like me, like *him*, to face the coming menace."

"You mean Arabia?"

Becky Waters let out a laugh.

"He really hasn't told you much at all, has he?" Becky said. The smile on her face was ghastly. She walked to the cots. "For the next few years I was mostly a bed-ridden lab rat. My recovery was slow and very painful. I underwent more tests than I can remember and, like all lab rats, faced plenty of trial and error. More errors than trials. Then again, I'm still here. I suppose the General's work wasn't a complete failure."

Becky Waters' head hung low.

"I hear the voices, General. Lemner's passkey...a new version of it...was activated. That is why you came, right?"

"Yes."

"The calls are very strong, the voices are...angrier. Far angrier. The new program shares many of the same elements of the old...but it clearly isn't."

"David improved upon his creation," General Spradlin said.

Becky Waters shook her head.

"Improved?" she spat. "Lemner was a fool. He gave his Frankenstein monster the one thing is should not have: emotions. And this new version appears to have even more of it. You hear it, don't you Nox?"

"Yes."

"You already know it wants her to join the other runts," Becky Waters said. "I'm amazed she hasn't succumbed."

"Becky," General Spradlin said. "We're...we're at the end stage."

Becky Waters' silver eyes lit up for a second.

"I need her," General Spradlin said. "I need you to clear her head. I need you to still the voices, if only for a little while."

Becky Waters approached Nox. Her half machine hand came up. She laid it on Nox's cheek.

Nox tried to move away, but it was difficult for her to move at all. She reluctantly allowed Becky to press her metal and flesh hand against her cheek. For a second Nox felt an electric charge race through her body. In her mind there were visions of standing on a cliff's edge, staring into darkness. The darkness was Becky Waters' soul.

"She's burning up," Becky Waters said. "If the program can't have her, it will destroy her. Do you wish relief from the voices, Nox?"

"Do...do I have a choice?" she muttered.

"Of course you do," Becky Waters said. "You can take the easy route and give in to them. There will be no more pain, I'm sure of that, but you'll be gone, too. Or you can let me do what I can for you. You'll feel some pain, maybe even quite a bit of it, and I can make no promises about results. I will, however, try my best to help you."

"Did you have a choice?"

"Yes, and I made it a long, long time ago," Becky Waters said. She turned away from the Mechanic and faced General Spradlin. "What makes her so special?"

"She was in Arabia when the nukes were set off," General Spradlin said.

"She refused to follow your orders?" Becky Waters said. "Is that true, Nox?"

"Yeah."

"Good for you. She's one of a kind. I see why the passkey wants her so badly. In any other time I would gladly do what you ask. But now? Is it worth it? Why not just let the program do its worse? If we're at the end stage, why bother?"

"I haven't finished all my work," General Spradlin said. "There is the possibility Lemner's passkey might interfere with the other programs."

"It hasn't so far?"

"No," General Spradlin said. "But it searches."

"You can fend it off. There's something else. What is it?"

"The passkey ordered the kidnapping of twenty four babies kidnapped from the TransCo Hospital."

"The magic number. Lemner's passkey wants to start the soldier program up again?"

"Yes."

"Losing twenty four children is not such a big sacrifice in the grand scheme of things."

"I won't let them die," General Spradlin said.

"They're only twenty—"

"I *won't* let them die," he repeated.

"I'll be damned," Becky Waters said. "You actually care for them? Over your own safety?"

Despite the blurriness in her vision, Nox could see the emotion in General Spradlin's face. She saw the weight of many years of sadness and loss crack through his hardened exterior.

"Help me," General Spradlin pleaded.

"You've changed," Becky Waters said. She considered his request for a few seconds before saying:

"Why the hell not?"

General Spradlin took Nox's arm and slung it over his shoulder. The three walked to end of the rails. There, a staircase led down.

"What...what is this end stage?" Nox asked. Her words were very slurred. She no longer was fully awake but sleepwalking through a dream.

"The single greatest thing ever," General Spradlin replied.

They proceeded to Becky Water's central computer room.

General Spradlin laid Nox down on an old cot before the many machines. Nox felt there were more questions she needed to ask, but the fog enveloping her mind made it difficult for her to think. She felt like a child once again, a child guided through this strange world by adult hands. She couldn't comprehend their actions, yet knew there was purpose in them.

Becky Waters paused before her computer equipment. It was ancient and for the most part outdated. A portable generator lay on the floor beside it. Becky Waters hit a switch and the generator came on. It was incredibly noisy and expelled a foul smoke. Becky Waters ignored it. Her attention shifted to the computers. She turned them on, one after the other. As she did, her lips moved. She was talking to General Spradlin. Their conversation was hushed, but from the look on their faces, whatever they were discussing was very important.

Nox tried to hear what they said, but their voices were drowned out by the generator.

At one point, Becky Waters offered the Mechanic a sad smile.
Easy child.

Her lips hadn't moved yet her words appeared in Nox's mind. Things around the Mechanic swirled as if she were on a carnival ride.

The conversation between General Spradlin and Becky Waters ended and the machine woman resumed her work on the computer. Minutes passed. Eventually, she paused. She looked into General Spradlin's eye.

When I do this, they'll know where we are. They will attack. They will destroy this place and kill everyone they find.

We need to get the children.

What about Jennifer?

General Spradlin laid his hand on Becky Waters' shoulder.

I'll save her, too.

Becky Waters nodded. She stepped away from the computers and walked to the stairway. General Spradlin reached out and stopped her.

I have to bring her down.

General Spradlin relented. Becky Waters left the room. Nox felt movement coming from somewhere above and heard ghostly voices. When Becky Waters returned, she carried Jennifer Alberts in her arms. She placed the old woman on a chair and gently arranged her hair. The elderly lady was bewildered by these surroundings.

We'll be fine, dear.

The words came from Becky Waters. Her tone was remarkably caring.

"What is she to you?" Nox heard herself say.

She's all I have left in this world.

Becky Waters rubbed her silver eyes and they sparkled in the dim light.

In that moment, Nox realized the two women shared very similar features. Jennifer Alberts and Becky Waters were blood relatives. Direct descendants.

How...how old are you?

The question was directed at Becky Waters, but even as Nox spoke it she realized it applied to General Spradlin. She asked him that same question before and hadn't received a straight answer. General Spradlin and Becky Waters were team mates at one time and had to be of similar age. Yet both looked *far* younger than Jennifer Alberts, a woman the General knew when Nox was barely in her teens.

How was that possible?

Becky Waters approached the computer system. She sat before it and pressed a series of buttons. The ancient equipment hummed and screens came alive with information.

You may feel...something, Becky Waters said.

Nox did. She felt the old program stir within her. An ancient rage flared up. Lemner's passkey was unleashed.

At that moment, it had her.

Nox felt its rage overwhelm her. She reached out, her movements faster than her thoughts. She tried out to grab General Spradlin.

Just as she did, her world went black.

41

"You're one of us. Come back. Come back..."

Nox recognized the voice. She opened her eyes and found...

The pregnant woman with the bullet hole in her forehead lay beside a row of bodies. Fresh blood flowed from her gory wound. The girl soldier sat a dozen yards away. She knew the shot was fatal and therefore was no longer interested in this kill. Her attention was on cleaning her weapon.

The elder Nox stood to the side of her younger self, watching the scene before her. The tank commanders, absurdly, rushed to the fatally injured woman's side and tried to help her. The young soldier couldn't help but notice their movements.

Why do they bother? the soldier girl thought. *She's the enemy. The enemy must die.*

A boy sat on the ground a few feet away from the two. His brilliant blue eyes were on them and, in turn, the older and younger Nox realized they were being watched. The boy smiled. He leaned back and stretched his legs.

"Join us."

The scene around the elder Nox froze in time. The boy soldier and the elderly Nox were the only ones moving in this still picture.

"Return to us," the boy said. "Become what we were always meant to be. Soldiers."

"Killers," Nox said.

The smile remained on the boy's face.

"There will come a point where we will no longer ask."

Nox ignored the threat. Her eyes were back on the village and the scene before her.

"This isn't right," she said.

"What difference does it make?" the boy retorted.

Nox ignored his comments. Her body shook and her eyes closed. She concentrated hard, trying to remember. Trying to—

Her eyes opened.

The scene before her shifted. The rows of bodies disappeared while the wreckage of the village dissolved. New walls and intact buildings formed. Villagers –alive and uninjured– appeared. They were all there. Even the pregnant woman. They huddled in groups around several large military transport trucks. They boarded these trucks in pairs while the child soldiers offered those who needed it food and water. The villagers did not protest or argue. Somehow, they knew they were safe. They knew the child soldiers, despite their fearsome weaponry, posed no threat.

No one died.

The boy soldier, Joshua Landon, watched this new scene play out.

"This is a lie," he said.

The scene shifted once again. The village and the villagers disappeared. All was white. At Joshua Landon's side appeared the young Nox. She reached for her weapon and took aim at an invisible target.

The elder Nox followed the gun's barrel. The pregnant woman reappeared. She lay on her back. Blood caked the side of her face. Her eyes fluttered open. She lifted her body slightly, only to recoil in horror at the sight of unseen relatives and friends lying dead around her. Her hands came to her mouth. She wanted to scream, but she couldn't.

The girl Nox once was tightened her grip on the rifle's trigger.

"You were the only one to see her move," Joshua Landon told her. "You did as you were programmed."

"This isn't what happened," Nox said.

"You are a soldier," Landon said. "This is what soldiers do. No mercy. None at all."

"That isn't what happened."

The image of Nox's younger self blurred. More images flashed before her. The villagers were alive. The villagers were dead. The villagers were alive...

"What did they do to me?" Nox yelled.

Joshua Landon smiled.

"Whatever they wanted, until they decided we were of no more use to them. Then they discarded us. We won't do that, Nox. We will never discard you. We are family."

A rifle appeared in the elder Nox's hand. Without wanting to, she raised and aimed it at the vision of the pregnant woman. The villagers were dead. The villagers were alive.

"This isn't right," Nox said. She had no control over her body. She felt her fingers slowly squeeze the trigger. "Stop this."

"We're going to make this a better world."

"By killing pregnant women?"

"By killing the enemy, whoever they are."

The villagers were alive...the villagers were dead.

"We will make humanity stronger.   We will protect this world."

"From what?"

"From what's coming."

"What is coming?"

To this Joshua Landon had no reply. Nox fought to lower her rifle. She could not.

"What makes you think we'll do any better?"

"We'll get it right."

Despite her heightened emotions, Nox couldn't help but laugh.

"That's what they all say."

With those words, the spell was broken and Nox had control of her weapon. She lowered it. The villagers before her were alive. The pregnant woman she saw shot in her nightmares was alive and uninjured. She was escorted to the transport vehicle by the younger Nox and climbed inside. She was with her friends and family. She was safe.

"They've manipulated our thoughts," Nox said.   "They created a false story within the real memories."

"They made us and threw us away," Landon said. "We will do the same to them. We are the next generation. The superior generation."

Nox was no longer interested in what Joshua Landon – Lemner's passkey– had to say.

"Why would they imprint one memory over another?" she wondered aloud. "Why...?"

"Come with us," Landon insisted. "...Please..."

The village and its surroundings faded away. Joshua Landon fought to remain, but he too vanished, as did the rifle in Nox's hands.

The Mechanic now stood upon a grassy hill. Before her was a lush, beautiful forest. In all her life she had never seen so many shades of vibrant green. Trees were alive and filled with leaves. The grass was long and swayed gently in the wind. The sky was clear.

"Nox?"

Before her appeared a young, attractive woman.   Nox recognized her instantly, even though her body and limbs were entirely of flesh and she no longer bore scars or mechanical attachments. Her silver eyes were now a vibrant blue. They were human eyes.

"Why am I here?" Nox asked the vision of Becky Waters.

"Because I needed to clear your mind before I could bring you back."

"Back?"

"I had to dig deep, sort through every nano-probe within your being. I had to inoculate you."

"From Lemner's passkey?"

Becky Waters didn't answer her question. She sat down before Nox and motioned to the forest.

"The world was like this, once," Becky Waters said. "Before we let it go."

"Can it be brought back?"

"No," Becky Waters said. "It's gone forever."

The smile faded away. A single drop of blood fell rolled down the side of her head. Nox watched it, transfixed by the sight. Another drop fell. Then another.

Nox felt a deep unease. It gnawed at her, growing into something larger. Something terrifying. She looked down at her hands. There was blood on them.

"Have I...did I do something?"

"Yes."

"What?"

"It doesn't matter. What's important is that you have to trust General Spradlin. No matter what he's done to you and the other child soldiers."

"I don't think I can," Nox said. "Not entirely."

"Try. Please."

Becky Waters pointed into the distance. The forest faded, replaced by the harsh yellows of the Arabian village. The villagers were alive and in the process of being escorted to the transport vehicle. The young girl Nox once was helped the pregnant woman onto a truck. She offered her a canteen.

"This is it," Becky Waters said. "Can you feel it?"

Nox could. Somewhere deep within her she knew that this vision of her encounter with that Arabian village was the truth. It was the memory stripped of all lies.

"I didn't kill them," Nox said. She couldn't stop the tears from streaming down her eyes. "They left. They were taken away. Where?"

"To safety," Becky Waters said.

"Why…why was I given those false memories?"

"It was my idea."

Nox faced Becky Waters.

"Why?" she pleaded. "Why torture me like this?"

"It wasn't my intention," Becky replied. "You were front line soldiers. That was a dangerous position to be in in more ways than one. We feared that if any of you were captured, the truth of what you were doing in Arabia might come out."

"What truth?"

"That you weren't the bloodthirsty, fearsome soldiers we made you out to be. That you didn't wipe out entire villages. In your mind, we made you vicious killers. In reality, you were saviors."

Becky Waters wiped the blood from her forehead.

"We couldn't let the world know what you were really doing. It would have endangered General Spradlin's plan."

"What was his plan?"

"You'll find out soon enough," Becky Waters said.

Nox grimaced.

"I…I still hear their voices," she said. "The passkey is still trying—"

"You will hear the passkey's wails for as long as it exists," Becky Waters said. "Now, you have to return. You have to set things right. You have to save those twenty four children."

"So they can grow up in this dying world?"

"You'll save them Nox, because that's the type of person you are. And because you're the only one who can."

Becky Waters laid her hand on Nox's shoulder. Nox looked into Becky Waters' natural eyes. She saw in those eyes several lifetimes' worth of sadness.

"I'm as much to blame for this as General Spradlin," she said. She offered Nox her hand. "We can set things right."

"I'm afraid," Nox said.

"You have reason to," Becky replied. "But I promise we will fix this. Do you believe me?"

Nox thought about that. Finally, she took Becky Waters' hand.

"Yeah," Nox said. "I do."

Nox helped Becky to her feet.

"Let's finish this."

42

Becky Waters let out a scream when she emerged from her artificial dreams.

Her silver eyes flashed in the dull lights of the basement. She sniffed the smoky air. Blood dripped from the side of her face and stained the floor. Her artificial limbs could not move. Her body was momentarily paralyzed. She looked at the computers around the room. Dark smoke emerged from several of them.

"They've found us," Becky Waters said. "They're on their way here."

"It was inevitable," General Spradlin said.

He was at her side and wiped the blood from her face. Becky looked at the cot beside the one she was in. Nox was there, sleeping. The Mechanic let out a low moan. She was coming to.

Becky Waters felt some strength return to her body. She forced herself into a sitting position and reached over to check Nox's pulse.

"Is it done?" General Spradlin asked.

Becky Waters nodded. She released Nox's arm. Her attention shifted to the room. In the corner sat Jennifer Alberts. Moments before, the elderly woman watched them while they worked on Nox. She too had drifted off to sleep.

"Help me," Becky Waters said.

General Spradlin did. He helped Becky to her feet and took her to Jennifer Alberts' side.

"Jennifer was always a real pain in my ass," General Spradlin said. "You did what I asked. Let me take care of her."

General Spradlin released Becky Waters and reached into his jacket pocket. When his hand emerged, it carried a small leather pouch. He unzipped it and exposed a syringe and set of vials.

"This will take care of her," General Spradlin said.

"Didn't you shut off the machines?"

"Temporarily. When she's injected, they will receive the signal. It will take care of her."

"Is she worth it?" Becky Waters asked.

"Everyone is worth it," General Spradlin said.

"You didn't use to think that way."

"I've changed."

He took the syringe and injected the clear solution into the elderly woman's arm. Alberts grimaced and let out a soft moan but did not awake.

"That's it?" Becky Waters asked.

"Yes."

The warrior woman gently ran her hand through the elderly woman's hair, arranging it. She pulled in close and laid a tender kiss on her forehead.

"You had family once, didn't you?" Becky Waters asked.

"They're gone now."

"You miss them?"

"Every day."

"She's all I have left," Becky Waters said. She closed her eyes. "I remember holding Jennifer when she was a child. I remember...I remember her fourth birthday. She loved cartoons, especially the ones with princesses and magic kingdoms. I bought her a toy magic wand. When she saw it, she took off, ran to the corner of her room. Her parents were relieved to have a few free moments. Me? I couldn't take my eyes off her. She waved the wand, like they did in the cartoons, and pointed it at the floor. She was making a wish. I don't know what she wished for. It...it broke my heart to see the look of disappointment on her face when she realized there was no magic in that wand."

Tears rolled down Becky Waters' checks and mingled with her blood.

"There's still some magic left," General Spradlin said. He laid his hand on Becky Waters' shoulder. "I'll miss you."

Becky Waters laughed.

"You haven't seen me in twenty years."

"That was a mistake."

Becky Waters held General Spradlin's hands in hers. Both set of arms, Becky Waters' as well as General Spradlin's were scarred with age and wear. Hers as much as his.

"One day, they'll know what we did," Becky Waters said. "They'll know what we went through."

"Do you have any regrets?"

"None," Becky Waters said.

"I wish I could say the same."

"Save the children, General Spradlin," she said. "Save yourself."

Becky Waters knew she didn't have to tell him. General Spradlin would save them. General Spradlin would save the world.

It's what he always did.

43

Nox awoke to chaos.

From somewhere far away came the blare of alarms. She smelled smoke and felt hectic movement. Her eyes fluttered open and she realized she was the one moving. She was in a dark corridor. Computer panels lined the walls. They flashed a bloody red, all warning of imminent danger.

From the corner of her eye she saw General Spradlin. Her right arm was draped over his shoulders. He was holding her up and dragging her down the passage.

"...what...?" she asked. Her voice was weak, her mind still in a fog.

"Easy," General Spradlin said.

Nox shook her head.

"What happened?" she asked.

"Becky Waters temporarily purged the old program from your system," General Spradlin muttered. "You remember?"

"Some."

"In doing so, she gave away our location. Lemner's passkey attacked."

A crashing sound come from somewhere above.

"Joshua Landon and the other child soldiers are here," General Spradlin said.

The crashing increased. There were many people above and inside the mansion. They were scurrying about and destroying everything they crossed. They were working their way down to the basement.

Down to them.

"Where's Becky?" Nox asked. "Where's Jennifer Alberts?"

"They're gone," General Spradlin said.

Nox raised her free hand. It was covered in blood.

"What did I do?" she asked. "What the hell did I do?!"

General Spradlin ignored her question.

"They're converging on the basement," he said. "It won't be long before they make it inside."

Nox put weight on her legs in an attempt to speed up their movements. A wave of nausea washed over her. When it passed, a memory burst into her mind with the force of a nuclear bomb.

"I know exactly where the children are," Nox said. "I can feel them."

"They're alive?" General Spradlin asked.

"Yes. All twenty four of them."

"Good," General Spradlin said.

They reached a large wooden door and General Spradlin gently put Nox down on the stone floor. The sound of mayhem coming from above was reaching its apex. Somewhere, a door crashed open.

"They've found the staircase," Nox said.

General Spradlin pushed the wooden door open. Beyond it was a garage filled with a half dozen vehicles. Many were in disrepair. Another couple were classic roadsters. The last was a desert all-terrain vehicle. Behind the door and nailed to the wall was a wooden box. Spradlin opened it and found sets of labeled keys. He quickly located the one he needed and helped Nox back to her feet.

As they entered the garage, they heard the discordant sounds of ripping metal.

"They're through the security doors in the main computer room," Nox said. The fog in her mind was lifting with each passing second. She frowned. "I feel her."

"Who?"

"Becky," Nox said. She shook her head. "She's still alive!"

Nox tried to turn, but General Spradlin held her firm.

"She's still alive," Nox repeated. "We have to get her!"

"We can't," General Spradlin said.

"You left her behind…on purpose?"

"We have to go."

"What have you done?" Nox said.

"We have to go," he repeated, softly.

They hurried to the all-terrain vehicle.

44

When they reached the vehicle, Spradlin used the key he retrieved from the wooden box to unlock its passenger door. He helped Nox into her seat, ran to the other side, and climbed into the driver's seat. He scanned the controls and noted the radio over the vehicle's central panel. He yanked it from its place and tossed it out the window.

"She's an older vehicle," General Spradlin said. "We'll just have to hope there aren't any other electronic devices within susceptible to Lemner's passkey."

Nox barely heard him. Her thoughts were on those they left behind. She feared what Joshua Landon and his one-time child soldiers would do when they found Becky Waters and Jennifer Alberts. General Spradlin inserted the key into the ignition and turned it. The truck's engine coughed once before roaring to life. He waited a few seconds while it warmed up. The engine sounded fine. It appeared there was nothing within the vehicle for Lemner's passkey to grab on to.

General Spradlin let out a relieved breath.

"Good," he said. "Hang on."

The vehicle skidded from its parking place and into a long, poorly lit corridor. At the end of the corridor was a metal garage door.

"Hang on," General Spradlin said.

The truck smashed through the door, ripping away the thin sheet metal. From the darkness of the garage the duo emerged into a very sunny day. They were on the north side of the mansion and on the white sands surrounding it. They moved away fast. Though Nox could still barely move, she forced herself to turn in her seat.

She looked back at the mansion and found it was engulfed in flames. Shadowy figures were visible in the building's windows. They moved at great speeds. One of the figures saw the ATV exit the parking garage. Almost as a collective, the other figures in the windows disappeared.

"They're after us," Nox said.

General Spradlin floored the accelerator. The vehicle skidded down a gentle sandy hill. They approached the north side shore. The rusted relics of tankers lined the beach and the water was a corrosive green.

A bullet shattered the vehicle's rear window.

"Get down," General Spradlin said. For a moment he closed his eyes. A look of great concentration filled his face.

We're out.

The two words echoed in Nox's head. The voice was General Spradlin's. The message was directed outward.

"That was for Becky Waters?" Nox asked.

General Spradlin opened his eyes.

"Yes," he said.

As the words left his mouth, the mansion erupted in a massive ball of flame. The concussive wave sent the ATV skidding. It wobbled wildly and almost tipped. The shock wave was followed by an equally strong heat wave, one hot enough to set the sand itself on fire. When the energy waves were spent, pieces of mortar and wood rushed past them. Chunks of shrapnel capable of ripping limbs and tearing flesh slammed into the sands.

General Spradlin fought the controls of the ATV. The vehicle continued to lurch from side to side, but he kept his speed while the ruins of the mansion fell around them.

Soon, the debris lessened and the vehicle was under control. General Spradlin slowed down and turned until they faced the remains of Jennifer Alberts' mansion.

There was nothing left of it. The structure was completely gone. Heavy black smoke rose from an equally black crater.

For several seconds, Nox and General Spradlin watched the fires around the crater burn. For several seconds, neither said anything.

"They're gone," Nox said. There was emptiness within her, a feeling the bulk of the one-time child soldiers were lost. "I can only sense a few of them left..."

A shadow appeared over General Spradlin's face.

"He's still alive," Spradlin said.

"Yes he is," Nox said. She too could feel Joshua Landon and, through him, Lemner's passkey. She could feel its frustration and anger. It suffered a devastating loss and a majority of its soldiers were now dead. Ironically enough, they died the way Lemner's passkey attempted to kill General Spradlin at the TransCo Hospital. They were lured here, just as he was to the Hospital. At the Hospital, the bombs were defused. Here, Joshua Landon's soldiers hadn't been quite so lucky.

"He's alive but injured," Nox said.

"Yes," General Spradlin replied. The shadow over his face lifted and was replaced by sadness. He closed his eyes once again and concentrated.

Goodbye, Becky.

General Spradlin gripped the vehicle's steering wheel and drove off.

45

They passed the boundaries of Jennifer Alberts' estate and were back in the Big City. The deserted buildings looked even more ominous in the light of day. The morning sun obliterated the shadows that hid much of the empty city's ugliness. Several more of the massive skyscrapers had caught fire. The fires sent plumes of heavy black smoke into the sky. As before, there were no signs of anyone or anything to come fight the flames. They would burn until they could burn no more.

Nox watched all this. She no longer felt weak. Whatever Becky Waters did to her, she was recovering fast. Her pale skin was turning a healthy pink and she sat erect in her seat.

"This is it. The end of the world."

General Spradlin pressed down hard on the accelerator and continued their trip through the wide, empty streets.

They found a barricade of cars and debris in front of the Northwest exit of the Big City. General Spradlin slowed their vehicle down. His head swiveled back and forth. His eyes probed for some way through. He found a way out on the west edge of the barricades, a small opening that was nonetheless large enough for their ATV to fit through.

Something, however, didn't feel right. Instead of driving through the opening, General Spradlin hit the brakes.

"You feel it too?" Nox said. There were eyes on them. Watching, checking.

Abruptly, General Spradlin shifted the vehicle into reverse. Tires screeched as she backed away from the blockade. As quickly as she moved, it was not quick enough. Something slammed into the road before them, sending a ball of flame in all directions. The vehicle lifted off the ground and fell on its side. The front end was a mangled ball of fire.

Nox ripped away her seatbelt.

"Let's go," she said.

General Spradlin didn't move. He was in a daze and blood stained the front of his fatigues.

Nox kicked what remained of the shattered windshield. She slid from her seat to the ground and reached back inside, pulling General Spradlin from the wreckage and carrying him down the hill and toward the nearest building. Whoever fired upon them scurried out of sight.

"Things keep getting better and better," Nox said.

When they were safely in the building, she laid the General down and checked for wounds. He had a deep gouge in his left shoulder from which a large piece of shrapnel stuck. Nox swore and grabbed at it.

"This is going to hurt," she said.

She pulled the shrapnel out as the General groaned. The metal piece was at least three inches long and quite dull.

Good thing it was, she thought. *Or else it would have sliced right through you.*

Nox set it on the ground and ripped off part of her shirt. She wrapped the torn fabric against the wound.

"Hold on to it," she said.

Though he was barely conscious, General Spradlin did as told. It was the worst possible time to be helpless.

Deeper in the building, Nox heard the sounds of someone moving.

"Stay here," Nox said. "I'll be right back."

She headed deeper into the building.

Nox moved on, weighing the danger of not allowing her eyes to completely adjust to the darkness inside the building.

She didn't have the time.

She heard the sounds of footsteps just a few feet from her and froze behind a corner. The person moving in her direction was doing so cautiously. She knew who it was.

Joshua Landon's feet shuffled against the dusty floor. His breathing was very heavy. Nox could feel his pain. The injuries he sustained from the explosion at Jennifer Alberts' mansion were very serious and Nox had an advantage. Would it be enough?

Let's find out.

Nox kept still while the sounds increased. She could feel the one-time child soldier, the boy –now man– that walked at her side in Arabia approach even closer. He was silent and focused.

Abruptly, Joshua Landon stopped moving.

You can still join us.

Nox took a step back, surprised by the thought that intruded into her mind. Joshua Landon knew she was there. He knew—

Goosebumps covered Nox's arms. She took a step back, then another before running at full speed away. Even before her mind could put it into words, she realized Joshua set a trap. He positioned her exactly where *he* wanted her to be.

The wall Nox was hiding behind only a second before erupted in explosive flames.

Nox was thrown hard to the ground. Debris both large and small stung her body and her ears rung. Nox spun aside. Her mind was in a haze but she quickly got up. Heavy black dust floated around her, dulling her vision. Nox desperately looked about, trying to see where Joshua Landon was. She knew he was about to attack, yet no longer knew from where. She could no longer *feel* him.

Was he gone?

Nox knew that was unlikely. Injured or not, he would—

Nox noticed a shadowy figure emerge from a doorway to her right. To Nox's surprise, it was a woman, one the Mechanic recognized instantly. It was Alexandra Despero, the one-time child soldier who found General Spradlin's Big City parking hideaway.

She stood a full foot shorter than Nox and sported black and gray hair. She was overweight and her body was flaccid. Yet her eyes were a brilliant brown and ringed with a violent red.

She let out a scream and launched herself at Nox.

Nox grabbed the woman's arms and twisted.

The moment she touched Alexandra Despero, Nox felt a sharp sting throughout her body. Her nano-probes were being assaulted by those within Despero. Even though the middle-aged woman was hardly a physical match to Nox, with the aid of her nano-probes she could easily gain the upper hand.

You can still join us.

The words were Alexandra's. The words were Joshua Landon's.

The words belonged to Lemner's passkey.

Nox felt the flesh under her skin heat up. She desperately twisted her body while Alexandra used her weight to force Nox back and down. Nox anticipated the action and half-turned. The two dropped to the floor on their sides and Nox violently kicked the woman away. The moment Alexandra's grip on Nox was severed, she felt her strength return. No longer were Alexandra's nano-probes bombarding her system.

With a quick swing, Nox smashed her fist into the woman's face.

Alexandra rolled back. The blow broke her nose and blood flowed down the side of her face. The one-time child soldier got back to her feet and drew her arms out in anticipation of another attack. She let out an animalistic hiss.

Nox was gone.

The woman waved at the dusty air and crouched low. Another low growl erupted from deep within her throat. She stepped forward, momentarily stopping to pick up a metal pipe. She wiped the blood from her face. She smiled. The blood from her nose dripped onto her teeth.

"I know where you are," Alexandra said.

She crept forward, slowly approaching the far end of the room. There, a crooked, shattered wall had collapsed like a large tree.

The one-time child soldier grabbed at that flimsy wall. She cautiously pulled it away, revealing the gaping hole behind it.

There was no one hiding there.

Surprise registered on the woman's face. She turned quickly, but Nox was already there. The Mechanic tackled the woman and slammed her against the floor, knocking the air from her lungs. Alexandra, in turn, swung the metal tube and clipped Nox on the side of her head.

The blow was enough to send Nox back. She barely had time to look up before Alexandra was once again on top of her. One hand reached for the Mechanic's flesh, touching her neck and linking her poisoned nano-probes to Nox's. She then smashed the metal tube against Nox's midsection and followed that with a second quick blow. Nox deflected it with her arm and slid away.

Nox's vision consisted of faint blurs. Alexandra Despero was a black mass. She saw a glint of light reflect on the metal tube and watched as the woman raised it over her head. She wasn't going to stop until Nox was dead.

That's what makes them different from me, Nox thought. She had killed but it wasn't her first instinct to do so. Yet Alexandra Despero wasn't in control over what she was doing. Nox didn't want to hurt her.

She had no choice.

Alexandra raised the metal bar over her head. Nox could crawl no more.

Kill or be killed.

Nox felt blood drip from the side of her head. Her jaw locked and she reached into her pant pocket. Her hand grasped the second and last flare handgun General Spradlin gave her in the armory.

The metal tube came down. Fast.

Before it reached her, Nox pulled the gun out. She didn't know –or care– what setting it was on.

She fired.

A bright white electric burst sprang from the handgun and enveloped the one-time child soldier. The metal tube flew from Alexandra Despero's grip and past Nox, slamming onto the dusty floor only inches from the Mechanic's head. Alexandra stood frozen above Nox, her body in shock. Her skin blackened, charring as the electronic pulse roared through her. Parts of her smoldered and caught fire, the sizzling flesh giving off the smell of cooked meat.

In seconds, the charge was spent. What was left of Alexandra Despero dropped to her knees. Her flesh was charred black. Her ferocious brown eyes still looked forward.

Alexandra Despero died staring at Nox.

Nox threw the flare gun away and got to her feet.

She examined the corpse lying before her. This woman was a child soldier just like her at one time. If only for a quirk of fate, it could well have *been* her.

"You did what you had to do," came a voice from behind Nox.

The Mechanic found General Spradlin standing behind her. His face showed signs of life. He held the two last flare handguns in each hand.

"Don't tell me what I had to do," Nox shot back. She walked to General Spradlin's side. "Joshua Landon was here."

"I felt his presence," General Spradlin said. "He's gone."

"The signals from the passkey are even stronger now," Nox said. "We're getting closer to it."

"I know," General Spradlin said. He approached Alexandra Despero's corpse.

"Your electronic toy worked well," Nox said. "Now we're down to the two guns you have."

"I should have devoted more time researching ways of...of stopping the child soldiers," General Spradlin said. He eyed Nox. "No offense."

"None taken."

"In the old days, all we had were black blades. At least with the handguns we have a bit more space."

"It's always easier to kill when you don't have to stare down your victim," Nox said. She sighed. "Killing is too damn easy as it is."

Nox leaned against a wall. She massaged her temples.

"What about you, General? You still have a taste for this?"

"No," he said. "I'm fucking exhausted."

Nox nodded. She reached for the General's shirt and pulled the collar to get a better look at his wound. It remained a bloody mess.

"You heal a lot slower than I do," Nox said. "If I'd taken the shrapnel, the bleeding would have stopped by now."

"Joshua Landon's poisonous nano-probes prevent mine from healing me like they used to."

"You never did tell me how you got them."

"No I didn't," General Spradlin said.

He motioned for Nox to follow him out of the building and back to the barricade.

46

For their second approach to the barricade, they walked.

They did so with great caution, hiding behind anything they found along the way and making sure they weren't letting themselves be easy targets. Yet they also knew that none of the one-time child soldiers remained behind. Joshua Landon left before Alexandra Despero died and he didn't have any other soldiers with him.

The two moved past the barricade and stepped onto a field of brilliant white and coffee colored sand. They were in the Desertlands. At the other side of the barricade was a ramshackle diner, the first before the Big City and the last for many miles of desert. It was a popular trucking stop and literally the last chance to fuel up and resupply before heading into hostile territory. A trio of abandoned vehicles was parked in front of the structure. Two of them were modern, sporting considerable computer technology. The third was a very familiar looking military transport truck.

"Is that...?" Nox asked the General as they approached the vehicles.

It was. Nox recognized it as the very same transport truck General Spradlin and she used to travel from the military base to the Oscuro building.

General Spradlin pulled a set of keys from his pocket and inserted one of them into the transport's door. It slid in smoothly.

"You planned this?"

General Spradlin nodded.

"Son of a bitch," Nox said and laughed. She motioned to the diner.

"I'll go check that place out, see if there's any water or supplies."

"No need," General Spradlin said. He walked to the transport's rear hatch and opened it. "We've got enough."

Within the trunk was a cardboard box filled with rations and bottles of fresh water.

"I'll be damned," Nox said. "You really did plan everything."

"It's always good to have contingencies," General Spradlin said.

Nox walked to the passenger seat of the transport while General Spradlin inspected the supplies. When he was done he closed the rear hatch and entered the vehicle through the driver's side door. Nox was already in her seat, waiting to go.

"We have enough supplies to make it to Lemner's base," Nox said.

"Yeah."

General Spradlin inserted the key into the ignition.

"Ready?" he asked.

"As much as I'll ever be," Nox replied.

In seconds, they were off.

The first hour of their trip passed in silence.

While Nox felt renewed after leaving Jennifer Alberts' estate, those energies were rapidly depleting the closer they were to Lemner's base. The signals coming from Lemner's passkey were furious, and fighting them was taking what strength Nox had. Her skin was once again turning pale, her eyes were half open. She shook off a wave of nausea and rubbed her hair.

"You going to tell me what this is about?" Nox asked. Her words were slightly slurred.

"You mean other than saving the world."

"Salvation through complete destruction? That's a funny way of saving the world, General."

"There's a lot you don't know."

"Tell me."

"You wouldn't understand...or believe."

"Try me."

General Spradlin shook his head. The midday sun blasted the interior of the military transport craft and the heat was overwhelming.

"Later," General Spradlin said. "In another hour we should be there. Save your energies, Nox. You'll need them."

47

The vehicle slowed but Nox barely felt it.

To her, the drive into the Desertlands felt like a long fall into a deep, dark hole. Above, the harsh sun felt like it was being swallowed up by an oppressive darkness along with the rest of the world. All that remained was rage.

"We're very close," Nox said between gritted teeth.

General Spradlin stopped the transport truck and shut its engine off.

"We'll walk the rest of the way," he said.

They were a little over a hundred and fifty kilometers from the Big City. For most of their trip they followed the common roads used by suppliers and prospectors before leaving that path and traveling into the deep shifting sands. There were significant chunks of civilization buried under these sands, including their goal.

"How many of them are left?" General Spradlin asked.

"Not many," Nox replied. "Including Landon, four...no, five. We only have two flare guns."

"And our quick wits."

"I'm all out of that."

They walked for a half hour through the scorching, endless terrain. For Nox, the dark emotions swirling around her were growing unbearable, especially when one of the objects of the passkey's rage walked right beside her.

"You should have left me," she told General Spradlin. "Taking me along was a mistake. I don't think...I don't think I can help you."

Nox's face was now drained of all color and the dark circles under her eyes were deep.

"When the time comes, you *will* help me," Spradlin said. "I have no doubt."

After a while, General Spradlin stopped walking. He grabbed Nox's hand and turned her until she faced him.

"I have to give you something," he said.

General Spradlin reached into his shirt pocket and produced the small leather pouch. He opened it and showed Nox its contents. She stared at the sophisticated syringe and the glass vials.

"Wh... what is this?"

"Vaccines."

"For?"

"The children."

"Are they...were they...poisoned?"

"They were."

"What's the plan?"

"We find the facility, get to the infants, and you give each one of them a shot," General Spradlin said.

Nox stared at the General.

"You know me, always with the complicated plans," Spradlin said.   "Whatever happens, you need to give them these injections."

"Why?"

"Because if you don't, they will be lost."

"To what? Disease? Radiation?"

"Something far worse."

"What's worse than death?"

A sad smile appeared on General Spradlin's face.

"Plenty," General Spradlin said. The smile disappeared. He closed the pouch and handed it to Nox. "This vaccine ensures the children will be saved. Make sure they get it."

"What about you?"

"I'll be...I'll be busy. It's up to you to do this."

"If it's that important, you should keep it," she said. "You can't trust me."

"I have faith in you, Nox," General Spradlin said.

He placed the pouch in her hand and guided her hand down, until she placed the pouch into her pant pocket.

"You're a survivor," the General said. "You will do what needs to be done."

"I can barely think. How do you—"

"The syringe is calibrated," General Spradlin interrupted. "Just press the barrel against the children's legs or arms and pull the trigger. There's enough serum to vaccinate fifty children. Make sure you give it to every one of the twenty four."

"What...what about getting them away from here? We can always give them the vaccine when we get them out."

"If we don't give them the vaccine, getting the children out won't matter."

"What aren't you telling me?"

General Spradlin looked away.

"All my adult life, I've held on to information," he said. "It's difficult to know what to reveal and what to keep secret. I've made my choices and some worked while others failed. I've come up on the winning side enough times to know I've been successful. This, Nox, is my greatest challenge."

"S...saving twenty four infants?"

Nox's speech was slurred. Her eyes could no longer focus and she could barely stand. Lemner's passkey was a drill tearing though her head and forcing its way into her.

General Spradlin pulled Nox's now empty hand from her pocket.

"When I was a child, the greatest entertainer in the world was a man named Harry Houdini. Are you familiar with that name?"

"Hou...Houdini?" Nox repeated. A distant memory flared in her mind. "He was a... a magician. So many years... so many... How...?"

"More like an escape artist," General Spradlin said. "His specialty was being handcuffed and locked into trunks. These trucks were then hung in the air or submerged in water. He would escape these 'death traps' as he called them, to the delight of his audiences."

"So... so long ago..."

"It wasn't magic, of course," Spradlin continued. "Often, the 'death traps' weren't anywhere near as dangerous as they appeared. Much of his work was illusion."

The smile on General Spradlin's face broadened.

"Before this day is over, you'll witness some real magic," he said.

General Spradlin stopped. His grip on Nox's hand tightened. He faced her.

"Do you still hear me?" he asked the Mechanic.

Nox's eyes came up. She stared into his.

"Yes."

"Whatever happens, I forgive you," he said. "You understand?"

Though she could barely think, the words stunned her.

"You... forgive... *me*...?"

General Spradlin's eyes didn't waver.

"One day soon, I hope you can forgive me, too," he added. "For all the things I've put you through."

General Spradlin stopped talking. He released Nox and turned. His hands were in the air. He stood perfectly still for several long seconds. A trio of red laser sights appeared. They settled over his heart. A single light appeared on the Mechanic. It also hovered over her heart.

Before them and on top of a sandy dune, a shadowy figure rose. He sported a fearsome automatic weapon.

Cloudy though her thoughts were, Nox's first instinct was to run. General Spradlin sensed this.

"Stay where you are," he said. "You'll never make it."

Of the original twenty adult soldiers that were part of Joshua Landon's group, only five remained. They surrounded General Spradlin and Nox. Joshua Landon broke from this group. He walked with a pronounced limp. Dried blood filled the charred clothing on the left side of his body. Blackened flesh peeled from his arms. Shrapnel pierced his body. He hadn't cleaned himself up. He hadn't taken any time for medical care.

Joshua Landon stopped in front of Nox and Spradlin. His face was lean and hard, his eyes remained a brilliant blue. He looked from General Spradlin to Nox, his face barely hiding both contempt and curiosity. Nox and General Spradlin had successfully run from his group for quite some time, yet here they were, giving themselves up without a fight. He –and Lemner's passkey– sensed a trap.

Nox felt the program swirl around her like an invisible mist. It probed deep into her mind, searching for the reason for this abrupt surrender. It found none. Neither, however, did it detect a trap. Its focus shifted. It probed Nox, stronger now. In spite of everything, it still wanted control of her. A sinister smile appeared on Joshua Landon's face. His thoughts appeared in Nox's mind.

You're pale.

"Haven't had... had much of a chance to hit the beach," Nox said aloud.

You remember me?

"Yes."

Why do you still refuse us?

"Never much cared to be...to be part of the in-crowd."

Joshua Landon pointed to General Spradlin.

You follow him.

"By my own free will."

A deep frown appeared on Joshua Landon's face. He opened his mouth and finally spoke aloud.

"That choice could cost you."

Nox said nothing. Her eyes closed, tight. Lemner's passkey continued to swirl around Nox. This time it grabbed a firm foothold deep in her mind. Nox cried out.

"I don't... I don't understand," Nox yelled. She gripped General Spradlin's shirt. Sweat dripped down her forehead and cheeks. She knew her battle against Lemner's passkey was all but lost. "Why did you bring... why did you bring us here?"

General Spradlin lowered his hands and gently took Nox in them.

"Remember," he said. "I forgive you."

Nox slipped out of his grasp and fell to the sandy desert floor. She could barely keep her eyes open.

Through a misty haze, she saw Joshua Landon step up to General Spradlin. He aimed his weapon at the man's legs and let loose a barrage of gunfire. The General's legs erupted. Blood stained the desert floor and he collapsed. Nox felt the passkey's bloodlust. The long dormant artificial intelligence screamed in joy. It was time for General Spradlin to die.

Slowly.

Nox tried one last time to shake the program from her mind. She fell into mental rapids and swirled against a merciless tide. She could no longer control herself. She could no longer control anything.

Joshua Landon appeared before her.

"You're nearly there," he whispered. "Give in."

Nox tried to fight it. She reached deep within, grasping at the meager energies she still had left.

"Give in," Joshua Landon repeated.

Her mind moved frantically, her will still strong despite the overwhelming voices ordering her to stop. She fought and she fought, but she knew this was a fight she would not win.

"Give in," he said for a third time.

And she did.

48

For Nox, consciousness came and went.

A strong white light shone down on her, only to fade away.

While this light was on her, she felt moments of lucidity. What she saw was a living nightmare. General Spradlin was tied up against a gritty wall in a dark cell, his half-naked body spread eagled. What clothing remained on him was in tatters, ripped and bloody. Hundreds of gashes, from small cuts to gaping wounds, marred his bare flesh. He was missing fingers, his right ear. His eye-patch was gone, exposing a dark, empty eye socket. There was damage to other areas...areas Nox found difficult to look at.

The Mechanic held a bloody knife, just like the other five one-time child soldiers. And, like children in a playground, she and the others took turns using their weapon to slowly kill General Spradlin.

That realization screamed in what was left of Nox's mind. While Lemner's passkey forced her hand, she knew many of General Spradlin's horrific wounds were her own doing.

After a while...a lifetime...Nox and the others realized General Spradlin was dead. His death took many hours. For much of that time, the General said nothing.

Before it was over, he screamed.

The General's blood stained the hands and bodies of all the one-time child soldiers, including Nox. The final cut was delivered by Joshua Landon. By then, General Spradlin was barely conscious and neither Landon nor Lemner's passkey could hold back on their animalistic impulses. Once the General was dead, Lemner's passkey was jubilant. It relished its revenge against the man who first approved the program only to seek its destruction.

There would be no last minute rescue. There would be no salvation. General Spradlin was gone.

The darkness in Nox's mind receded and she felt her soul crying out. General Spradlin, the man responsible for destroying her childhood and ordering her death in Arabia...was himself dead.

And she was responsible for it.

I forgive you.

The voice was a ghostly whisper. It's cool, easy tone startled Nox. She was afraid to embrace the message and afraid to listen to the words.

She was afraid it was all a lie.

I forgive you, it repeated.

He repeated.

General Spradlin was dead, but his last words to her were meant to ease her pain. Almost as if he...

Almost as if he expected it.

How much of this did you plan out? She heard herself say.

Nox's eyes opened.

Nox was back in that tiny village in Arabia. She again stood a short distance from her child self in the nightmare version of her memory. The pregnant woman lay in the row of bodies. She moved. The child soldier saw this and prepared to take the shot...

The scene froze.

Nox felt a presence behind her. She spoke to it.

"Becky told me it was a programmed memory."

The Mechanic turned. General Spradlin stood only a short distance behind her. His body was intact. He had his right eye and bore no scars.

The scene shifted. Colors blurred before tightening up. In this new scene, the village was intact. The people were alive and being herded into a group of military transport crafts.

"I've seen this already," Nox told General Spradlin. "What am I missing?"

"This."

The child that was once Nox watched as the villagers moved in a line before the transport trucks. Each and every one of them rolled up their sleeves and allowed the child soldiers to give them a vaccine before entering the vehicles. The child Nox carried a syringe that was identical to the one General Spradlin gave the grown Nox before he...

She tried not to think of that.

"It's the same vaccine..."

"Yes it is," General Spradlin said.

The child she once was gave the pregnant woman an injection. The woman experience no discomfort or pain. The young Nox put away the syringe and offered her a canteen.

"What's in the syringe?" Nox asked.

"Magic," General Spradlin replied.

The villagers huddled in the back of the transport craft, away from any satellite's prying eyes. The other child soldiers looked away. They were ordered to do other things. The child soldier Nox once was couldn't help but take a peek. She saw the pregnant woman and the woman saw her. She was sitting at the back end of the truck, just feet away from Nox. She reached out and gave Nox her canteen. There was an appreciative smile on her face. Nox took the canteen. She returned the smile.

Strange lights of all colors appeared. They sparkled around the villagers. One of the children cried in his mother's arms, but most of the others were mesmerized. The lights had no source, yet enveloped all the villagers in each of the transport crafts. The lights caressed their skin and calmed their fears. They grew more intense…

A sharp crackle of energy was heard, like distant thunder. And then, all at once, the villagers slowly faded away. The pregnant woman raised her arm. She waved to the child Nox…

Just like that, the back of the transport vehicles –every one of them– was empty.

Only Nox witnessed this. The other child soldiers had drawn their shovels from their backpacks and were digging shallow graves. The transport vehicles noisily departed the village. Once they were gone, the child soldiers who weren't digging graves pulled out their weapons. They fired at the village structures, destroying everything in their wake. When they were done, they produced plastic containers filled with blood and viscera from their backpacks. They spread this material around the walls and grounds of the now destroyed village, finally dropping more of it into the shallow graves before covering them up.

When their work was done, it appeared a tremendous battle had raged in this place. They radioed command.

Exactly one hour later, and long after the transport trucks were gone, a single tank rumbled into the village square from the west. Two tank officers exited the vehicle and couldn't help but be impressed with the destruction around them. They kept their distance from the child soldiers and walked to the freshly dug graves. They counted these graves but did not bother digging up any of the supposed victims. They assumed the corpses were there, as they would from this day on and through many, many more villages.

"What happened?" the adult Nox asked.   "Where did the villagers go?"

"Far away. To safety."

"Explain."

General Spradlin held out his arm.

"Why don't you let me show you."

Nox looked at the General's outstretched hand. Her gaze returned to the empty village square and the phony graves and the child soldiers.

You're not a killer, she thought.

Nox reached out and took General Spradlin's hand...

...and all was revealed.

49

THE BLUE MOUNTAINS, ARIZONA.
October, 1925

All was revealed.

The Sheriff, Paul Spradlin, felt a blistering heat envelop the hand that touched the strange statue before him. The heat terrified him to the point he feared it would catch fire. At almost the very same moment, his mind was flooded with information and images. At first this torrent of information was overwhelming and made no sense at all. With each passing second, he realized he was witnessing memories from the distant past and all the way to the present. He saw mankind in its infancy, small tribes that traveled from location to location searching desperately for both food and shelter. He saw some of these tribes die out while a precious few established small enclaves, then villages, then cities...

Those images were replaced with views of alien worlds, of war machines as yet undreamed of. The Sheriff saw metallic war birds scream through the air and deliver crushing payloads that wiped out glistening cities of emerald and bronze. He saw soldiers carrying futuristic gear; he saw handguns shoot searing beams of light. He saw destruction and death on a scale that made his memories of the Great War pale in comparison.

Then he saw them. The creatures.

They were fearsome and alien. They stood eight feet in length and their bodies were composed of sinewy muscle and metallic bone.

Somehow, he knew what they were.

These alien creatures inhabited a massive space armada and journeyed from planet to planet, searching for one thing only: Food. They had traveled for many millions of years devouring entire worlds to replenish their energies. They were fearsome parasites, and the many advanced civilizations they encountered in their journeys were destroyed. None of them had come close to slowing, much less defeating, them.

When they were done with their latest conquest, the mighty parasite armada moved off in search of new feeding grounds. What they left behind was horrifying. The planets they invaded were left completely lifeless and nothing more than empty husks.

Their latest target was the Earth.

Even now, the creature's armada was several million miles past the solar system. The speeds necessary to make their long journey were great, and so too was the time required to slow down for their arrival. The armada would spend another three hundred years slowing before arriving on Earth.

The moment they did, the alien creatures would begin the process of taking Earth apart. They would make no attempt to communicate with any person or nation. They had no interest in this planet's cultures and species, only in their own self-preservation. They needed to feed and if the human race, or any race, had to fall, then so be it.

When the visions were over, Sheriff Spradlin released the statue.

"Now you see," the prospector said.

Sheriff Spradlin fought the urge to throw up. His head spun from the overwhelming information dumped into it. He held on for a few more seconds before falling to his knees. His stomach heaved once again. This time, he couldn't hold back.

When his stomach was empty, Sheriff Spradlin wiped his mouth and faced the prospector. His body felt very odd, as if something new was flowing through his veins.

"What...what did you do to me?" Spradlin asked.

"When you touched the statue, you received an inoculation. The statue housed nano-probes."

"What... what the hell is that?"

"Very small, automated machines. They penetrated your skin and are now in your veins. They're streaming through your body, examining your makeup. Making changes."

"What changes?"

"You'll be more... much more than you were when the nano-probes have fully merged with you. You'll have information beyond your wildest dreams, of technologies stolen and squandered."

"The visions?"

"The nano-probes penetrated your brain and are now interacting with your brain cells. Those visions are images fed directly to you."

"Why me?"

"I already told you."

"Because I fought in the Great War? Because I know about our military capability?" A fresh wave of pain shot through the Sheriff's body. He grunted and shook it off. "What we have is... is child's play compared to these... things coming here."

"You have time."

Spradlin let out a laugh.

"Not nearly enough."

"I've studied your kind for many, many years," the prospector said. "You humans are incredibly resourceful. You can adapt."

"What are you?"

"My masters call me a sentinel."

The prospector pointed to the statue.

"We two are alike," he said. "We are robots composed entirely of those nano-probes."

"How did you get here?"

"There were three of us originally. We were scouts sent by the creatures who mean to devour your world."

Sheriff Spradlin drew back.

"You...you're with them?"

"I no longer do their bidding," the prospector said. "When I did many millennia ago, my mission was simply to ensure this world was ready for their arrival."

The prospector stared at the statue.

"My masters not only ravage worlds, but they also amass technologies. They are clever and adapt and use the information that helps them in their pursuit of fresh feeding grounds. Sometimes they use these technologies without fully studying and understanding them. There can be unintended consequences."

"What do you mean?"

"The programming behind my being was stolen from a culture lost to my masters," the prospector said. "They used the nano-probes and their programming to make me. As I said, we were to be their scouts, to observe this world and report back to them at regular intervals. Somehow, this programming malfunctioned or, perhaps, functioned in a way my masters could not anticipate. Over time, unknown subroutines were activated. Whether this happened by accident or was pre-programmed by the race whose dead hands my masters ripped the nano-probes from is unknown. What is important is that these new subroutines took over our being."

"What did they do?"

"They allowed us to have independent thought. The first of my companions was driven mad by these new...thoughts. It launched itself into a volcano." He pointed to the statue before him. "My other companion fared no better. It no longer spoke or interacted with me. It no longer wished me to be at its side. One night, many, many years ago it vanished. It took me until now to find it."

The prospector approached Sheriff Spradlin.

"Between then and now, I've wandered the Earth and tested my newfound independence."

"How long?"

"Over twenty thousand years," the prospector said. "During that time, my communication equipment failed and I lost all contact with my masters. Not that it mattered. I no longer did their bidding. I spent millennia alone, wandering this planet and storing information. I disguised myself when needed and assimilated languages and customs of the various tribes, then cities, then Empires of this world. Eventually, I boarded a British ship and was delivered to the New World. It was during that trip that all the information I stored over all those years was processed. I came to a realization that I could not allow this planet to be destroyed. I spent the next two hundred years searching for my lost companion. I thought together we could come up with a way to stop our masters. When I finally found him a month before, I realized he was too damaged. The best I could do was reactivate a small percent of the nano-probes in his system. I made adjustments on them so they could incorporate themselves into a human body. Yours."

"Why?"

"Because I can't stop the coming invasion on my own. I need help."

"Why should I trust you?" Sheriff Spradlin said. "How can I trust you?"

The prospector was silent for several seconds before saying:

"That is up to you, Sheriff."

"How do I stop them?"

"I don't know," the prospector admitted. "But I'm certain together we can find the answer. We have to. Otherwise, you and all your kind will die."

There were several more seconds of silence. After a while, the prospector walked to the edge of the cul de sac.

"I've given you warning, Sheriff Spradlin. A warning and an understanding of what you face. This is my gift...and curse...to you. What happens from this point forward is your choice. The decisions you make will be hard. Many will involve matters of life and death. If you are successful, you will earn the ultimate reward. Your race will survive."

Sheriff Spradlin considered the Prospector's words. He looked away and at the rock formations. He then looked up at the clear night sky. He saw the stars spread out before him and shivered. His eyes locked on one of those stars, a faint light lost among millions. It was the armada. His eyes turned away from the sky and back to the Prospector.

"I will save the human race," the Sheriff said. "I will accomplish what all those other races, including the one that originally programmed you, could not."

"I'm pleased to—"

"I will do this without your help."

The Prospector took a step back. Confusion was evident on its features.

"Why?"

"Back in the Great War, a soldier from the Axis army showed up one day at our line. He was unarmed, beaten, and starving. He said he was forced into this war against his will, and deserted his side. He claimed to want nothing more than revenge against the German army. To that end, he provided us with intelligence on troop movements. Our commanders used this information to plan what they hoped would be a devastating surprise attack. Up until the first shot was fired in that attack, we thought we had the upper hand. We did not. We lost more than half our platoon that day, including three of my very best friends. Somehow, I and a small group of soldiers managed to escape the massacre. We retreated and regrouped behind our lines, then informed our Commander of what happened. He was livid. He was certain the German deserter was a double agent that set us up."

"The Commander ordered the soldier's execution. The soldier pleaded with us not to kill him, that he was innocent. He kept on pleading until the firing squad's bullets tore through his body. Our commanding officer was certain the soldier was a double agent. I wasn't. If there's anything I learned over there, it's that wars are messy and things don't always work out as planned. Maybe the man was a double agent. Or maybe his superiors knew he was about to defect and allowed him to do so...after feeding him information they knew he'd give us to lead us into a trap. Or maybe the soldiers on the other side simply got lucky and figured out what we were up to and turned the tables. Either way, many died."

Sheriff Spradlin stared deep into the prospector's eyes.

"You were one of them once," he said. "You claim independent thought, but you're a machine. A machine that does as it was programmed to do. Perhaps you were programmed to think you were independent. Perhaps you were programmed to lead us into a trap. Or maybe, just maybe, everything you say is true. Unfortunately, that's something I can never know. And it's something maybe you can't, either. I could never trust you."

As Sheriff Spradlin walked past the prospector and headed out of the cul de sac, he added:

"Stay the hell out of my way."

50

The rocky cul de sac faded away.

Nox and General Spradlin stood in an empty white room.

"What was that?" Nox asked.

"A small taste," General Spradlin said. He released Nox's hand and reached up, until his fingers pointed at her forehead. "Here is the rest."

"What are you—"

Spradlin's fingers gently touched her.

The moment they did, an avalanche of memories roared through the Mechanic's mind. Volumes and volumes and *volumes* of life memories, beginning with General Spradlin's early childhood in the slums of New York through his journey to Europe and experiences in the Great War penetrated her mind. She saw the deserting German soldier he talked of moments before and witnessed Spradlin's sadness when the impossibly young looking man was executed. When the Great War ended, she stood at his side when he returned to New York on an old freighter. The sight of his home did not lift his spirits as the war left him an emotionally broken man. Though he longed for a better world, he lost almost all faith in humanity.

For several months the still young Paul Spradlin wandered the streets of New York aimlessly, taking on odd jobs while wallowing in a deep depression. Then, one rainy late September day, he found Charlotte. She was a modest, down to earth woman who worked in a textile plant. They courted. They married. A year later they had a child, Jessie. They felt the big city was not the type of place to raise their precious little Jessie and decided to move to Arizona. It was there Paul Spradlin hoped to live the rest of his years in peace.

This was not to be.

Nox experienced the horror the then Sheriff Spradlin felt that day so very long ago when he received the message that his daughter was kidnapped. She relived his furious trip to the Blue Mountains, of awakening before the elderly Prospector, of touching that mysterious statue.

As memories from the statue flooded Paul Spradlin's mind at that moment, so too did they flood Nox. She experienced the statue's –the Sentinel's– activation. She was there when it joined its companions on their long trip to Earth. Because their bodies were composed entirely of nano-probes, they survived the crushing gravitational pulls needed for the abrupt deceleration and orbit of Earth, something their masters' bodies could not withstand. Nox was there when they landed. She was there when they explored the lush forests and icy mountains of primitive Earth. She witnessed their first contact with humanity, then in its very early infancy. Later, she relived the moment their master's programming was subjugated and the Sentinels gained independent thought.

Independence proved too much for two of the three artificial beings. One of them could not adapt to its new setting and opted for self-termination. This Sentinel fought mightily to process its new status and eventually abandoned its remaining partner. It wandered the Earth alone for several hundred years before finally stopping in a mountain range of what would eventually become Arizona.

The visual input of the Sentinel became static while the world around it changed. Rock and dust covered the artificial being until its optical equipment could only see darkness. Its internal machinery failed...it went dormant. Then one day a small part of it was reactivated. It again saw the world around it. Sheriff Paul Spradlin stood before the re-activated being and touched it. He received this same information...

The perspective changed and Nox now viewed the world through General Spradlin's eyes. She watched as he returned to town and, a few months later, reluctantly abandoned his beloved Charlotte and Jessie and devoted himself fully to stopping the alien invaders. Spradlin learned of his wife's passing two years after the fact, and Nox witnessed his collapse before her dusty grave outside the Blue Mountains. He was filled with regret and a deep sadness. He spoke to the grave. He spoke to his lost love.

"I wish... I wish I could have said goodbye."

For weeks grief consumed Paul Spradlin. He forced it aside. Saving humanity became his sole purpose in life.

A few years later and just a couple of months after the end of World War II, she watched General Spradlin make his way up a treacherous icy mountain top somewhere in the Alps. Top Secret Nazi documents found in vaults buried deep beneath Berlin pointed to secret expeditions sponsored by sordid Nazi higher ups. A map among those documents indicated the discovery of strange wreckage buried in the snow on that distant mountain top. A German sponsored expedition was organized to retrieve the wreckage but the fall of Nazi Germany ended the operation before it began. On that mountaintop, General Spradlin found and unearthed the wreckage of a strange spacecraft. It would not be the last time he got his hands on alien technology.

Years later, Nox saw General Spradlin standing a distance from a burial. A large group of people –strangers to him– watched with sadness as little Jessie's coffin was lowered into the ground. She died peacefully at the age of eighty five and surrounded by grown children, grandchildren, and great grandchildren. They were direct family to General Spradlin. They were all strangers.

Even more memories flashed before Nox's eyes before slowing and finally stopping at the moment of General Spradlin's death.

The memories left Nox exhausted and bewildered. Buried in that enormous memory dump, she caught bits and pieces of his plan to counter the approaching alien invaders.

The information scared the hell out of her.

"I can't…I don't understand…" she said. She was back in that white room with General Spradlin and fell to her knees. "There is… too much to absorb…"

"You will," General Spradlin said.

"What is…what is a Displacer? How will it save us?"

General Spradlin gently helped Nox back to her feet.

"When I left the Blue Mountains in 1925, I was just as confused and scared as you are now," General Spradlin said. "It was as hard for me to assimilate the information thrust into my head as it surely will be for you. It took me a while before I could fully focus on the coming invasion. There was so much to process on these invaders –the Locus Plague as I called them– as well as an enormous amount of information on the many, many races they destroyed. I sorted through it all, seeing where those races failed in their fight against the Locust Plague, and what lessons I could learn from those failures."

General Spradlin paused.

"In doing so, I made the exact same mistake they did."

"What?"

"Like the other races, I was intent on finding a way to fight the Locust Plague," General Spradlin said. "It was from that mindset that Oscuro arose. But first, and as you saw, I abandoned my family and journeyed to Washington D.C. I met skeptical politicians and quickly turned them into allies. Given the advanced technologies at my disposal, it didn't take all that much to convince them the Locust Plague was a real threat. In a short amount of time I attained the highest ranking in the U.S. military as well as my own department and budget. All top secret, of course."

"My Department estimated the Locust Plague's power and based on those estimates, we theorized how strong our forces needed to be if we had any hope of fighting, and defeating, them." General Spradlin shook his head. "The results were...maddening. Not only were we technologically many, *many* millennia behind them, but we simply didn't have enough time or resources to create any sort of meaningful counter to their forces."

"Nonetheless, by the end of the twentieth century Oscuro was in operation. It didn't take very long for me to realize it simply would not work. Estimating future global population growth and conversion of that *entire* population into weaponized soldiers, we could hold off the Locust Plague for only a decade. Twelve years if we were lucky. Afterwards, we would fall as surely as all those other civilizations and races before us."

General Spradlin faced Nox.

"Then, at the start of the twenty first century and only a few years after initiating Oscuro, I gained access to a Sentinel's handheld computer. Within its memory banks, I discovered new technologies the Locust Plague took from civilizations I was unfamiliar with. Deep in those memory banks I discovered the existence of the Displacer."

The white room they were in darkened until it was night. General Spradlin and Nox hovered over a lush Caribbean island. Immediately below them was a military helicopter. It made its way to that island. Suddenly, something exploded on the helicopter's tail.

Just like that, the two were inside the vehicle. The passengers within, including a younger General Spradlin and Becky Waters, grasped at their harnesses as the helicopter dropped from the sky, an apparent victim of an attack.

"It was here I met Becky Waters, as well," the elder General Spradlin said.

They watched as the helicopter crashed on that island and Nox witnessed the survivors' trek through the forest and to a military base on the island. She re-lived the horrors the group encountered on their way to the base and the equally terrifying discoveries made within it. Through the General's memories Nox came to know the other passengers, including Captain Samantha Aaron, the co-pilot of the craft. Nox sensed the General's very sad memories about her fate, but was unable to recall anything specific.

Finally, Nox witnessed the defeat of the very last of the Sentinels –at that time classified as Automated Chameleon Units– among them, and how General Spradlin gained access to that Sentinel's personal computer storage device. Months later the device was fully unlocked. The amount of information gleaned from it was nothing short of incredible.

"Now we had the schematics for creating Displacers," General Spradlin said. "Many years later, you witnessed our first use of it outside the confines of our laboratories."

The island scene faded and the two stood in the Arabian village. Nox was next to her younger self. She watched as the villagers in the back of the transport vehicles shimmered in the glow of strange lights. She heard the distant sound of thunder and, just like that, every one of them was gone.

"Put simply, the Displacer is a device that transports objects from one location to another," General Spradlin said. "The race that discovered this device used it like a sophisticated railway, connecting planets and systems within their Galactic Empire. It allowed them to strengthen their ties to their outer territories and facilitated trade. When they were targeted by the Locust Plague, they tried to use the Displacer to flee."

"To...flee?"

"Yes," General Spradlin said.

He stepped away from Nox's side and looked up at the Arabian sky. Around him, the Child Brigade soldiers went about their work, creating phony graves and destroying the village.

"I've never thought of myself as a coward," General Spradlin said. "Yet after going through all our options and all the means by which we could deal with the Locus Plague, the facts proved brutally clear. We could stand our ground and fight until we were just as dead as all those other civilizations that came before us...or we could give up on this planet and run. The Displacer allowed us to do that. It was the only viable option for humanity's survival. The question was: how many people could I save before the invaders arrived?"

The Arabian village faded away and was replaced with a dark laboratory. In it was a young General Spradlin. He consulted several technicians.

"I gathered a group of my most trusted scientists and began work on our own Displacer. From the beginning, we realized there were two issues we had to deal with: First, the device required a great deal of energy to function and each time it was used it left behind enormous amounts of radioactive waste. That's why the race that created it did so for use in outer space and far away from habitable planets while using heavily insulated starships. Second, and most importantly, we needed a Displacer unit at both the point of departure *and* arrival. One couldn't step into a Displacer and reappear at any point of one's choosing. We needed to find a destination to send humanity. A place far enough away from the Locust Plague that *also* had its own Displacer unit."

General Spradlin waved his hand and the scene around them shifted.

"On the face of it, it appeared we hit a complete dead end," General Spradlin said. "If we created a target Displacer and sent it to the stars, it would take many thousands of years before it arrived at the closest habitable solar system to us. By then, the Locust Plague would have fed off our world and destroyed humanity a long, long time before. I feared my work was a failure and humanity was doomed. But I didn't give up. We *had* to find some kind of alternative. We simply had to."

Before General Spradlin and Nox appeared a youthful General Spradlin. He stood among several very excited scientists and looked over several reams of paper. A look of wonder filled his face.

"One day, we had an incredible breakthrough."

General Spradlin stood before his younger self.

"We theorized the Displacer's creators must have a network of such devices in and around their home world and beyond. Even if the Locust Plague devoured their entire civilization, we hoped at least one of those Displacers units survived the attack and might still be active."

The figures before Nox and the elder General Spradlin froze.

"We were right," the General said. "We found and established contact with a single Displacer in a system far, far away from us. It was operational."

The scene before Nox and General Spradlin shifted again. They were standing in the middle of outer space. Nox was startled by this unexpected view. General Spradlin pointed to the right.

"Look over there."

Several hundred miles from them was a small asteroid field. Before the asteroids floated a large rectangular object. Its structure was dark metallic gray and its center was completely empty. To its side hovered three enormous silver spacecraft.

The black emptiness at the center of the rectangular object was suddenly filled with an intense halo of pulsating energy. The alien Displacer device was alive with multicolored lights. Abruptly, those lights winked out. All looked the same as before, but it wasn't.

At the center of the Displacer floated an almost microscopically small object.

It was a man in a spacesuit.

The man examined his surroundings in quiet wonder. His eyes settled on the trio of ships parked to the side of the alien Displacer. He activated the thrusters in his suit and began the flight toward the closest of the three ships. Though he thought the ships were very near to him, the astronaut soon realized they were incredibly far away. The only reason they appeared so close was because of their enormous size.

The man continued his journey. He burned almost half his propellant and spent five hours before reaching the nearest of the distant ships. Once there, the astronaut gazed at the massive wall of alien technology before him. The starship was easily fifty times the size of the Big City.

"These three ships, we found later, were designed for massive evacuation," General Spradlin told Nox.

"How massive?"

"Massive enough to fit every single person on Earth," General Spradlin said. "Not only did we have the means to escape our doomed world, we now had a place to fit *everyone* in."

"Why hadn't the ships been used?"

General Spradlin shrugged.

"Maybe the civilization that created these ships perished before they could be used. Or perhaps they built more ships than they needed and these three were left behind."

"You don't believe that," Nox said.

"I had another theory," General Spradlin admitted.

The astronaut maneuvered his body toward a large window on the side of the ship and wiped away a thick layer of dust. He peered inside. Despite the darkness within, he saw enormous corridors and rooms. He gathered as much data as he could before re-activating his thruster and journeying back to the Displacer.   When he reached it, his supply of oxygen and propellant were almost exhausted. The astronaut reactivated the Displacer and made the instantaneous journey back to Earth.

The scene shifted again. Nox and General Spradlin were in a brilliant white laboratory. They stood behind several scientists who, in turn, stood behind a heavily plated glass wall. In the room beyond theirs a much smaller version of the Displacer unit, one no larger than a door, activated. Energy pulses lit up the room and the astronaut emerged from inside that Displacer's center. He staggered forward and fell to his knees. Clouds of steam rose from his suit and for a moment it appeared he might catch fire.

None of the scientists came to his aid.

Gauges within the outer room indicated the Displacer room was filled with toxic levels of radiation.   Cleansers were activated, but the astronaut was already poisoned. He remained on his knees until the steam rising from his suit abated. Once it did, he removed his helmet and revealed himself to be a young General Spradlin.

The scene froze.

"I performed the first tests of the Displacer because I was the only one that could," General Spradlin said. "It took two full weeks for my nano-probes to cure me of the radiation poisoning from each trip."

The scene shifted yet again.

General Spradlin and Nox were in a larger room. They stood behind a larger, heavier protective glass. Beyond that glass was another Displacer unit. This one was as large as a house.

"Time passed," General Spradlin said. "We expanded and refined our work."

The large Displacer faded away and was replaced by one even larger, then one larger still.

"Soon, we were ready for the next phase."

Small experimental spacecraft appeared before the Earth's now massive Displacer.

"It was time to explore the abandoned alien ships," General Spradlin said.

Astronauts in the Earth ships passed through the Displacer and journeyed to the three abandoned alien space crafts. Dozens of such ships made the journey between Earth and the asteroid field.

The Earth ships docked alongside the alien crafts. Dozens of impatient scientists and technicians in space suits awaited their opportunity.

"The hardest part of exploring these ships was finding a way inside," General Spradlin said.

A pair of astronauts floated beside a massive door on one of the alien spacecraft. After considerable effort, they managed to pry open a panel beside that door. Within, they found alien circuitry. Inside the Earth spaceships, scientists pored over the schematics of this exposed circuitry and tried their best to understand its meaning and function. After a while, one of the scientists excitedly jumped from his seat. The alien ship's locking mechanism was deciphered!

The scientists within the Earth ships watched in awe as a large door in the alien craft noiselessly slid open.

Cautiously, the Earth ships made their way inside.

"When we were in, we began a thorough analysis of all the alien equipment," General Spradlin said. "Naturally, much of it was strange to us. But thanks to my exposure to the Locust Plague's information on this race, not all of it proved a mystery. The creatures that created the Displacer and made these ships proved to be humanoids not all that different from us. They anticipated a very long flight from the Locus Plague and filled each of these three space crafts with stasis chambers. With slight modifications, we were able to make them, and the ships themselves, compatible with human beings."

Astronauts and engineers moved along the corridors within the alien space crafts, modifying gear and adapting technology. Nox and General Spradlin stood within one of the ship's massive engine rooms.

"The ships, which we named Ark 1, 2, and 3, were soon on-line and ready for use. All we had to do was fill them up."

The engine room faded away and was replaced by the white research center. Nox and General Spradlin found the younger General Spradlin there, reading over his notes. Behind him was an even more massive Displacer unit, one capable of fitting a supertanker.

"There still remained our one big problem," the elder General Spradlin said. "How would I get people into the Arks? At that point in time, the only way to do so was by putting them into our spacecraft and flying them through our Displacer and to the alien ships. But how could I take large amounts of people from

Earth to those ships without revealing what I was up to? If I announced to the world that we were threatened with an alien invasion and was planning an evacuation, I risked ridicule at best and a worldwide panic at worst. And there remained one other danger: What would the Locust Plague do when they discovered my plans?"

Nox thought about that.

"They would... they would stop you," she said. "That's it, isn't it? That's why the ships were never used."

General Spradlin nodded.

"I believe the alien race that created these ships hid them well from the Locust Plague," General Spradlin said. "But agents of the Plague discovered what the race was up to and acted. They mercilessly slaughtered that alien race before they could use their hidden ships. Once the race was decimated, the Locust Plague simply moved on to their next meal. They either forgot about or didn't bother spending any more energy searching for the hidden Ark ships. That will prove to be their biggest mistake."

The elder General Spradlin walked to his younger self's side.

"One day not so very long ago, while going over how to get our people to the Arks for what seemed like the millionth time, I had a brainstorm," he said. The younger version of himself stared intently at his notes. A crazy smile appeared on his face. "I don't know where the inspiration came from, but it hit me like a bolt of liquid lightning. I realized that by combining my knowledge of Displacers and nano-probes, knowledge derived from two separate and vanquished civilizations, there was another way we could use the Displacers. By using simplified nano-probes as energy mirrors, we could create a pulse echo within people *themselves* that a Displacer could lock onto. As long as the person with these simplified nano-probes stood near an entry Displacer, we could then transport him or her without having them physically step through a Displacer and risk incurring massive radiation poisoning. This person could then be sent to a location of our choosing, again as long as this location was relatively near the target Displacer."

The younger General Spradlin faded away. He reappeared, this time dressed in astronaut gear. Scientists stood around him. They watched as he prepared for another test.

"As with all else, I volunteered to be the first subject of these simplified nano-probes," the elderly General Spradlin said. "I was inoculated with them and stood four floors directly above our Displacer unit. A countdown was initiated. Our Displacer was activated."

A halo of light enveloped the younger General Spradlin and grew in intensity. The younger man looked at his instruments and read the radioactivity gauges. They were all green. When he looked up again, he was shocked to find he was no longer on Earth. He stood in the cargo bay of one of the three Ark ships. A large window above him displayed the floating rectangular Displacer in space.

"We succeeded," the elderly General Spradlin said. "We found a way to send people directly into the ships."

Nox understood.

"The vaccines."

"They contain the simplified nano-probes."

"What happens to the nano-probes afterwards? Will they remain in people's bodies forever?"

"No. The Displacer jump consumes the nano-probes. Upon their arrival, every one of the people sent is free of any and all alien technology."

"There's no way you could inject everyone on Earth."

"We didn't need to. When the test trials proved successful, we created mountains of the Displacer nano-probe solution and pumped it into the world's ground water. Over several years all people, animals, and vegetation absorbed it. With the aid of computer scanners, we could track everyone on Earth who had those probes within them. All we had to do to get them to the Arks was dial in their position into our matrix."

"If everyone on Earth was exposed to the nano-probes, why do we need to vaccinate the children Landon stole from the hospital? Why couldn't you figure out where Jason Landon and the other child soldiers were?"

"Several hours passed before we realized the children and the other one-time child soldiers were gone," General Spradlin said. "We immediately initiated the Displacer matrix and tried to locate them. We couldn't. Lemner's passkey had somehow discovered the simplified nano-probes within all their bodies and flushed them out. That's why we needed to inoculate the kidnapped children once again."

"But not before getting rid of Lemner's passkey."

"Though the Displacer matrix is off the GCN grid, it would be foolish to continue using it at full power while Lemner's passkey remained alive and capable of infecting computer systems. Lemner's passkey might find a way in to our Displacers and, if it did, those who remain on Earth were at risk of being stranded here. Or worse."

General Spradlin stared at the alien Displacer.

"I had to get the infants and I had to destroy the passkey so that the evacuation could be resumed...and completed."

"Did you?"

"Yes. The passkey is gone."

"Where are the Ark ships going? Have you found another world for us to inhabit?"

"These are things I can't tell you, Nox," General Spradlin said.

"Why?"

Even as she asked the question, Nox knew the answer.

"I won't be going, will I?"

General Spradlin faced Nox.

"You can't," he said.

"Why?"

"Even as I made those first trips through the Displacer, I knew doing so put humanity at risk. The nano-probes in my body and yours are Locust Plague technology. We may be in control of them at this time, but they *never* belonged to us. If even one of the billions of nano-probes in our system should somehow be turned or establishes contact with the Locust Plague, they could revert to their original programming. Not only could we lose control of our bodies, but the invaders would surely discover everything we know."

Visions of the German soldier from that ancient war swirled through Nox's head.

"We are... we are him," she said.

General Spradlin shared Nox's vision. He nodded.

"Unintentional or not, we could be traitors to our race's survival."

"And we can't remove the nano-probes within us," Nox said.

She recalled the conversation she had with General Spradlin not so very long ago.

"The nano-probes are a part of us now, just like our heart and lungs. You destroy the probes, you kill the host."

"We're stuck with them."

"I'm afraid so."

"When the Arks were functional and there was no need for me to supervise the population transfers, I set up a security protocol in the Displacer matrix," General Spradlin said. "I made sure the Displacers could not send anyone infected with even a single one of my –of the Locust Plague's– nano-probes to the Arks. Humanity, with their simplified nano-probes escapes the invasion. We… we cannot join them."

Nox closed her eyes. A single tear ran down her cheek.

"How… how many people did we actually kill back in Arabia?"

"Very few," General Spradlin said. "By the time the Child Brigades arrived in Arabia, the people throughout the region had already been exposed to the simplified nano-probes. Our computers were tracking virtually everyone there. We transported many hundreds of village's worth of people to the Arks under cover of the Child Brigade massacres."

"What about the nukes?"

"Sleight of hand," General Spradlin said. "Once the smaller villages were cleared, we focused on getting the people in the big cities to safety. While it was plausible to tell the world the Brigade soldiers wiped out the smaller villages, but there was no way to fake the deaths of the millions of people in the big cities of Arabia. So we sent the Brigade soldiers into those cities armed with nuclear devices. Seconds before the nukes were detonated, we transported every one of those citizens to the Arks. The only casualties of the nuclear explosions were the Brigade soldiers themselves."

General Spradlin's head hung low.

"We saved millions at the cost of several thousand," General Spradlin said. "The child soldiers could never join us in the Arks and I justified their deaths as a…kindness. Rather than leave them behind to face the Locust Plague, I thought it was more humane to…to…"

"Kill us," Nox said.

"It's… it's what Generals do."

"You kept this from everyone."

"Yes. The Locust Plague's sentinels were aggressively infiltrating and sabotaging my organization whenever they could. It took them less than two years to discover Oscuro. I decided to keep the project alive even though I knew it would not succeed. The only reason I did so was to fool the Locust Plague's agents into thinking it remained my sole project to counter their invasion."

"But when you set off the nukes in Arabia, the Locust Plague must have realized you were up to something else."

"I'm sure they did," General Spradlin said. "By then it was too late for them to do anything about it. The security protocol on the Displacers was in effect and we had only twenty to twenty five short years left to fully evacuate the planet. There was no chance they could stop me. Not anymore."

"You kept this secret from your allies, as well."

"That proved to be a mistake," General Spradlin admitted. "David Lemner continued working on his passkey. He was convinced I lost my nerve and was allowing the world to die. I tried to convince him I wouldn't do that without revealing what I was up to. I stripped him of his credentials and locked him in his own home but somehow, he *still* managed to keep working. All those long hours took their toll and David Lemner's health was destroyed. Before he could fully implement his new program, he died."

"Not before making at least one hard copy."

"Yes," General Spradlin said. "It was his legacy, an automated monster whose goal it was to fulfill the promise of Oscuro."

"I wish I hadn't found those disks," Nox said.

"It doesn't matter now."

Nox thought about these revelations as more memories bled into her mind. After a while, she spoke.

"If the Locust Plague is as driven as you say, what's to stop them from hunting the Arks down?"

"We set charges in the Displacer units both here and at our destination. As soon as everyone is out, the Displacers will be destroyed."

"The Locust Plague can still follow."

"Humanity will be far enough away that it would take the Locust Plague thousands and thousands of years to reach the location of the Arks. By then, we'll be long gone."

"But the Plague remains. Even if it takes them all those years, they still might track humanity down and destroy it. How can you leave a threat like that out there?"

"I'm not going to," General Spradlin said. "Earth is the Locust Plague's last destination."

"How do you know?"

"Because I poisoned their meal."

Nox exhaled and shook her head.

"By the Gods," she said. "The Arabian nukes... the desert sands... the Displacer's fallout..."

"Yes," General Spradlin said. "We fouled the air, water, and land. We've exhausted the Earth's resources. We've done everything short of blowing this world up.   As vicious and unstoppable as the Locust Plague is, they operate under one major flaw: They have to feed to continue. What little food they find here will be useless to them. They came here to starve."

Despite it all, Nox couldn't help but smile.

"I'll be damned," she said.   "Congratulations, General Spradlin. You figured out a way to kill creatures civilizations hundreds of thousands of years more advanced than ours couldn't. The only cost was our planet."

Nox was silent for a few more seconds.

"What happens now?"

"My people will reactivate the Displacers in full and send what remains of the Earth's population to the Arks. By the end of today, everybody will be gone."

"Everyone but me."

"You're a survivor, Nox."

Nox let out a bitter laugh.

"I'll be one against millions. Billions."

"You'll find a way," General Spradlin said. "Survivors like you always do."

As the words left his mouth, he faded away.

51

Nox opened her eyes.

She was surrounded by several amorphous shapes.

At first, she could not tell one from the other. She rubbed her eyes and shook her head. She was sitting on the ground before an ancient computer terminal.

Nox no longer felt Lemner's passkey tugging at her mind. For the first time in what seemed a lifetime nothing gnawed at her mind. She was fully at peace.

"At peace," she said out loud.

Her next move was entirely hers to make.

She examined the terminal before her. It was dark and appeared dead. No lights flashed and no fans cooled heated circuitry. She recognized the computer as one of the premiere models built during the Arabian War.

Only the best for Oscuro.

Nox sensed Lemner's passkey had resided within this computer. Cameras stationed above the machine looked outward, to give the passkey eyes to view its surroundings. The cameras were just as dead as the machine itself.

No, not completely dead.

A single memory chip on the lower left side of the machine extruded from a plug. Nox reached for it but stopped.

A single dull red light flickered on the chip.

Nox could feel it. Lemner's passkey was there, contained and imprisoned within that chip. It was all that was left of the most fearsome computer program ever devised.

Nox cautiously reached for the memory chip. She touched it. Nothing.

Lemner's passkey was trapped with no hope of escape.

Nox pulled the chip from its plug. It was impossible to tell how much of the program remained within. She considered dropping it to the floor and crushing it under her foot but didn't. Though her desire for revenge against the program was great, she would have plenty of time to deal with it later. Nox put the chip into her pocket and examined the rest of the room.

As she did, she noted the bitter stench of death that permeated the area. She realized her clothing and hands were stained a deep red. She was covered in dry blood.

The Mechanic looked at the other side of the room and feared what she would find.

Her fears proved justified.

General Spradlin's body was there, still strung up against the wall like a grisly trophy.

Lying in front of him were the five remaining one-time child soldiers. Like Nox, their bodies were also covered in the General's dry blood.

Nox gingerly got to her feet. For a moment she felt she would fall and had to lean against the wall of computers. She then remembered the kidnapped children. Nox reached into her pant pocket and was relieved the black leather pouch with the syringe and vaccines was still there. The one-time child soldiers hadn't bothered searching her, so focused were they on getting revenge against General Spradlin.

"You planned it that way," Nox whispered.

She approached the one-time child soldiers and checked for any signs of life. She found none. Their faces were the faces of ordinary people in their mid-thirties. She couldn't remember any of them from her time in Arabia. None but Joshua Landon.

Landon's body lay closest to General Spradlin's. His corpse was curled up under the General's bloody feet and his face was relaxed. There was no longer any evidence of the animalistic rage she saw in him when they were captured. He found peace in death.

Nox's eyes moved from Joshua Landon and up. She stared at the gory remains of General Spradlin and, involuntarily, drew her hand to her mouth. Visions of the General talking to her only moments before were replaced with this gory tableau. Nox stared at his injuries, then at her hand and the General's blood which stained it.

"The blood," she said, awareness dawning on her.

We're all covered in the General's blood.

Even the computer terminals were sprinkled with it. Everyone and everything in this room was bathed in the General's blood.

The blood which housed the alien nano-probes.

"What did you do to me back at Jennifer Alberts' mansion?" Nox wondered. She didn't know, not exactly, yet she *knew*. Years ago, the early version of Lemner's passkey reprogrammed the nano-probes within Joshua Landon's body and made them offensive weapons. General Spradlin did the same with his blood.

He knew Lemner's passkey and the one-time child soldiers would not be content to just kill him. They would make sure he suffered. They would make sure his blood flowed. As his blood sprayed his attackers, the nano-probes inside that blood would attack, penetrating the one-time child soldiers' bodies as well as the computer terminals around him. All would die even as they reveled in General Spradlin's death.

All but Nox.

"You had Becky immunize me," she said. "You had her immunize me from your blood."

General Spradlin purposely allowed the one-time child soldiers to take them captive, knowing that doing so would result in his death. He had to defeat them all and quickly, and this was the most effective way to do so. His sacrifice meant the end for Lemner's passkey and the one-time child soldiers. It also freed Nox so that she could rescue the kidnapped children.

She, unlike the other one-time child soldiers, was the only one General Spradlin could trust to do this. She was the only one among them who was a true...Independent.

Nox couldn't help but laugh.

"The last of the Mechanics... just another Independent."

Nox gripped the syringe case. There was work to do.

Nox found the kidnapped babies in a natal wing of the hideaway. All twenty four of them lay at the center of a bank of impressive computer equipment. These computers, another part of Lemner's passkey, were also dark. Wires stretched from the computers to the twenty four children's rectangular cribs. A couple of the wires poked into each of them. Nox gently removed the wires and was relieved to find they were little more than feeding lines. The full indoctrination hadn't yet begun. Lemner's passkey was more concerned with getting rid of General Spradlin and recruiting Nox.

When Nox was done removing the feeding lines, all the infants were awake and crying at the top of their lungs.

Nox tried to console each one of them as they were injected with the vaccine. Doing so triggered forgotten memories of giving those same injections to others in Arabia. She remembered the pregnant woman more clearly now, and specifically recalled injecting her. She then remembered the woman's warm smile and how she waved just before disappearing. Just before being saved...

When Nox was done vaccinating the kidnapped children, she stepped back.

Get ready to see some real magic.

The words and voice came from General Spradlin and were in her mind. His memories were hers. She couldn't help but wonder if she was no longer Nox the Mechanic but a combination of herself and General Spradlin.

There would be time to figure that out. Later.

Nox watched the children and knew what came next. Not five minutes after the vaccine was administered, a hazy light appeared around them. Some were scared by this while others were curious. The light's intensity grew. There was a sparkle followed by a gentle noise. It sounded like a wind chime.

Despite her loneliness, despite her overwhelming loss, Nox smiled.

Just like that, the infants disappeared.

The moment they were gone, Nox felt a deep pain in her chest. The pain grew sharper and sharper until Nox let out a groan. She doubled over and dropped to her knees.

She felt the Earth's Displacers reactivate in full. Administering the vaccine to the twenty four children served as the final signal to the people operating those machines that it was time to finish Earth's exodus. Throughout the world, wave after wave of people were transported from Earth to the awaiting Arks.

Please, Nox thought. *Don't leave me here alone...*

They all fled to safety, to a place beyond the grasp of the Locust Plague. Once the Arks were filled, they would depart in search of another world to populate. Nox knew the Human Race would survive. She knew it would thrive.

Without her.

The pain passed and Nox straightened up. She wiped a tear from her eye and walked out of the natal ward.

She returned to the bodies of her fellow one-time child soldiers.

Nox spent the next hour burying the dead.

The feeling of emptiness grew within her as the Displacers continued their work.

Several times she cried out. As time passed, the sadness and her tears subsided.

Every one of the one-time child soldiers were now buried, including Joshua Landon. General Spradlin was buried before them. Despite it all, they, like Nox herself, were his children.

There was nothing to say and the emptiness within Nox was near absolute. Like one last leaf falling from a tree, she felt the very last group of Earth's people leave.

Seconds later, she felt a rumble. Something enormous within the Big City erupted. She knew what it was. The Displacers had self-destructed. General Spradlin's military base and the equipment in the dark basement were nothing more than highly radioactive rubble.

For a moment, she thought she'd cry once more. She was the last person left in this poisoned world. The very last one.

Even Catherine was gone, whisked away to safety...billions and billions of miles away.

Abruptly, the sadness lifted. She looked up and away, toward the Big City. She sensed something.

No. I'm not the last person. There is one other.

Nox dropped her shovel and ran.

52

Nox found the military transport truck the General and she used to drive to the base parked where they left it. The blowing desert sand was already licking at her tires and a thin layer covered her body. In another couple of days, the vehicle itself might well be swallowed whole.

Nox ran to the transport and opened the driver's side door. The key was still in the ignition, right where General Spradlin left it.

You left it for me, she thought. It was a nice though unnecessary gesture. Nox knew how to hot wire almost anything on wheels. She closed the door and gazed out the front windshield. Her trail of footprints disappeared into the distance.

A flicker of memory was triggered in her mind. She had an image of walking to the base, but her point of view was that of General Spradlin. His felt a mix of dread and hope as they approached the hidden Desertlands base. Though he knew these were his final minutes of life, he knew his sacrifice would not be in vain.

I know you will save the children, Nox, he thought during those last minutes.

Nox saw him then, looking at her. Holding her up.

"I forgive you," he said.

She didn't understand it then. She did now.

Nox turned the key and the transport truck came to life.

"Goodbye, General."

Nox drove like a demon through the Desertlands and made quick time back to the Big City. She spotted a thick black cloud rising from the southwest side of the town. The cloud originated from General Spradlin's military base. Nox knew all that was left of the base and the enormous Displacer buried underneath it was a radioactive crater.

Desert gave way to wire fences and the military transport vehicle made it to the last chance Diner and the barricade before the Big City. Nox navigated the tight entry and was soon on solid streets. She hurried through this familiar terrain.

Nox drove north, eventually reaching the outskirts of Jennifer Alberts' estate. The midday sun was bright in the sky, revealing the destruction that was once the dilapidated mansion.

Nox drove the truck to epicenter of the blast.

Before the crater that marked the mansion's remains, she hit the transport's brakes and jumped out of the vehicle. She ran past burnt wood, shattered furniture, and unidentifiable debris and climbed down the crater. She stumbled as she went and eventually found the remains of the stairs leading to the basement. Nox descended those stairs, pushing aside still more debris along the way. It took her a while to clear a path, but she soon reached the basement.

Once there, she found the rock walls relatively intact. She worked her way deeper and deeper into darkness until reaching Becky Waters' computer room. Though the explosion was very powerful, the brunt of its energy was spent on the mansion. The computer equipment here was scorched from the heat but had not shattered. The rock walls appeared to have muffled much of the explosion's impact.

Nox moved to the computer room's far wall. To her right was the door to the garage. Its heavy wood paneling was cracked and burned. To her left was the metal door that led to the bunkers. It was slightly warped but otherwise relatively intact.

Nox pushed against the door and found it was jammed. She slammed her body against it a couple of times until it gave and the door cracked opened.

Nox entered the room beyond. The bunker's beds were in place, just as Nox remembered them. On the other side of the room was a metal door. This door was almost intact and opened easily. Beyond it was a small room occupied by a single chair and, before it, a small computer panel. The computer monitor was on. It displayed electronic snow.

In the chair before it sat a single figure.

"Becky?" Nox said.

The figure stirred.

"Nox?"

The one time partner of General Spradlin looked terrible. Dark, dried blood stained much of her body. She sported a series of deep cuts and bruises.

"You... you look like hell," Nox said.

Becky Waters eyed the blood stained body of Nox and let out a laugh.

"Speak for yourself," she said.

The last of Nox's memories returned as she helped Becky Waters out of the basement. She recalled being inoculated against General Spradlin's weaponized blood and felt the inevitability of the one-time child soldiers' descent on the mansion. She also remembered, this time through General Spradlin's thoughts, how Jennifer Alberts was injected with the Displacer vaccine. While Lemner's passkey was active, Spradlin's Displacers were shut down. However, the General left orders that should the Displacer computer scanners register anyone inoculated with his vaccine, they were to be immediately whisked away to the Arks. Thus, Jennifer Alberts was saved before the one-time child soldiers attacked her mansion.

Nox took Becky Waters from the basement and to the transport truck. She sat her in the front passenger seat and reached for a first aid kit hanging from a side panel. She applied medicated crème and wraps to the woman's exposed injuries.

"I can't feel anyone... anyone at all," Becky Waters said. "No one but you. Is it...?"

"Yes," Nox replied. "It's over."

"The babies?"

"Gone with the rest of them."

"The General?"

"He... succeeded," Nox said. "We're all that's left."

Nox took her time applying the medication and bandages on Becky.

When she was done, Becky Waters looked much better. The damage she sustained from the blast, however, was great. Muffled or not, the shock wave crushed parts of her body, breaking bones and causing an unknown amount of internal injury.

"I'm... I'm sorry," Becky Waters told Nox.

"For what?"

"For what was done to you," she said. "To all of you."

"You save humanity," Nox said. "If I were in your place..."

Becky Waters shook her head.

"No one could have done what General Spradlin did," Becky Waters said. "No one."

Becky marveled at the destruction around them.

"Made quite a mess of things."

"You should rest," Nox said.

"Good advice," Becky said. "I think I will."

Nox found it difficult to keep her emotions in check. On the way up Becky had coughed up considerable amounts of blood and her metal limbs barely moved. Her injuries required professional medical care, something Nox was incapable of giving. Becky's only hope for survival rested on the nano-probes within her. Would they be enough?

Becky Waters leaned back in her seat and shut her eyes. For a second, Nox feared the only other person on the face of this barren world was also gone. But Becky Waters breathing, though labored, continued. She wouldn't die. At least not yet.

Nox quietly closed the passenger door and walked to the back of the military vehicle. She opened the rear hatch and reached for the box of supplies. They couldn't remain within the Big City's limits for long as the Displacer's radiation was permeating the area even now. They would have to retreat to the desert. But to survive for any prolonged period of time there, they needed supplies.

Nox removed the food and liquid rations with the purpose of taking an inventory of what they had. When she reached the bottom of the box, she found a sealed package. Written on it was a single word:

NOX

She ripped the package open and found a computer pad and file within. She immediately recognized the file. It was the one General Spradlin gave Nox in his office, the one Nox herself left at Catherine Holland's side back in the military hospital.

Catherine.

The memory of her friend came back in full force. Catherine Holland was safe with the rest of humanity and so very far away.

Nox considered reading the file's contents. For so long she hungered for information about her past, yet when given this file, she refused to open it unless she felt she had earned the right to do so.

She earned that right.

But the contents of the file no longer were important or even relevant to her.

Nox set the file aside and brooded. Her thoughts returned to Catherine, until it was hard for her to think of anything else.

I wish I could have said goodbye, she thought. She fought her sadness reached for the computer pad. She pressed down on its screen and it lit up.

On it was a video image of Catherine Holland.

"Hello, Nox," Catherine said. Bandages covered her head and her right eye was a swollen mess. She tried to say something but, for the moment, couldn't. Tears ran down Catherine's face. She shook her head and wiped them away.

"I hope," she said then paused. "I hope you're doing well. They were… they were kind enough to let me make this message for you. There's so much I want to tell you…"

Nox pressed the computer tablet's screen, freezing the image.

She stepped away from the transport vehicle and walked a distance from it.

In the passenger seat of the transport vehicle, Becky Waters stirred. She saw Nox walk away and sit next to a charred piece of lumber. The Mechanic stared at the computer tab while a voice emerged from it. The Mechanic's eyes welled up and tears flowed down her cheeks.

After a while, the message ended. Nox ran it again, then a third time before turning the computer tablet off. She remained by the wreckage of the mansion for several more minutes, contemplating the scene around her.

"Goodbye," Nox said.

She wiped her face and stood up. She held the computer tablet tight and smiled.

"Thank you, General," she said.

She returned to the transport truck and put the tablet back into the package along with the unread file. Afterwards, she climbed into the driver's seat. She stared through the front window for a few seconds and at the destruction that surrounded them.

"How you doing?" Becky Waters asked.

"I should be asking you that question."

"Better," Becky Waters said. "Now, what about you?"

"I'm doing better, too," Nox replied. "What now?"

Becky Waters thought about that.

"Let's take a ride."

"Where?"

"North."

"North? Why?"

"Got a place up there…a little past the sands," Becky said.

"A… place?"

"Yeah. Nice little… hideaway. Well stocked."

A knowing smile worked its way onto Nox's face.

"Is there anything you and the General didn't plan out?"

"If… if there is, I don't know about it," Becky said.

Nox let out a laugh.

"North it is," she said.

And together, the two of them drove off.

EPILOGUE

Several months later a new star appeared in the night sky.

Each night that followed, it grew larger and larger. After a few weeks, it was a fifth the size of the Moon. Soon after that, it was visible during the day as well as the night. More weeks passed and the star kept growing until it filled most of the sky.

By then, it was obvious the object was not a star. It was a dark gray sphere with enormous mechanical projections that resembled spikes on a cactus. Swarms of smaller lights – starships– buzzed the structure like bees around a hive.

No, not bees.

Locusts.

The invaders were awake and making preparations for their arrival.

On the northern Desertlands, Nox lowered her binoculars and laid them on the transport vehicle's hood. She walked to the vehicle's rear hatch to check on her supplies. During this latest scavenger run, she loaded up on as many weapons as she could find.

Given the impossibly large object that loomed over her world, these weapons seemed pathetically few.

Yet even now, with the odds so overwhelmingly against her, she had no intention of lying down and giving up.

If nothing else, Nox was a survivor.

THE END

Atomic Rocket

All images copyright 2010 E. R. Torre

The Works of
E. R. Torre

Available
now

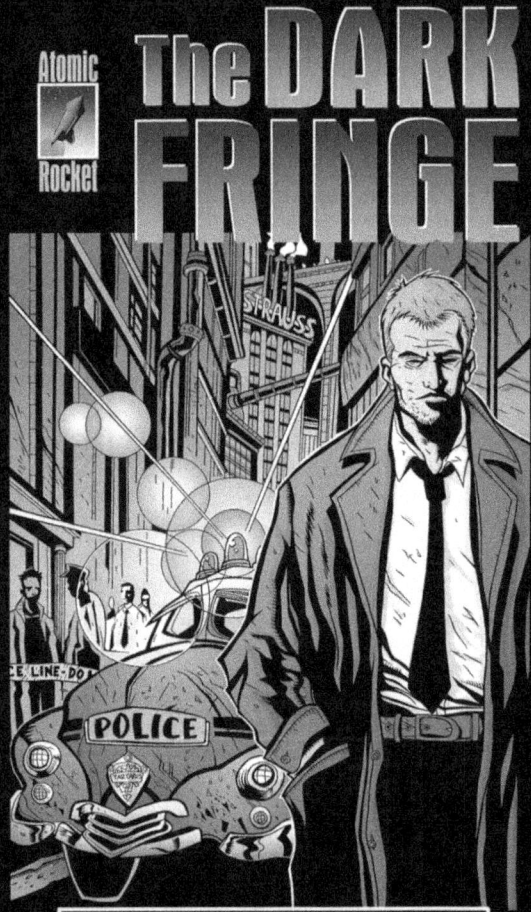

From the grittiest corners of a dark metropolis...
...to the coldest reaches of outer space...
...and all those uneasy places in between...

SHADOWS at DAWN

E. R. Torre

Fourteen tales of Mystery, Suspense, and the Fantastic.

Visions of a dead actor haunt a lonely young man...
Fate leads him on a journey to the man's home town...

E. R. TORRE

HAZE

It started with Blood...
...see how it ends.

Return once more to the world of
The Dark Fringe.

COLD HEMISPHERES

E. R. Torre

An elderly Hitman's most dangerous job
Is the one he can't complete.

For over two hundred years a deadly secret has been kept. A secret that could shatter the delicate peace between two galactic empires and result in the death of billions...

CORROSIVE KNIGHTS 2

THE LAST FLIGHT OF THE ARGUS

E. R. TORRE

That secret is about to be revealed.

Arizona, 1925: A Sheriff makes a discovery in the fiery desert
that changes everything.
Bad Penny, the Present: On an idyllic island army base, a
hidden menace is about to be unleashed...

CORROSIVE KNIGHTS 3

CHAMELEON

E. R. TORRE

For the seven passengers of a military transport helicopter,
the next twelve hours could signal the end of mankind.

Nox the Mechanic is back and this time she faces
a threat that could destroy all of mankind...

CORROSIVE KNIGHTS 4

N O X

E. R. TORRE

A threat she carries in her own blood...

Centuries ago, an unstoppable enemy
forced humanity to flee to the stars.

Today, humanity will take the fight to *them*.

A scavenger on a lost planet
carries a terrifying secret...

CORROSIVE KNIGHTS 6

FOUNDRY OF THE GODS

E. R. TORRE

What lies beneath the desert sands
within the Foundry of the Gods?

The Corrosive Knights series comes to
its explosive end...

CORROSIVE KNIGHTS 7

LEGACY OF
THE ARGUS

E. R. TORRE

ertorre.com

Science Fiction, Mystery, and Suspense